THE INDEPENDENT PRODUCER

Film and Television

Amanda Harcourt
Neil Howlett
Sally Davies
Naomi Moskovic

faber and faber
LONDON · BOSTON

First published in 1986 by
Faber and Faber Limited
3 Queen Square London WC1N 3AU

Printed in Great Britain by
Butler & Tanner Ltd, Frome and London
Reprinted in 1987

British Library Cataloguing in Publication Data

Harcourt, Amanda et al.
The independent producer.
1. Cinematography
I. Title
778.5'3 TR850

ISBN 0-571-13971-X

AUTHORS' NOTE

The law is stated as at 1 January 1986 to the best of the authors' abilities. However, the law changes constantly and a volume of this size cannot provide comprehensive coverage of what is a complex area of the law. You are advised to seek specialist legal advice in the event of a dispute.

Although this book is written in good faith, the authors hold no responsibility for any use or purpose to which information or advice in this book might be put.

ACKNOWLEDGEMENTS

Throughout the researching and writing of this book the authors have received nothing but encouragement and support from those approached for advice. In particular we would like to thank Alan Parker for his wonderful cartoons. We are grateful for the help of Gilly Ruben; Richard McD. Bridge, partner in the firm of Bartletts, de Reya (solicitors); Roxana Knight; Mark Devereux, partner in the firm of Simon Olswang (solicitors); Channel 4 Television, in particular David Scott; Carol Topolski; David Huckfield; Simon Slee; Jenny Woodley; Judith Higginbottom; Willis, Faber & Dumas (UK) Ltd; Eureka Ltd; Jo Howlett; David Lascelles; Colin McCabe; Steve Pinhay; Matthew Crampton; Nigel Urwin, partner in the firm of Brown, Cooper (solicitors). And Alice Watts at the City Desk.

CONTENTS

Put it this way – 5 million quid buys you 12 weeks filming, 20 weeks of post production, a six week run at the Empire and four years litigation trying to figure out where the profits went.. or I can bung the whole lot on the red and go home early..

Alan Parker

FOREWORD

Since Channel 4 began transmitting in late 1982 there has been a considerable increase in the number of professional film-makers and independent production companies in response to the new outlet. Cable stations and satellite broadcasting bring the possibility of further new markets in both Britain and Europe. The largest potential English-speaking market for your film is America, the so-called 'domestic market', but without experience it can be difficult for the independent to penetrate.

Film-making is an expensive and complex process beset with technical problems. A group of people with a variety of skills working together under pressure can be a difficult situation. Once you go into production the problems are often ones that can be solved by the combined expertise of those that are there at the time. But for you, the producer/film-maker, there are plenty of headaches in the pre-production stage. Dr Johnson said: 'Knowledge is of two kinds. We know a subject ourselves or we know where to find information upon it.' The solutions to problems that are often of a legal or financial nature will possibly require outside specialist help, and in your discussions with a specialist an understanding of the terminology being used may ease the communication of *your* ideas.

As smaller regionally-based production companies spring up, more bankers, lawyers and insurers with no previous experience of the film industry will be brought into the pre-production process for their particular skills. Your relationships with them will be more fruitful if they understand the nature of the business in which you are involved, as well as your appreciating the constraints under which they operate.

The advice of a specialist is expensive. Whilst this book cannot provide the answers to all the problems you may encounter in all aspects of production, it may help to alert you to some potential difficulties. As you put together your pre-production package you will find, or may well have already discovered, that the pieces of this particular jigsaw seldom come together to form a nice neat picture. Information abounds about the technical side of film and video production. What seemed to be missing was information about the law as it affects you, the independent film-maker, and some explanation of the trade practices within the industry. There will be information here with which you are already familiar, but increasing knowledge reveals increasing ignorance and that ignorance need not cost you money or waste valuable time.

The phasing out of first-year capital allowances leaves few attractions in the form of tax advantages to the foreign financier wishing to invest in British films. Funding for indigenous productions has been affected by the abolition of the Eady Levy, and the grant-aided sector of film and video is facing cuts from central government. It remains to be seen what support from public funds the British film industry will receive in the future through tax-based incentives, grants or subsidies. It is a subject of much current debate. But the fact remains that Britain has an internationally respected film and television industry, and a wealth of skilled technicians and artists. The fast-growing independent sector is in a very good position to turn some of its creative energy towards the problems of fresh financing sources and structures. This book is designed to be part of that process.

A basic grasp of legal concepts and an understanding of the jargon of the film industry will give you greater freedom in translating 'money into light'.

1

LEGAL BASICS

1.1 Contract

Whenever you make a contract there are two things you should always bear in mind:
- How can I prevent things going wrong?
- How can I be sure that I can enforce my rights if something does go wrong?

1.1.1 What is a contract?

A contract is an agreement between two parties enforceable by law and recognized by a court. You make contracts every day when you buy a cinema ticket or a copy of the *TV Times*. However, not every agreement that you make is a contract; a contract must contain particular elements, discussed below. If it does you can ask a court to enforce the contract: to order the individual who has not performed what it agreed to perform, to do so, or to pay you a sum of money in compensation. (See Seeking legal advice, p. 34.)

You may think you only need to worry about ensuring that the agreements you make are enforceable by a court if you do not trust the people you are dealing with. This is not the case, however. Mistakes and misunderstandings can cause as many problems as dishonesty. With a basic understanding of contract law and common sense you should be able to avoid ever having to go to court. At least you will be aware of your rights to get individuals to do what they contracted to do.

1.1.2 Elements of a contract

Before a court will recognize an agreement as a legally enforceable contract it will look for four elements:

– that the individuals who made the agreement had the capacity to do so. Individual people and companies are able to make contracts on behalf of themselves. When you are dealing with a company you can assume that a director is entitled to make a contract on behalf of the company. However, do not assume that other people from the company are authorized to make a contract or vary its terms. The doorman at a firm's West End headquarters may say he has the power to clinch a deal, but would *you* believe him? Individuals may also make contracts on behalf of other individuals. (See Agency, p. 23.)
– that the individuals who make the agreement intend it to be legally enforceable, and not merely a friendly agreement. Normally there is no difficulty with this. However, if an agreement contains a clause which says, for instance, 'this is an informal agreement only', the court may refuse to enforce it. Do not mistake an agreement to negotiate about specified terms for a contract which includes those terms.
– that one party has made an offer to make the contract on specific terms, which the other party has accepted unequivocally, and has told the offering party of this acceptance.
– that the party accepting the terms has given some valuable 'consideration' for the offer when accepting it. There must be two sides to a contract, and if one party offers to do something the party who accepts the offer must do something in return. Consideration basically means payment and valuable consideration can be payment in money or in kind. There is much argument about what constitutes value. The word 'valuable' does not mean that the payment reflects the worth of what is bought but it must be worth something. Brighton Pier, for instance, was sold for £1, and certain leases are even granted for a peppercorn. Consideration is often a promise to do something in the future if the contract is performed, usually to pay a sum of money.

1.1.3 Making a contract

Unless you are buying land or shares, any contract can be made by word of mouth. However, as the late Sam Goldwyn put it, 'a verbal contract isn't worth the paper it's written on'. As far as legal theory is concerned this is not true, but in practice Sam was right. If you are relying only on words, how do you prove what was said? Even if there are witnesses, there will always be some uncertainty about exactly what was said. This can cause two problems:

- The court may decide that there is no contract unless there is certainty about the terms, i.e. about the essential terms of the contract, like the price. There is nothing to stop you making a contract which leaves some things to be determined, but there must be some mechanism for settling any undecided terms in such a way as to bind both parties. An example of this is the payment of royalties where the total amount is not specified but the method of calculation is. There is an exception to this. If you are negotiating a very complex contract, and after a long period of negotiation finally reach an agreement on the main terms, it will be assumed that you will continue to negotiate in good faith the terms which remain. You should not rely upon this, and should always try to settle all the terms, or if you cannot, write in some independent mechanism for settling them if agreement cannot be reached.
- If the court decides that there is a contract there may still remain uncertainty about what the parties intended the terms of the contract to mean. If there is uncertainty the court will not try to work out what each party intended. It will decide what each party was entitled to assume the other party meant, and will hold both parties to this. Remember, this may not be what you actually assumed the terms to be. It is therefore very important that when the contract is made both you and the other party are sure what is expected of you both. The best way to do this is to make a written memorandum of what you have agreed, and to get it signed. You can do this on anything which comes to hand. If this is not possible, write a letter as soon as you can setting out what you understand the terms to be. If you receive such a letter, and it is not exactly what you understood the terms to be, write back immediately setting out your view. If you do not you might be held to the terms of the letter which has been sent to you.

1.1.4 What can a contract do?

Except for some restrictions, which are discussed below, you can make a contract to do anything. This is called 'freedom of contract'. When a court looks at a contract it will not make any decision as to whether the terms are fair or not. The court assumes that both parties are equally free to accept or reject any term which is proposed or the contract as a whole. Unless there are exceptional circumstances, the court will not alter the terms of even the most one-sided contract. There have, however, been cases where young and innocent artists have been released from the terms of oppressive long-term contracts where they did not receive adequate legal advice before they signed (for example Gilbert O'Sullivan, Elton John and the Sex Pistols). However, these are exceptional cases. It is very important to remember this when you are negotiating your terms, especially if the other party is a large company and they present you with a standard form contract.

Always remember two things:

- If you sign a contract you will be held to its terms, even if you did not actually read every clause, *because you should have*. Many clauses are long and complicated. Do not be put off by this, nor allow yourself to be put under pressure. You always have the right to take your time, or to take the proposed terms away and get independent advice on them. In particular you should never rely on a verbal comment that a particular clause will never be enforced. If it is not necessary, cross it out. If terms are altered at the last moment do not be afraid to write on a typed contract to record these alterations, and initial them when you sign the contract. You should be especially careful with insurance contracts. They always include clauses that release the insurance company from liability if you breach some terms of the contract, or even if you failed to reveal something about yourself or your intended action before you made the contract. (See Insurance, p. 86.)
- If you decide that you do not like any of the terms of the contract, you are always entitled to negotiate. If you do not like a particular term you can always score it out. Even printed contracts are negotiable and should not be treated as sacrosanct simply because they are neatly printed. Most people are prepared to negotiate on terms. However, do be sure when you agree to change something that the person with whom you agree it has the power to make such a change. Also, make sure that

the change is recorded at the time that the contract is made. Again, insurance contracts are an exception to this. If you want to make an unusual insurance contract, then look around and find a company which has or will draw up a special contract that is tailored to your particular requirements.

1.1.5 What can a contract not do?

At various times since the middle of the last century Parliament has imposed restrictions on what terms may or may not be included in a contract. For example, there are many restrictions about terms which may be included in a contract of employment. These are mainly intended to protect employees, who are in a weaker bargaining position than their employers. (These are dealt with in Chapter 5.) Regardless of what you agree with the other party to the contract you cannot:

- make a contract to commit a crime or to do anything which is contrary to 'public policy'. A court will not enforce a contract which is for an immoral purpose.
- exclude your liability in a contract for death or injury which is caused by your negligence. You can only exclude liability for damage to property or financial loss to the extent that it is reasonable. What is reasonable will be decided by the court, which will take into account the relative bargaining power of the parties, the availability of insurance, and the possibility of making a similar contract with someone else. This may be important if your shoots put your artists or technical personnel in situations where they might be injured. You should make sure that you have adequate insurance cover in any situation in which liability may fall upon you.
- as a trader, exclude an implied term that anything sold is fit for the purpose for which it is normally used, or any special purpose for which it is known it will be used. As a person who is more likely to be buying than selling, this provision can be very useful to you. If you are uncertain about whether something that you want to buy will do what you want, then ask. If in fact it does not, then you will be entitled to take the supplier to court for compensation. If you want to do something unusual with equipment, such as filming in the Arctic, make sure the

person you buy it from knows this, and confirms that the equipment will work in sub-zero temperatures.

1.1.6 Remedies for breach of contract

Knowing your rights can help avoid problems. If you think that someone with whom you have a contract might break that contract, letting them know that you know your rights may persuade them to carry out their obligations. However, it is not always possible to prevent things going wrong. If they do, what recourse do you have?

Specific performance

You can take the other party to court and if you can prove that they have broken their contract with you the court can order the other party to carry out their obligations under the agreement in the way which was originally agreed. In law this is called ordering 'specific performance'. The court will only order specific performance if money will not compensate you, and if it is still possible for the contract to be performed in the way in which it was originally intended to be performed. Frequently this will not be possible. The court will not order specific performance if it would require supervision by the court to ensure it is properly carried out. Thus, for example, the court will not order specific performance of a contract where there has been a failure to provide artistic services.

Damages

The court can also order the party who has broken the contract to pay you a sum of money – 'damages'. The amount of damages is intended to compensate you for the loss which you have suffered as a result of the other party's failure to carry out the contract properly. You can still get damages even where the contract has been partly carried out, or if it has been fully carried out but not to the standard it should have been. There are two limitations on the amount of damages which the court may order to be paid:

- The other party will only be ordered to pay for losses which, at the time the contract was made, could be foreseen to follow as a consequence of failure to carry out contractual obligations, or which were drawn to their attention at the time. If you have a complex shooting schedule and one individual fails to perform their contract, your losses could be enormous. Make sure every party involved knows about this, and if they appear likely to default, remind them of how large their liability might be. It may persuade them to carry out the contract, or to find someone else who will do it for them.

- You may have a duty to do everything which you can be reasonably expected to do to reduce your loss. This is called 'mitigating' your loss. Whether you mitigate your loss or not, the court will only order that you be compensated for the loss that you would have suffered had you mitigated your loss. If you have all of your crew ready to shoot a banquet but your caterers do not turn up, you should make an effort to find the food they would have brought from other sources before you abandon shooting. You will be entitled to recover the extra cost of finding the food but not the cost of losing a whole day's shooting, unless you cannot replace the missing food at short notice with a suitable substitute. If you are running an Elizabethan banquet you do not have to make do with a Chinese takeaway! Notwithstanding, you should be careful not to incur expenses which you cannot later justify.

Time is of the essence

In the interpretation of contracts there is a rule that, unless specified to the contrary, time is not of the essence. This means that someone that carries out their part of a contract, but not at the time provided for in that contract, is not in breach of contract, and cannot thus be sued for damages. It is clearly useless if all your performers and technical personnel turn up at different times saying 'here I am, let's go'. Contracts should provide not for what is to be done, but where and when, and the hours and times at which personnel are to be available.

1.2 Agency

Agency is a contractual relationship between two parties, the principal and the agent. The agent acts on the principal's behalf to form a contract between the principal and a third party. At the point when the contract is made the agent drops out in law and is not a party to the agreement. If the agent signs a written contract he must sign 'for and on behalf of' to indicate his status. In casting your film you are likely to be dealing with an artist's agent or personal manager. When it comes to distributing your film you may wish to appoint a sales agent to act on your behalf. In the first instance you are a third party contracting with a principal through an agent. In the second instance you are the principal on whose behalf the agent is contracting. The law attaches particular duties to both parties to safeguard them.

An agent:

- cannot delegate unless authorized by the principal. A distribution contract may include a provision allowing an agent to employ others.
- must carry out any duties with appropriate care and skill.
- has a 'fiduciary' duty to the principal. That is, in occupying a position of trust in relation to the principal, the agent cannot, for example, accept a bribe, and must not allow circumstances to arise that cause a conflict between the interests of the principal and the personal interests of the agent. If you are considering two artists, both of whom are represented by the same manager, the manager, as their agent, has a duty to disclose to those artists the potential conflict of interests, and will require the artists' consent to negotiate on behalf of both of them.
- must hand over to the principal all profits from the agency except the agreed fees. Within your contracts with performers you should ensure that there is a clause stating that the agreed payment made to the agent or manager on behalf of the principal is full and final settlement of any money due to the performer. Otherwise you may be liable if the agent fails to account to the performer.
- cannot benefit or make a secret profit from the agency and must keep the principal's money separate from its own.
- must keep accounts and make them available to the principal on request.
- must hand over all monies received on the principal's behalf.

In return the principal:

- must pay to the agent an agreed payment for services.
- must indemnify the agent against liability the agent might incur in the course of the agency.

The usual law of contract applies between the principal and agent. Someone can be an agent by express appointment, or by implication from the parties' conduct and their relationship. An unauthorized contract made by an agent can subsequently be approved or ratified by the principal. Just as the principal and the agent must have the capacity to contract, so too must the principal and the third party.

In your dealings with an artist's agent or personal manager you will be forming a contractual relationship with the artist as principal. Check, if you can, the agent's capacity to contract. Some agents only represent an artist in a particular territory. While it is most unlikely that you will have access to the agreement between artist and manager, it is worth remembering that many artist/manager contracts specify the area in which the agent is empowered to act. If you are led to believe that you can contract with the artist through the agent in an area that turns out to have been outside the scope of that agent's contract with its principal, and you suffer loss or damage as a result, bear in mind that you can bring an action against the agent. This may be no substitute for the chaos that probably resulted. Where the contract is quite specific, any act done within the scope of the agreement is binding on both the principal and the third party. The law also entitles an agent to do anything which is necessary or reasonable to carry out the agent's obligations. Fraud and misrepresentations made by the agent within the scope of the agency will be actionable against the principal. A third party can take action against an agent if the agent is found to have exceeded the scope of its authority.

The agent normally incurs no personal liability under a contract unless the agent is acting for an unnamed principal and does not tell the third party before the contract is made. In this case, the third party is entitled to treat the agent as principal, and, in the event of a breach, may sue either the agent or the undisclosed principal if their identity has become known. The decision to sue must be made within a reasonable time, and the third party cannot change its mind once it has decided which to claim from.

For general points on dealing with artists' agents see page 148, and on sales agents, see Chapter 8.

1.3 Your business base

Unless you intend to work entirely on your own you must think about the form in which you will collaborate with other people. This can have very important consequences, especially as to how your profits will be taxed. Even if you have not thought about this question the Inland Revenue will when they come to assess your liability to tax. If you do not beat the Inland Revenue to it there will be nothing you can do to reduce your liability to tax. The form of organization which you adopt will also affect your liability for any trading losses you might suffer or your legal liabilities. Finally, it will make a difference to your ability to raise money from various sources.

If your production involves a substantial amount of money you must get professional financial advice right at the beginning. Even if a small sum of money is involved you simply cannot afford not to think about this question. As with everything else planning is the key to success.

This book cannot deal with this problem in detail, but the following outline should give you some idea of what form of collaboration will be most appropriate for you.

1.3.1 Partnership

You can be a partner and not even know it. All that is necessary for a legal partnership to exist is for two or more people to be carrying on business together with the intention of making a profit. You do not have to make a profit, but if you do the Inland Revenue is likely to assume that you intended to do so. If you intend to be non-profit-making you should declare this in some form of agreement or constitution right at the beginning. There is no need to have a formal agreement to create a partnership, you simply have to set up a business venture with someone else. However, unless you make a formal agreement the partnership will be subject to the provisions of the Partnership Act 1890. These are numerous and complicated, and since they have been around for nearly one hundred years not all of them are what the modern entrepreneur would choose.

Among the provisions of the Partnership Act is a rule that partners will share profits, and any losses, in equal shares. This is fine if that's what you want, for instance where you are all contributing equally to the production. However, this may not be what you want. Unless you have some evidence to the contrary, the Inland Revenue will tax you on the basis of the Partnership Act. As with contracts it is vital to record in writing any agreement which you make with your partner(s), both to avoid disagreements between yourselves and to show to the Inland Revenue.

The taxation of partnerships is complex. Basically the profits which the partnership makes are taxed as the individual incomes of the partners in the proportion in which the Inland Revenue assumes they share profits. The calculation of the taxable profit, and in which year it is taxable, are both subject to complex rules. There are also provisions whereby losses made in one year can be offset against profits made in other years to reduce liability to tax. This may be very important to you if your production is to spread over two tax years, which run from 6 April to 5 April. In the first year you will have little if any income from the production, and will make a loss, but later you will have little expenditure but hopefully considerable income. As we said before, you should take financial advice, and take it early.

The risk which you take as a partner is that if the partnership makes a loss, or is sued and does not have adequate insurance, you are liable to make good the loss to the whole extent of your personal wealth. Proper financial control and full insurance cover is absolutely vital. You cannot literally lose the shirt off your back but you could lose your business, your car, your house and your furniture.

As a partnership you can do business under any name you want, provided that it is not too close to the name of a person or organization already established in a similar field of business. If you do this you are likely to be sued by them in what is called a 'passing-off' action. This is a claim that you are taking advantage of their reputation to increase your trade by implicitly suggesting some connection with them, or acting in such a way that other people might think you were connected. If you trade under a name which is different from the names of all the partners, all of your business stationery must show the names of the partners, and they must also be displayed at your 'principal place of business'. This is so that the people you do business with will know where they can send letters, orders, cheques, final demands and writs.

1.3.2 Companies limited by shares

The risks involved in starting a business venture as a partner were believed to be a discouragement to enterprise in the early years of the Industrial Revolution. Many countries in Europe developed forms of business enterprise which allowed entrepreneurs to limit their liability if their enterprise should fail. In Britain the form which developed was the limited liability company. There are two forms, companies limited by shares and companies limited by guarantee. All limited companies are legal entities separate from their members, who have the final say in their management. Thus if the company fails, the members cannot be sued by its creditors.

In a company limited by shares each member buys a share in the value of the company. If the company fails, the most that the members can lose is the amount which they paid for their shares. When the company is set up the shares have only a nominal value. After the company has traded for some time a value can be calculated from the accounts, based on the value of the company's assets and its likely future trading profits. If the company is very successful it can go public, and offer its shares for sale on the unlisted securities market, or on the stock market. Until then it is usual for there to be restrictions on the sale of shares to people who are not already shareholders. Shares are a way of raising money for the company. Instead of interest being paid, like a bank loan, the company rewards the shareholders by distributing some of its profits as dividends on the shares. The shareholders can also benefit from the increase, if any, in the value of their shares. Thus the shareholders only get a reward if the company is successful, which is the risk they take.

A company limited by shares has various advantages where profit is the motive. The money paid by the first members for their shares gives the company capital with which to begin its operations. It is not necessarily expensive or complicated to set up, although it is something which you should get advice about from an accountant. It is possible to buy a 'ready-made' company off the shelf if you are in a hurry and your requirements are simple. There need be only two members to start the company, a director and a company secretary. It is not unusual for the members to be the director and secretary, and for any new members to be made directors too. The directors deal with the day to day management of the company, although the members have ultimate power to determine policy. In a small company it is obviously sensible for the directors and members to be the same people. Directors are officers of the company, although they can also be employed and paid by it, and almost always are.

Companies are liable to corporation tax on their profits. The current rate of corporation tax is 52 per cent. Any income which is received from the company by the employees as pay or by the members as dividends is liable to income tax. Any increase in the value of the shares is liable to capital gains tax, although there are many exemptions which can be used to avoid this. As you can see, the taxation of companies is complicated and you should take professional financial advice as soon as, if not before, any company is set up.

A company must have a registered office to which letters, orders and writs can be sent. A company must also have a name. You can choose any name you want, provided that:

- it is not the same as or similar to the name of a company which already exists. You should also beware of the possibility of 'passing-off' actions.
- it is not offensive or misleading. In the past, 'Jesus Jeans' has been refused.
- it does not inaccurately suggest a connection with royalty or the government, or exaggerate the geographical extent of the company's business.

Limited liability is not a complete protection from risk. The company has to raise money to finance its business. Lending institutions whom you ask to lend money to your company will want to see you invest some of your own money in it. Unless you have a proven record you cannot expect anyone to invest in a project which you are not prepared to invest in yourself. Apart from anything else they will wonder why you are missing such a wonderful opportunity. Almost invariably lending institutions or others to whom the company will be in debt will ask the directors to enter into personal guarantees for the liabilities of the company.

Under such guarantees the directors may be made liable for limited or unlimited amounts. Often these guarantees are in the form of second mortgages on the directors' homes. If the house is owned jointly by the director and the director's spouse the spouse will also be asked to sign the guarantee. Too often they do so without realizing how much they could lose. Never sign a guarantee without taking independent advice on its effect.

1.3.3 Companies limited by guarantee

If you want the protection of limited liability but you do not intend to make a profit, or want a co-operative form of enterprise, then a company limited by guarantee is a more suitable form. This is subject to the same rules as a company limited by shares, and is taxed on the same basis (see above). The difference is that the members do not actually pay for their shares, but they guarantee that should the company fail they will pay a certain amount to its creditors, up to the value of their shareholding. As the company has no capital from its shareholders it does not pay them any dividends. A company limited by guarantee is appropriate where you want to encourage wide membership, and you can set up a co-operative structure where all the members are active in the management. If you have been operating a loose voluntary organization with quite a few members, a company limited by guarantee can be a charity, with major tax advantages.

Co-operatives

An alternative form for a co-operative, which is more suitable where you want a co-operative form of management but want to make profits, is an industrial and provident society. An industrial and provident society registered under the Industrial and Provident Societies Act 1965 with the Registrar of Friendly Societies is commonly called a registered co-operative.

The members of a registered co-operative have the benefit of limited liability, based on their shareholding. They also have a right to participate in the management of the co-operative. The difference between the members of a co-operative and the members of a company limited by shares is that the members of a co-operative cannot increase their voting power by buying more shares.

To become registered a co-operative must have at least seven members, and its constitution must comply with the Industrial and Provident Societies Act 1965. The rules must include provisions that:

- the co-operative will be run for the benefit of those members who participate in its management.
- each individual member will have one vote in the management of the co-operative.
- there must be no artificial barriers to stop new members joining.
- at least 50 per cent of the workforce must be members of the co-operative.
- profits must be distributed in proportion to the members' participation in the co-operative.
- the amount of interest payable on the share and loan capital must not be more than is necessary to allow the co-operative to attract funds.

Most co-operatives also include provisions in their rules which prevent the co-operative being wound up, and its assets distributed to the members as a speculative gain.

Registered co-operatives pay tax on their profits at a rate of 40 per cent, which is lower than the rate paid by limited companies. A co-operative can be a charity, but if you want to achieve charitable status you must be careful to frame the rules of your co-operative in such a way that the public, as well as the members, benefit from its existence. There are model rules for co-operatives produced by the Industrial Co-operative Ownership Movement, and also by the Co-operative Production Federation, which make it easier and cheaper to register. These organizations, and also the Co-operative Development Agency, can help you with advice if you want to set up a registered co-operative.

Charities

Charitable status is not a particular form of organization but is recognition that an organization benefits the public or some part of it. Being recognized as a charitable organization confers enormous financial benefits. If your production will be of benefit to the public then it will be sensible to try to get your charitable status recognized. The normal method is to register with the Registrar of Charities. This is not possible for an industrial and provident society. If you are not able to register as a charity you may be able to persuade the Inland Revenue that you are still entitled to the benefits available to charities, although this will be difficult.

Organizations whose charitable status is recognized by the Inland Revenue (registration is conclusive) pay no income or corporation tax on their profits or on their income from land and other investments. They are also exempt from capital gains tax, though not from VAT. If they own land they are entitled to 50 per cent relief on the rates they pay, and at the discretion of the local authority may also get relief on the remaining 50 per cent.

Charitable organizations are able to receive money from charitable foundations which are unable under their constitutions to give money to non-charities. They can also make use of their exemptions from tax to increase the value of money which is given to them. Schemes which do this use legal devices to transfer money from the donor to the charity before it becomes taxable. This avoids the taxation of the gift as the income of the donor, and as the charity pays no tax the gift is tax-free. For instance, if a company whose income is subject to tax at 50 per cent wants to give £100 out of its income after tax it will have to make £200 in profits before tax. If the gift can be made before it becomes taxable as the income of the company no tax will be deducted. These schemes are not difficult to set up, and there are many books which can help you. As always you must make sure that your information is up to date, as the tax system is always changing.

If you need extra pairs of hands there is useful exemption from the supplementary benefit and unemployment benefit regulations which assist charities. Volunteers can work for you without losing benefit, provided they are able to leave on twenty-four hours' notice, as they will still be classed as available for work.

The advantages which charities are granted are because they are of public benefit. Charities also have to accept restrictions.

They cannot involve themselves in party political activity or the promotion of Acts of Parliament. This limitation is now interpreted liberally and charities are allowed to provide information for MPs promoting new legislation, and to lobby for legislation which has already been introduced.

Workshops

If you want to engage in grant-aided or non-commercial film and video production you may be able to take advantage of the terms of the Grant-aided Workshop Production Declaration. This has been drawn up by the Association of Cinematograph, Television and Allied Technicians (ACTT) after consultation with Channel 4, the British Film Institute (BFI) Regional Production Fund, the English Regional Arts Associations and the Welsh Arts Council. Enfranchisement by the ACTT and use of the Workshop Declaration can reduce costs of production. Before 'franchising' a workshop the ACTT will want to approve the structure of the workshop, its funding, personnel and programme of work.

The workshop must have a collective structure, with rights in productions being retained by the collective, although this can be a partnership, co-operative or company limited by guarantee. Profits from work should be returned to the workshop and not distributed to members or funding bodies. Under the Workshop Declaration funding can come from any source, provided that the funding bodies have no entitlement to rights in the productions. In practice most workshops rely on funding from Regional Arts Associations, Channel 4 and the BFI, with additional revenue from the private sector. Where funding is not yet secured the ACTT will grant a provisional franchise which can be of assistance in seeking funds.

The Declaration insists on a minimum of four ACTT members regularly employed. While the Union recognizes that community-based workshops also undertake exhibition, distribution and education, it favours production-oriented work.

Enfranchising under the Workshop Declaration is based upon the assumption that productions from workshops will not be exploited commercially. The emphasis in existing workshops is on non-commercial, innovative or experimental work. Some have a very clear political direction which influences both the form and content of their work. If a workshop production is considered for commercial exhibition the ACTT may require the payment of an amount equivalent to the saving made from using the terms and conditions of the Workshop Declaration in place of the usual ACTT agreement. Channel 4 has an annual quota limiting the number of hours of grant-aided regional production broadcast annually.

1.4 Seeking legal advice

1.4.1 Assistance with the law

A problem? The best general advice is to get assistance as soon as you can. This does not mean that you have to go and see a lawyer. You may be able to find a solution in a more specialized book, or from the advice available from one of the independent producers' associations. There is a list of other useful books and associations in the appendices. If you cannot find the answer there then you should seek professional advice as soon as possible. It is dangerous to ignore the problem in the hope that it will go away. It might, but if it does not, the longer you leave it the more difficult, and expensive, it will be to solve.

It need not be expensive to see a lawyer. Many solicitors offer a half-hour interview for a fixed fee of £5. If this is not enough time you may be eligible for legal aid. This is a means-tested government-funded scheme which has two parts:

- The Green Form Scheme: this enables a solicitor to give advice and assistance on any matter of English law. Advice and assistance can include writing letters, drafting documents or obtaining specialist advice from a barrister. It will not normally cover representation in court. There is a financial limit on the amount of work which a solicitor can do, which can be extended in some circumstances. There are financial limits on eligibility, with a maximum limit on savings, and a sliding scale for income, with allowances for dependants. In some cases you will be asked to pay a proportion of your legal aid costs.
- A Legal Aid Certificate: there are several schemes covering both civil and criminal proceedings. They are also subject to a financial qualification, but they allow a solicitor to do anything

which is appropriate to take or defend proceedings, including representing you in court, or instructing a barrister to advise or represent you. If you are liable to make a contribution to your costs you will be told at the outset the maximum amount which you may be asked to pay. Legal aid is intended to enable people of limited means to get legal assistance. It is not intended to put them in a better position than people who have to pay their own legal fees. If you lose you pay your maximum contribution, but if you win, your legal aid costs will be deducted from any money or property you recover.

A specialized problem relating to copyright or specific aspects of entertainment law may need to be referred to a specialist lawyer. Finding one is not necessarily easy. Friends or producers' associations may be able to recommend lawyers they know of or have used. Unfortunately such specialists are usually expensive, and are unlikely to do work under the legal aid scheme. Unless you have legal expense insurance, or your problem involves a very large amount of money and you are prepared to pay whatever the cost, you should be careful of the possible cost of a specialist. As with all things, specialist advice costs what the market will bear, and until recently the market has been almost entirely large corporations who are accustomed to paying steep fees. Some trade associations provide specialist legal advice to their members at reduced rates or free. If you are a member of a trade union or trade association you should find out whether such a service is available, and make use of it.

1.4.2 Arbitration

Some contracts provide for an optional or compulsory reference to arbitration if disputes arise over specific matters. This generally means that the problem is presented to an independent third party, whose decision is final. This can be a cheap, quick and simple mechanism for resolving disputes. However, you should never accept a provision for compulsory reference to arbitration or refer a matter to arbitration, before checking that the arbitrator is independent and that the procedures for presenting the cases of either side are fair. If you do not you may find yourself bound by a decision which was made without your having a proper opportunity to state your case.

2

COPYRIGHT AND UNDERLYING RIGHTS

Your film is not only a physical entity on which time, effort and money have been expended, it is also the result of your original creative work and that of others.

The law offers protection to this creativity, allowing you to benefit from the film by identifying it as your work and property, giving you control over it, and preventing other unauthorized people from claiming it as theirs and exploiting it for their profit and reputation instead of yours. The law also protects those who contribute their original creative work to the film so that their work is acknowledged financially and in other ways. It is important that you understand the principles upon which the law operates not only to protect your own rights, but to know what other rights you may need to acquire. The following is an outline of the applicable law and trade practices. The reader should note that this is a basic guide and does not deal with the more complicated issues. Statutes and legal sources will be referred to, for those who wish to know more.

The main topics covered are:

- Confidentiality: your idea and how to protect it before it is recorded in permanent form.
- Copyright: an outline of the law, its application to the production and use of a film and the protection of your film through copyright and other legal remedies.

The acquisition of the rights to use existing musical compositions in films and the commissioning of new music are dealt with in a separate section, because of their complexity.

In general, litigation is very expensive and unless you have no alternative going to court is a terrible waste of time as well. It should only be contemplated as a last resort. Knowledge and awareness of the relevant law can be protection in itself, because people are much less likely to take advantage of you if you make it clear from the outset that you know your rights and the dangerous areas that you might encounter. Throughout this section it will be indicated what legal remedies are available, but although you must be conscious of these, they should not be your first concern. Of more immediate importance are various preventive measures which are listed where appropriate. These are very often simply a matter of common sense and it will cost you nothing to include them at the time that you are having discussions and making transactions. It is worth bearing in mind that the combined complexities of a film in progress and the applicable law can throw up circumstances which no one can predict, or for which there are no immediate answers. This is not a comprehensive study but a basic guide through what can be a very confused terrain, as you will see.

2.1 Confidentiality – your idea and how to protect it

2.1.1 Breach of confidence

Turning an idea into a film is a process which inevitably requires the continual exposure of your original thoughts to other people and organizations. At this initial stage, it is important that you are able to develop the idea by discussing it with relevant people such as financiers, co-producers, broadcasters, a director, etc. without allowing others to use your idea themselves and benefit from it.

The following is an outline of the law that protects your idea while it is still in that initial stage. It need not have been developed in great detail or even put in writing. Ideas that have become embodied in writing or put in other permanent forms are protected by copyright law.

In order to be protected by the law of breach of confidence an idea must be:

- disclosed in a relationship of trust.
  This exists when you reveal information which is of commercial value which at the time is regarded by you as confidential and recognized expressly or by implication as such by the recipient.
- confidential.
  An idea cannot be protected if it has been disclosed to so many

people that it has become general knowledge, but an idea known to an identifiable and cohesive group of people can be protected.

- clearly identifiable, original, potentially commercially attractive and capable of being fully developed.

  Originality is always hard to define. Your idea should contain some significant element which is not public knowledge even if it is in the form of a new angle on a well-known concept.

If these criteria apply, and your idea is used by somebody else, your remedies through the courts are either or sometimes both of the following:

- An injunction.

  The court would prevent disclosure for an unlimited period or until the idea has become general knowledge, thus allowing you to use and benefit from it. Unfortunately by the time that anyone knows that confidence has been breached the idea has often been used already and so is of no value to its originator, so the courts more often award damages.
- Damages.

  This is compensation paid by the defendant which should put you in the same position financially as if you had successfully developed the idea yourself. This kind of exercise is often speculative and therefore damages are hard to assess.

How can you avoid the likelihood of having to go to court?

- Say at the beginning of your discussions and before you disclose anything that any information disclosed is, of course, given in confidence and keep written records of the discussions, however informal they may have been.
- Follow up your discussions with a letter confirming their content and headed 'in confidence'.
- Keep copies of all correspondence.

In this way everyone you deal with will understand the significance of these initial meetings and conversations and will be aware that you understand it too.

As a final safeguard, until your idea has passed this sensitive and developmental stage and has reached a point where commitments have been made by others, you should not discuss your idea with anyone who does not really need to know about it.

The leading case in this area of the law arose from the 'Rock

Follies' series produced by Thames Television. Thames Television were taken to court by the members of a rock group who claimed that Thames had based the series on an idea which they themselves had developed, and with which they had approached Thames with a view to appearing themselves in a series. Discussions took place with a producer and scriptwriter from Thames, although no script was produced at this stage. An option was granted by the group for the use of their services in 'a possible new series' in which they were granted first refusal on the parts, and by implication on the use of the idea. A script was then produced and the group agreed to participate under the option but because of conflict with other commitments they could not do so at the time required by Thames. Thames went ahead with the series using different actresses, and the group took them to court. The court held that because of the circumstances in which the discussions had taken place, the idea remained confidential to the group and that even though it was not protected by copyright, Thames were not entitled to use it. The court also held that Thames had failed to honour their option. It was reported in the newspapers that the damages awarded to the group were in the region of £250,000.

The hearing took place in 1982 and lasted eight weeks because such a large number of witnesses were called to give evidence about the course of the negotiations eight years earlier in 1975. There was considerable conflict between the witnesses about what they remembered as having been said, and the only contemporary written record was a letter sent by Thames Television which both sides agreed did not accurately reflect the terms of the verbal option. Much of the disagreement could have been avoided if either side had kept records of the discussions at the time, and the length of the hearing and the legal costs could have been reduced.

2.2 Copyright

Copyright law in the United Kingdom is governed by the Copyright Act 1956 which came into force on 1 June 1957. This is the main statute and all references will be to this unless otherwise stated.

The Copyright Act has been amended by the Copyright

Amendment Acts 1971, 1982 and 1983, the Cable and Broadcasting Act 1984 and the Films Acts 1960 and 1985.

The United Kingdom is also a member of the Universal Copyright Convention and the Berne Convention.

It is worth noting that the principal act that governs copyright was enacted in 1956 and came into force the following year. A great deal has happened since then, particularly in the way of technological developments, and the law is now generally acknowledged to be out of date. There are now proposals that full-scale reform should be considered, and at the time of writing, it is expected that a Government White Paper will be produced shortly. The EEC has also published a Green Paper, 'Television without Frontiers', in which the problems of reconciling different national laws to the Common Market and the increasing difficulty of enforcing copyright internationally are considered.

2.2.1 What is copyright?

Copyright is the right of the owner of an original work to have exclusive use of it and prevent others from benefiting from it in certain ways without authorization. Note that copyright is not a monopoly; if someone writes the same tune or story as you completely independently, he is not infringing your copyright. Copyright is, among other things, the right to prevent others from copying your work, and it protects the property in an original work. This is, of course, completely separate from the property in the work as a physical entity. For example, the author of a book may donate the manuscript to the British Museum while retaining the copyright. The master negative in a film can be in the laboratory, or anywhere else, but the producer, or whoever else may own the copyright, can prevent the illegal copying of it.

Various qualifications surround the protection given by copyright. Copyright exists only in certain works and subject matters. It lasts only for a fixed and limited period of time, and only certain unauthorized acts (the restricted acts) are infringements of copyright, while other uses may take place without its owner's consent. The identification of copyright in something, who owns it, for how long it lasts and what can and cannot be done with it is essential in order to understand its use.

What is protected?

This section outlines the function of copyright, and shows how it can be acquired in the elements that make up your film, and how to use the copyright in your film.

Copyright can exist only in:

– the following works:

Dramatic, Literary, Musical } and adaptations of these three

Artistic

– the following subject matters:

Sound recordings

Cinematograph films (this includes all methods of moving images, including videos as well as celluloid)

Sound and television broadcasts

Cable transmissions

Published editions of works

It is important to distinguish between works, which can be thought of purely in terms of the words, notation or visual images of which they are made, and the subject matters in which they can be embodied. Subject matters, while often requiring creativity in their own production, are always physical reproductions of existing things and/or events outside themselves, including copyright works and other subject matters.

A film has potentially at least two layers of copyright. It uses all sorts of elements in its construction, such as script, choreography, music, etc. which may be copyright, and it is also a copyright object itself.

Individual works and subject matters will be discussed separately, but there are some general rules.

– Originality. To be protected, a musical, dramatic, artistic and literary work has to be original. This does not mean that it must have any aesthetic merit; it just has to be the result of independent thought or judgement. Thus an arrangement of existing information is copyright, such as telephone directories or the listings of television programmes. There is currently great controversy over whether the *Radio Times* and *TV Times* should retain their monopoly over television listings. Both the

Sunday Times and *Time Out* wish to publish weekly listings in full, but are prevented from doing so by the recent judgment that the *Radio Times* and *TV Times* own copyright in these listings.

- Material form. To be copyright a literary, dramatic, artistic or musical work has to be fixed in writing or some other material form. Interpretations of this vary but it is generally understood to include choreographic and musical notation. It follows that certain sorts of creative expression are not copyright because they are not fixed in material form such as:
  - Ideas. Ideas, especially as expressed orally, may be protected by the law of confidentiality.
  - Live performances. These are separately protected by the Performers Protection Acts 1958–72. Bootlegging the recording of a live performance without authority is not protected by copyright law but under the Performers Protection Acts. Improvisations, such as a live jazz recording, will give the player protection under the Performers Protection Acts and the recording company copyright in the recording, but the music itself, the work, will not be copyright unless it is subsequently transcribed.

2.2.2 Who owns copyright?

Qualified persons

For a literary, dramatic, musical or artistic work or published edition to be protected under UK copyright law, its creator must be a qualified person for the whole or substantial part of the period of its creation. A qualified person is a British subject or British protected person or a person domiciled or resident in the UK or in another country which recognizes UK law, or a UK registered company or one recognized by UK law. Note that the only qualifying bodies for sound and television broadcasting are the BBC and IBA and the qualifying bodies for cable transmission are the licensed cable operators.

Reversion of copyright

It is an interesting point that if an author has assigned or licensed rights in his work before the commencement of the 1956 Act on 1 June 1957, those rights automatically revert to his estate twenty-five years after his death, and may have to be renewed from it. This legislation may have been a paternalistic attempt to prevent the feckless writer from squandering all his work to the detriment of his survivors, but it also acknowledges the fact that an author's work is often not recognized to its full commercial potential for a long time after its creation and possibly not even until after its creator's death. The work is sold too cheaply and subsequently benefits only the purchaser. This legislation attempts to allow the author's survivors to benefit from any increase in fortune that posthumous public acclaim may bring.

Joint ownership of copyright

Copyright can be owned jointly in a work or subject matter if two or more people are responsible for creating it. Joint copyright implies that each owner must approve of the other's use of the work. Copyright in these cases expires fifty years after the end of the year of the death of the last surviving author. In addition the Act also applies to signatories to the Berne Convention and the Universal Copyright Convention.

Territorial division of ownership

Copyright can also be divided territorially and a work which is owned by someone in certain countries may be owned by someone else somewhere else. This most commonly occurs with films in which two or more large organizations have invested. The owners can then do what they wants with the work but only in their own territory.

2.2.3 Copyright in particular works and subject matters

WORKS

Dramatic, literary and musical works

There are no exhaustive definitions but dramatic works include choreography, and literary works include arrangements of existing information such as telephone directories. Note that a play in its written form is both a dramatic and literary work.

- The first owner of copyright is automatically the author or composer unless it is made during the course of a contract of employment.

- The period of copyright lasts for fifty years from the end of the year in which the author or composer died (this is a very useful formula as it saves having to remember exact dates).

If the work is not published or performed in any way to the public before the death of the author then it remains copyright until fifty years from the end of the year in which any of these events first takes place. This leads to some rather curious anomalies. Some music by Handel was recently discovered in a manuscript department of the British Museum. (It is used in the background music to a film.) Jane Austen's unfinished novel *Sanditon* was recently published. Both these works are still in copyright.

Restricted acts include:

- Reproducing the work in any material form including photocopying it, making a film of it or including it in a film.
- Publishing the work. The definition of publication in this context is not precise but it is generally agreed that the publisher is the person responsible for bringing the work before the public. This may not always be the retailer and is more likely to be the wholesaler. Publishing does not take place where a work is exhibited in the home or a similar context.
- Performing the work in public.
- Broadcasting the work and/or including it in a cable programme.
- Making any adaptation of the work.

As an adaptation is in itself copyright, any of the above are also restricted acts in respect of adaptations.

Acts that are not restricted:

Some uses of copyright works are permitted without the consent of or consultation with their owner. These are generally referred to as 'fair dealing' and are not infringements of copyright. 'Fair dealing' in literary, dramatic and musical works includes:

- Private study.
- Criticism or review if done with sufficient acknowledgement. This only applies to published works.
- Reporting for current affairs either in a newspaper or magazine with sufficient acknowledgement, or by film or broadcasting or cable programme.
- Reproduction for the purpose of judicial proceedings.

- Extracts for use in publications for schools (with sufficient acknowledgement).
- Making rough edits on film or video in preparation for a broadcast which is not reproduced and which is destroyed within twenty-eight days of the broadcast.
- Supply of these works to libraries and use by people for private study.

Sufficient acknowledgement means that both the title of the work and the name of the author must be given unless the author has agreed otherwise or the work is anonymous.

Adaptations of dramatic, literary and musical works are themselves copyright under the same rules as the original work. Adaptations are:

- A conversion of a non-dramatic work into a dramatic one, for example, a novel into a screenplay.
- A conversion of a dramatic work into a non-dramatic work, for example, a novelization of a film script.
- A translation of a work.
- A version of the work in which the story or action is conveyed wholly or mainly by means of a picture in a form suitable for reproduction in a book or magazine, newspaper or periodical, for example, a comic strip version of a novel.
- An arrangement or transcription of a musical work.

Adaptations of literary, dramatic and musical works such as translations and arrangements are also copyright in their own right if they are sufficiently original. A translation is automatically copyright. The author would need the consent of the author of the copyright original before publication was possible.

Artistic works

Artistic works include paintings, sculptures, drawings, engravings and photographs, architecture or architectural models and other works of artistic craftsmanship.

The first owner of copyright in an artistic work is generally automatically the artist unless the work is a commissioned portrait, printing or photograph (in which case it generally belongs to the person who commissioned it) or is provided during the course of the artist's employment (in which case it belongs to the employer).

The period of copyright is generally fifty years from the end of the year in which the artist died, but engravings remain in copyright for fifty years from publication if not published before the artist's death. This anomaly exists presumably because the law was made before cheap reprographic techniques made the publication of paintings as posters very common and profitable. Engravings have always been made to be reproduced and therefore require greater protection. Photographs are copyright for fifty years from publication, whether or not in the lifetime of the photographer.
Restricted acts include:
- Reproducing the work in any material form.
- Publishing the work.
- Including the work in a television broadcast or cable programme.

Acts that are not restricted include:
- Fair dealing with artistic works, for the purposes of research, private study, judicial proceedings, criticism and review, etc.
- A representation or inclusion in a film or broadcast or cable programme of a work that is permanently on public view or a piece of architecture is fair dealing if the work or architecture is purely incidental and not the principal subject of the film, television broadcast or cable programme. Note that unlike dramatic, literary and musical works it is not an infringement to adapt an artistic work.

SUBJECT MATTERS

Sound recordings

This means sound recording in any format other than as part of a cinematograph film. A recording of the soundtrack separate from the film must be protected as a sound recording.

The first owner copyright belongs to the producer who is usually a record company.

The period of copyright is fifty years from the end of the year of first publication.
Restricted acts include:
- Making a record including the recording.
- Causing it to be heard in public.
- Broadcasting the recording or including it in a cable programme.
- Causing it to be transmitted to subscribers of a diffusion service.

Statutory licence for records of musical works

A statutory licence exists which allows a record manufacturer to produce a recording of copyright music without the consent of the copyright owner if:

- the music has already been published as a record in this country.
- the manufacturer notifies the copyright owner of his intention to produce the record before doing so.
- the manufacturer intends to sell the record by retail and
- the manufacturer pays the copyright owner the prescribed royalty of 6¼ per cent of the retail selling price of the record (this is collected by the Mechanical Copyright Protection Society).

Cinematograph films

This covers all means of producing moving images including videotape and disc as well as the obvious celluloid. It includes the soundtrack and any music on it if they are part of the cinematograph film.

The first owner is the person responsible for the arrangements necessary for making the film. This is usually a production company.

The period of copyright: films that were registered under the Films Act 1960 are copyright for fifty years from the date of registration. The Films Act 1960 has been repealed and while this does not affect the copyright term of registered films all other and subsequent films are now copyright until fifty years from their first public exhibition. Restricted acts include:

- Making a copy of a film. This applies even if you are just taping a broadcast film at home.
- Causing the film to be seen or heard in public.
- Broadcasting the film or including it in a cable programme.

Broadcasts and cable transmissions

Sound and television broadcasts are covered by the 1956 Copyright Act. Cable transmissions have only recently been licensed in the UK and their copyright is protected by the Cable and Broadcasting Act 1984. Any television or sound broadcast that is made by the BBC or by any company licensed by the IBA, is copyright. So too are transmissions of cable programmes made by UK operators licensed under the Cable and Broadcasting Act and also by authorized foreign operators.

Copyright in television and sound broadcasts is the property of either the BBC or the IBA. Cable transmissions are the property of the licensed operator unless the transmission is made of BBC or ITV programming which is received by the operator for immediate re-transmission, in which case the cable transmission is not copyright and the copyright in the programme remains the property of the BBC or ITV company.

The period of copyright is fifty years from the end of the year in which the broadcast is made, or the cable programme is first transmitted. Restricted acts include:

- Making a copy, except for private use.
- Showing it to or letting it be heard by the paying public.
- In the case of a broadcast, re-broadcasting it.
- In the use of cable programmes, broadcasting or showing them on cable except authorized re-transmission under the Act.

There are no exceptions or fair dealing provisions for sound recordings, films, broadcasts or cable transmissions.

Published editions

Published editions are copyright but only if they do not reproduce the typographical arrangement of a previous edition. This means, for instance, that a piece of music which is out of copyright may be the subject of a new edition by the publishers, there is copyright in that edition and reproduction of it may take place only with the publisher's consent, but the music itself is out of copyright and reproduction performance or transcription from other sources may not be an infringement of copyright.

The first owner of a published edition is the publisher.

The period of copyright runs for twenty-five years from the end of the calendar year in which it was first published.

Restricted acts:

- Making a reproduction of the typographical arrangement of the edition.

Exceptions are made for certain library uses.

OVERSEAS RIGHTS

The UK is a party to the Berne Convention and the Universal

Copyright Convention (UCC). These conventions provide that each acceding country will protect the copyright works of the others. Most countries have now acceded to one or other of the conventions and many are members of both. Only provisions under the conventions which are specifically adopted in UK law are recognized in this country. The Copyright (International Convention) Order 1972 provided for recognition of copyrights in foreign broadcasts.

2.2.4 Practical application of the law

Underlying rights

As we have seen, a film is protected by copyright but so are many of the elements that are used in it. The copyright in these elements is known as 'underlying rights'. Examples of these are:
– Script. This is a literary and dramatic work and could also be a

copyright adaptation of a literary work.
- Novel. This may also be copyright.
- Choreography. This is also a dramatic work.
- Sets and costumes (and the designs for them), and masks and lighting diagrams. These are artistic works.
- Camera script. This is a literary work.
- Music. This may be a copyright arrangement of other copyright music.
- An existing sound recording, which may in turn incorporate copyright music or literary or dramatic works.
- A piece of existing film, which could incorporate any of the above.

Use of any copyright material without the owner's consent is an infringement of copyright because film reproduces copyright work or subject matter in a material form. In order to use these elements legitimately you must acquire the right to do so by obtaining the consent of the owner and usually paying for this consent. This process is known as 'clearance of underlying rights' and can be very long and complicated, as a film can contain all or any of the elements listed above in different combinations. A documentary about a dancer could contain copyright music, choreography, a script and archival film, all of which will need to be cleared. The following are the steps in the clearance process that you need to follow to make sure that you can use your film in the way that you want to.

IS THE WORK COPYRIGHT?

Some details of what is protected by copyright and for how long are given in the previous section. However, it is worth noting that some underlying material will contain a multiple copyright, for example, a script may be an adaptation of a translation of a novel. Each of these elements may be copyright and the copyright may be owned by different people.

If your film is to be shown outside the UK, the UCC or the Berne Convention will determine the application of copyright. Each country has its own limitations. A work that is out of copyright here may therefore not be in certain other countries and it is worth investigating this very carefully for anything that may be distributed abroad. Some European countries have had the period of copyright extended beyond the usual fifty years from the year of the death of the author to compensate for the period during the First and Second World Wars, when the benefit from exploiting copyright works was significantly reduced. This can increase the period of copyright in a work by as much as an additional twenty years.

WHO OWNS THE COPYRIGHT?

Details of the first owner of copyright material are given in the previous section. It is usually the person who made the work – author, composer, producer, etc. – but not always. Since the repeal of the Film Act 1960, there is no registration of copyright in this country, as there is, for instance, in the USA. This means that discovering who owns rights and who to deal with can be difficult. Sometimes it is impossible to trace ownership of a copyright element. There is no way around this. If, after a lot of detective work in, for example, Somerset House, the British Library, and with the Society of Authors, you are unable to find the owner then you must look around for a substitute work. Remember also that the first owner of the work may have assigned their rights to someone else. For instance, the publisher may own the copyright or just the publication and film rights, in an author's book. Many individuals are represented by agents who will negotiate the terms of any agreement for the use of the work. If the work is the result of joint authorship then the consent of both or all the authors involved must be obtained.

ARE THE RIGHTS AVAILABLE?

Before committing yourself, or any money, to the use of a particular piece of copyright material, make sure that the rights to use it in a film are available. The commonest reason for rights not being available is that the owner has granted exclusive rights to someone else. That person or body will then have to be approached, and may or may not wish to grant the rights. You will probably have to pay the exclusive licensee as well as the owner. Another reason why rights are not available is simply that the owner does not wish to grant them under any circumstances for personal or other reasons. There is nothing to be done about this kind of thing and you must find alternatives. The fact that you cannot assume that rights will be available means that careful research must take place before commitments of time and money are made.

2.2.5 Acquisition of underlying rights

Copyright generally automatically gives its owner the exclusive rights to use the work or subject matter and prevents others from using it. A copyright owner can either assign the copyright to someone else, in which case all his rights cease, or he can merely grant a licence to use the work in a particular way, while retaining the copyright in the work and the control over it.

If you are the first owner you own the copyright in a work automatically. Otherwise you can acquire it if you have commissioned the work. In order to acquire copyright in a commissioned work you must specify this in the contract (unless the work is a portrait of you or a photograph). If you do not own the copyright you must acquire it or the right to use it. You may not want to acquire the copyright itself or be able to afford it. Whether you acquire copyright itself or a licence to use it depends on the history of that material, what use you want to make of it and what is available.

Licences

A licence is a contract granting a right to use the copyright in a work or form within specified limitations. There are many reasons for acquiring a licence rather than copyright. Take the example of a well-known play that you wish to use as a script. The publisher owns the copyright but either they do not want to assign the copyright or it would be too expensive. Besides, you want to make a film with it, you do not want to publish it as a book. With a licence you can acquire and pay only for what you need, which is the right to make a film and then exploit it in all the relevant ways. The important thing is to make sure that you get all the rights you need at the right price.

EXCLUSIVITY OR NON-EXCLUSIVITY

A licence can be non-exclusive, in which case the owner can grant others the same licence, or it can be exclusive, in which case no third party can acquire those rights. Exclusivity is very expensive, and whether or not you should acquire it in an underlying work depends on how central it is to the film. Exclusivity is usually only acquired in the script and the rights of the literary work on which it is based, because that is usually the element on which the rest of the film hangs and for which there is no substitute. Other elements, although significant, can usually be substituted, and often are.

Apart from the integrity of your work it is also important to acquire this exclusivity for commercial reasons, and it may be impossible to raise finance without it. Special arrangements are usually made for the acquisition and protection of exclusivity of film rights in literary works. Most other underlying rights are licensed non-exclusively as this is more economical.

In acquiring underlying rights you are putting together a package which can be put to a number of uses. How you are able to exploit your film depends in the end on what rights you have been able to buy. Since the grant of rights by others can be limited to particular periods, territories, media and uses it is essential that you assess how much of all these you must acquire. Ideally, you should acquire all that is available, which would then enable you to sell the film in any way, over however long a period, and wherever you want. This is not as silly as it sounds. It is always cheaper and easier to acquire rights before the production of a film than afterwards, and it is easier to sell a film which is pre-cleared than one with potential problems. However, budgets are limited, and compromises must be reached with care.

You should build all your copyright and other contracts around your main deals (for instance, the co-production agreement, union agreements, pre-sales, etc.) as these represent the main investment by you or someone else. Limitations on the supporting contracts such as copyright clearance should never be more restrictive than these. Apart from your immediate markets you should try to acquire as much as possible as early as possible or persuade your pre-purchasers or co-producer to do so.

Licences can be granted for the full period of copyright (known as perpetuity) or they can be limited to a specified period. Do not accept a limited period unless there is a very good reason for this. In any event individual pieces of copyright should never be granted for a period less than that covered by your main deals.

There is no point in, say, having ten years of performing rights from certain unions for broadcast television and only seven years from a copyright owner. If rights are granted for a limited period then their expiry should coincide with any limitation in your main deals so that renegotiation of an extended term can be done with an overall view of its cost. If you do not do this you may end up with a film in which many elements are only licensed for different short periods, and the administration of the renewal, to say nothing of the expense of purchasing the extensions, becomes a burden that may well make the exploitation of your film commercially unviable.

Whether you make your film on celluloid or videotape you should be able to distribute it on or through any available medium and for all available uses. You should consider its distribution as a combination of four distinct elements, all of which must be taken into account in the purchase of your rights.

- Medium: that is, the system by which your film is delivered (film, videogram, television in all its configurations).
- Use: the context of the exhibition/delivery of your film, that is, in a cinema to a paying audience (theatric), to a non-paying public audience (non-theatric) or at home.
- Territory: usually defined in terms of national borders but sometimes as a language group or television broadcast system.
- Period: a licence can be granted for the full period of copyright (known as perpetuity) or for specified limited periods.

More detailed definitions of the above are given in their distribution context in Chapter 8.

A licence of copyright should contain as well as the usual contractual terms:

- Adequate definition of the rights you are acquiring in terms of media, territory, use and period.
- A warranty by the licensor that he has the right to grant you the rights that you are purchasing and that the work *is* in copyright.
- A provision for payment that is contingent on the production of the film. Unless you have taken out an option on certain rights (see below) you will not have used any of the rights if the film is abandoned before production.

– A provision for assignment of your contract to a third party. If you are obtaining finance for your film from a bank, you may need to charge your rights to the bank. This works rather like a mortgage and offers the bank protection against its loan. If you default, the bank must be able to take possession of the copyright in the film and hence the need to make it assignable.

Options

An option is the contractual right to acquire something in the future. It is used in films particularly in connection with the underlying literary rights. Film and television rights in literary works can be very expensive. If, as a producer, you wish to develop an idea based on a copyright literary work, say a novel, you need time to organize the film and get finance for it, and you need to know that other people are not also trying to adapt that novel for a film as well. An exclusive option on the film and/or television rights of that novel costs a fraction of those rights and gives you the opportunity to get the film to a stage where commitments can be made without paying in full for something that may not be made. In order to be effective and legally valid, an option must:

– be for a specified limited period of time, for example one year. It can be renewable for a further period on payment of a further specified sum.
– set out all the terms on which the eventual purchase of the rights must be made. These must therefore be negotiated at the time you negotiate the option. This is usually done in a separate document referred to in the option which will contain all the usual terms of a copyright assignment (if you are acquiring the copyright) or licence (if you are acquiring only certain rights).
– contain some sort of mechanism for you to let the copyright owner know that you wish to take up or 'exercise' the option. This is usually done by writing to the copyright owner within the operative period of the option and means that the terms set out in the assignment or licence document then apply. If you do not renew your option or do not exercise it within the given time then it will lapse and others may use the work. Your payment for the option is then forfeited.

– grant the exclusivity in the option as well as the rights eventually purchased.

An option must also contain the following terms which should be the same as those in the assignment or licence:

– The nature of the rights that will be granted.
– An undertaking that the copyright owner has the right to grant those rights.
– The option must be assignable to any third party. A bank may take out a charge on your film against its loan and must if necessary be able to take possession of the rights if you default.

As with all the rest of your documentation, it is very important that your option contains all the right provisions, particularly as it may be central to the raising of finance for your film.

There is really no straightforward advice to be given on how much you might expect to pay for a licence or option, except to talk to agents, publishers and others who might have experience.

2.3 How to protect your film

The commercial and other less tangible benefits, such as reputation, of a film can easily be eroded by its unauthorized use. The following describes the various legal sanctions available that can protect a film from unauthorized exploitation, not all of which are under copyright law. The most appropriate remedy will depend on the sort of use that has taken place. However, it will surprise no one that increasingly cheap and efficient methods of reproduction, even of something as technologically sophisticated as a film, have sometimes made the law ineffective and obsolete.

Under the Copyright Convention published works and subject matters must have the symbol ©, and the name of the copyright owners and the year of the date of first publication to serve as copyright protection. This only matters in those Universal Copyright Convention countries that are not also covered by the Berne Convention, which does not carry these obligations, the most significant being the USA and Russia. In practice you should always put this information on your film (usually as an end credit and on any videogram labels and packaging).

In order to issue an action for infringement of copyright, the restricted act must be clearly identified. Establishing whether or not a work has been copied is not always easy or straightforward but a good test is whether the reproduction is the result of the skill, labour and judgement that went into the original.

There is generally only infringement if a substantial part of the work is reproduced, but the vagueness of the application of this word and its lack of definition allows for considerable variation. It is usually enough that a piece of a work recognizably belongs to someone else. Special care should be taken with the use of very short extracts in a film. There is no allowable minimum, and no matter how short it is, anything by someone else that is used in a film must be cleared.

2.3.1 Civil Actions for breach of copyright

In a civil action there need be no intention to infringe or knowledge that a dealing involves infringing goods for the action to succeed. The court may grant either or both of the following:

- An injunction preventing the exploitation of the infringed work. This is very often too late, unless it is likely that the breach of copyright will be repeated, as in video piracy, so the court is more likely to award damages, either instead of or in addition to an injunction.
- Damages: these normally reflect the financial loss to the copyright owner resulting from the breach of copyright. Sometimes the court will award exemplary damages if the breach of copyright has been flagrant, and the person in breach knew that what was done would be a breach of copyright, but still went ahead.

2.3.2 Criminal proceedings for breach of copyright

The law on criminal proceedings is set out in the Copyright Amendment Act 1982 and the Copyright Amendment Act 1983. For criminal proceedings there must be intention to infringe copyright. Breach of copyright is either a civil wrong or a criminal offence. Basically it is a criminal offence to exploit anything which infringes copyright for commercial purposes. While copyright subsists in a work, it is a criminal offence for any person to knowingly:

- make copies for sale or hire, or
- sell or hire copies or offer for sale or hire, or

- import copies into the UK, other than for private and domestic use, or
- distribute copies for purposes of trade, or
- distribute copies for other purposes, but to such an extent as to affect prejudicially the owner of the copyright.

The 1983 Act provides a penalty in the magistrates' court of a maximum fine of £1,000 or two months' imprisonment. However, if a defendant elects to stand trial in the crown court and is found guilty, then an unlimited fine can be imposed and/or a maximum of two years' imprisonment.

2.3.3 Piracy, counterfeiting and passing off

Under the law as it stands now, taping a film or recorded music for private purposes is a breach of the criminal law. Taping a broadcast or cable transmission whose content is *not* copyright, for example a sports programme or a chat show, is not an offence if it is for private purposes.

It is generally acknowledged that this law is unenforceable and many believe that it is also unjustifiable. They argue that home use of taped films or music does not harm the market as most people use it for 'time shifting' to free themselves from the broadcasting schedules and watch or listen at a time convenient to themselves. Others argue that people would buy more records and videograms if the facility for making home recordings were not so readily and cheaply available. The government has contemplated introducing provisions for a levy on blank video and audio tapes which would offer some compensation for these alleged losses. So far these proposals have not come near enough to the statute book to warrant further discussion here and their merit and effectiveness is still the subject of controversy.

Copyright owners are undoubtedly at risk of considerable financial loss from deliberate unauthorized commercial exploitation of a film, especially in video form by piracy, counterfeiting and passing off.

Piracy and counterfeiting

Both piracy and counterfeiting of video tapes have become widespread since the mid-1970s because of the commercial develop-

THE VIDEO PIRATES.

ment and enormous growth in the world market for video cassette recorders and the increasingly cheap methods of reproduction available. In 1983 it was estimated that total losses to the industry were assessed at about US $700 million of which at least US $180 million were attributable to the UK. Video pirates and counterfeiters became notorious as the markets were flooded with copies of popular films available much more cheaply than they could have been if copyright had had to be paid for. Such unauthorized use may enable the copyright owner or manufacturer to make use of various civil remedies, based on the following civil wrongs:

- Piracy is the illicit copying of a copyright work and as such is an infringement of copyright. It is also sometimes a criminal offence as an infringement of copyright, or as theft where a print is stolen to make infringing copies, or under the common law of conspiracy to defraud, where it is shown that a number of people conspire together to infringe the copyright.
- Counterfeiting is the presentation of an infringing work so that it represents the original. Counterfeiting can also be a criminal offence under the Trade Descriptions Act 1968, which makes it an offence to give a false description of the manufacture. Trading Standards Officers have power to seize goods and arrest the offender.

The distinctions are significant because different remedies apply to each case.

Passing off

Passing off is not an infringement of copyright, it is 'a misrepresentation made by a trader in the course of trade to prospective customers or ultimate consumers of goods or services supplied by him which is calculated to injure the business or goodwill of the trade, by whom the action is brought'.

In passing off, the offending traders pass their goods off as those of someone who has already established a reputation in the market place, so that it can be inferred that they intended to deceive the public into believing that the plaintiff's goods, business or title were their own.

Marketing a pirated copy of a videogram under the label of its legitimate distributor is a good example of such an offence, which is a civil one. The remedies are injunction and damages.

Anton Piller Orders

A major problem with coping with piracy is the fact that by the time the investigations have been made, the pirates have taken off. In 1976 the courts offered a way round this known as an Anton Piller Order, after one of the first cases in which it was granted.

An Anton Piller Order can be applied to sound recordings and other goods as well as videos. It allows a copyright owner to apply to the court *ex parte* (i.e. without the knowledge or presence of the other party) for an order allowing the inspection, photographing and seizure of all relevant material in the defendant's control. The plaintiff must show to the court that:

- there is a very strong case that the rights have been infringed.
- the actual or possible damage is very serious.
- there is clear evidence that the defendant has incriminating documents or things in its possession which it may destroy if it were warned of any action.

Copyright: the future

New communication technologies present potentially enormous copyright problems. The ease and cheapness with which a video pirate can reproduce films are well known. In addition, high-powered terrestrial transmitters and satellite broadcasting compound the difficulties involved in controlling the use of a copyright work. For example, the large area covered by a satellite's down signal or 'footprint' does not fit into given national boundaries. Signals which are intended to be received by the television services of one country may easily be received by several others and then re-transmitted. The same applies to signals from high-powered terrestrial transmitters. Even encoded signals can be decoded. The EEC's Green Paper on 'Television without Frontiers' suggests payment to copyright owners in some circumstances of an equitable remuneration which is not directed to the actual use of the programme. This is part of a continuing debate between those who believe that information of all sorts should be freely available if the creators are appropriately rewarded and those that believe that owners of copyright should be able to control the use of their work as if it were some kind of tangible property. There is no immediate answer to this, but it is now increasingly important that those who are responsible for the creativity that is enjoyed by so many are properly rewarded for their work.

2.4 Music

2.4.1 Acquiring rights

The use of music in films is complex, partly for historical reasons. The usual law of copyright applies to music, but in addition certain trade practices dominate the acquisition of licences and use of the relevant rights. This has resulted in a division of the rights into different sections, which have to be acquired separately. The following does not apply to music if you own the copyright but only where you are acquiring licences.

Mechanical and synchronization rights

Traditionally, separate payments are made for use of the music in the film and for the exhibition of the film with the music to the public. The right to record music is known as the 'mechanical rights'. The right to record music in synchronization with visual images as a soundtrack to a film is known as the 'synchronization rights'. These rights must be acquired for the production of the film and for its use in all necessary media, uses and territories. You may also want to acquire 'sound only' rights if you want to exploit the soundtrack separately, for example, on record, and 'simulcast' rights if there is to be a simultaneous radio broadcast. These rights do not include the right to exhibit the film in public.

Mechanical and synchronization rights in most music available in this country can usually be acquired through the Mechanical Copyright Protection Society (MCPS). This is an agency which establishes minimum rates for the composers and publishers who are its members, and can usually but not always negotiate on their behalf. The Mechanical Rights Society (MRS) represents music publishers in negotiations with the MCPS for synchronization licences and minimum royalties payable for the use of music in films when released on video. The MRS publishes rate cards through the MCPS which cover film, television and videogram use. The rates depend on whether the music is background or featured, as well as the medium used, and the length of the programme.

If you are using recorded music, as well as acquiring the necessary rights in the music itself, the recording is copyright and you must acquire rights in that separately. This can also be done through the MCPS. Although the MCPS may act as agents for the copyright owner, it may ask you to negotiate with these copyright owners directly. If you are dealing with music publishers directly, rates may be assessed on the basis laid down by the MCPS or in accordance with an existing agreement between a UK broadcaster and the Music Publishers' Association, but these may not always be applied, in which case the amounts payable are entirely negotiable.

Performing rights

The right to perform music in public, which includes cinema exhibition and broadcasting, is known as the 'performing rights'. The responsibility for payment of these rights usually rests with the exhibitor or broadcaster and not with the producer, but you should be aware of their existence so as to inform distributors. These rights are handled by the Performing Rights Society (PRS). This is a collection agency. Its members are composers, lyricists and publishers who are required to assign the public performing rights in their music, current and future, to the PRS. The PRS keeps records of all public performances of their members' music and collects fees from the organizations who perform it. It administers rights not only in the UK but also through affiliated organizations worldwide. These are not only cinemas, broadcasters, concert halls, etc. but also shops, hotels and so on where broadcast or recorded music is played to the public. As so much music is performed in this way all the time, it is impractical to keep accurate records of how many times each particular piece of music has been performed. Therefore, although some types of performer are accounted for individually, others are estimated on a pre-determined scale. The PRS accounts to the copyright owner on a regular basis, the payment being determined on a formula which reflects the relation of the PRS receipts to the overall use of their music during that time.

As well as purely musical works, the PRS handles lyrics to songs but it does not deal with arrangements of copyright music.

You should also remember that an arrangement of a piece of music may also be additionally and separately copyright.

The PRS has a very useful index which catalogues all music that is copyright in this country. Details of the copyright and the ownership of it can be given by telephone.

Grand rights

Grand rights are the same as performing rights, that is, the right to perform a work in public, but they exist in dramatic musical works, mostly opera, ballet and musicals. The significant difference between grand and performing rights is that grand rights are not handled by the PRS. The publishers must be approached directly by the performing organization. However, if the music is used out of its dramatic context, for example, as an accompaniment to something else or alone, or if an extract less than five minutes long is used in its dramatic context, then the PRS will administer it.

Phonographic Performance Limited (PPL)

The PRS collects payments for the public performance, including broadcasting, of copyright music, etc. on behalf of composers and publishers. The PPL performs a similar function in respect of recorded music on behalf of the record producers. Remember that there is separate copyright in original music and in any recording of it. The PPL distributes fees among its record producer members and also pays a percentage of its receipts to the Musicians' Union and to the music publisher.

British Phonographic Industry (BPI)

The BPI is a body that represents record companies.

Music hire fees

Music hire fees are often payable to a music publisher for the use of the printed music. This will occur irrespective of whether any copyright exists in the music or not and will be a completely separate charge. As this charge is only for the use of physical material and not for the use of copyright you should be careful that your music hire agreement does not impose any restrictions analogous to copyright on your use of the music. The charge itself should only be what is reasonable for the use of material that is expensive and difficult to produce.

2.4.2 Commissioning the composer

This section is designed to give general guidance to you when you are commissioning a composer to write original music for your film. You should always consult with legal practitioners before issuing a contract, particularly if you have plans to release a soundtrack album to complement the film. As you will see, a large number of individuals may become involved in dealing with the various rights which you will need to acquire.

The owner of the music copyright controls the publishing rights to the music. The composer will generally be the owner of the music unless he is under an existing song writing agreement where the copyright in all his compositions belongs to that party. Financiers generally require you to acquire the copyright in the music; however, if your budget is not sufficient you may only be in a position to acquire limited rights. If you acquire the copyright then the right to use the music in 'synchronization' with the film is assured, subject to payment of the composer's agreed fee. If you do not secure the copyright the contract should specify in detail the rights in the music which you are licensed to use.

Included in the publishing rights is the so-called public performing right which is the right to do or authorize other persons to perform the work in public, to broadcast the work, or to cause the work to be transmitted to a diffusion service. These performing rights will almost invariably be owned and licensed by the Performing Rights Society and therefore you need not concern yourself with them further *unless*:

- the film is intended for exhibition in the cinema in the USA.
- you acquire the copyright in the music, in which case the division of the Performing Rights Society royalties between you and the composer will be a matter for negotiation.
- the composer is not a member of the Performing Rights Society.
- the subject matter of the commission is a dramatico-musical work.

Performing Rights Society

A composer who is a member of the PRS is bound by the Society's rules of membership. The PRS grants licences to broadcasters and cinema owners in the UK, among others, and thereby authorizes the public performance of musical works, including those works synchronized with films.

The PRS divides the licence fees it receives, the formula for divisions taking into account the following:

- The amount of music, divided into unit lengths and weighted in value on the basis of being classified as background, visual, vocal, vocal visual. The purpose of the music cue sheet is to provide this information to the PRS and help determine these factors. You will find a sample cue sheet on page 274.
- How often it is used/played, from detailed records kept by the cinema owners and broadcasters and returned to the PRS.
- If there is a music publisher, the divisions of royalties between the composer and publisher. The PRS will automatically pay to the composer 50 per cent of the royalties received from the public performance of the music. The composer cannot grant to a publisher a greater proportion than 50 per cent without being in breach of its obligations to the PRS. If you acquire copyright in the music therefore you can only collect a maximum of 50 per cent of the PRS royalties. To collect these royalties a publisher must be a publisher member of the PRS. To do so the publisher must have at least fifteen works of which ten have been commercially recorded. In practice you will almost certainly need to appoint a commercial publisher to collect any royalties due to you.

PRS – Theatrical Performance Licence

As a result of USA anti-trust legislation, public performance licences cannot be collected by the American equivalents of the PRS – the American Society of Composers, Authors and Publishers (ASCAP) and Broadcast Music Inc. (BMI). Therefore no fees are returned to the PRS in the UK for disbursement to its members. To compensate for this loss of income the PRS demands an additional payment from the producer in the UK for these rights. The method by which the PRS achieves this is to acquire from its writer members the *film synchronization rights* in specially commissioned music. In the commissioning agreement with your composer there should be a clause placing an obligation on the composer to procure the grant of the necessary licence by the PRS. The PRS will grant these rights when you enter into its standard form USA Theatrical Performance Licence. The terms of this licence include an undertaking on your part to notify them when the film opens theatrically in the USA and thereupon to pay the appropriate lump sum fee. The fee is calculated by reference to the amount of music used in the film, subject to a minimum payment.

The composer as conductor/performer

Just to baffle you further, you will probably employ the composer to conduct the recording of the music or as a player of an instrument; that is, as a performer. This is not to be confused with the public performing right in the music referred to above. In this capacity the composer will be employed as a musical director in accordance with the appropriate Musicians' Union agreement. The proportion of the composer's fee paid to cover these services should be clearly identified in the contract so that any residuals that may become payable can be computed from the appropriate base level.

The commissioning contract

The following guidelines are based on the assumption that the copyright is retained by the composer. The commissioning contract should contain clauses to cover the following:
- The composer's services.
- Payment for those services.
- Grant of rights, 'synchronization licence'.
- Credits (see Chapter 8).
- General points.

THE SERVICES OF THE COMPOSER

A composer is usually commissioned to write the score, to arrange it, orchestrate it and advise generally in relation to the use of the music. The composer will often advise as to the hiring of the musicians, the choice of recording studio and give assistance during the dubbing sessions.

The timing of these services is obviously very important. The contract should include a delivery date for the score with a dated stipulation that 'time is of the essence'. The composer will expect some flexibility in the contract so that he is free to work on other projects at the same time. This is usually catered for by specifying a period when the composer is on 'first call', which means that your film takes priority over all other projects, and 'second call' when your film does not have the same precedence.

PAYMENT

The composer usually receives consideration in the form of a lump sum to include payment for the following:

- The services referred to above.
- Daily expenses.
- The rights granted (see below under Synchronization licence).

The contracts will usually provide for a proportion of this fee up front with the balance on delivery. The amount paid is of course subject to negotiation. Composers are prepared to negotiate, like other contributors, for a lesser fee up front, in return for payments later. In the composers' case the methods by which they receive these additional payments are rather different and more difficult to comprehend. They may be derived from all or any one of the following:

- The net profits from exploitation of the film; in this respect the composer is like any other profit participant.
- Payments for the performance.
- The use of music in the film.
- Royalties received via the PRS when the film is exhibited.
- Because extra payments may be due when the film is sold to the different media, to clear additional synchronization rights automatically.
- The use of the music independent of the film itself, for example, if it is used in other films, re-recorded for release on record, etc. This is discussed separately under Music publishing below.

The composer will take into account all of the above when fixing the original composition fee.

Synchronization licence

In this example the composer retains the copyright in the music, therefore you must acquire the right in the contract to use the music in synchronization with the film. In the same way as you approach the Mechanical Copyright Protection Society (MCPS) or a music publisher to acquire the rights to use published music for specific purposes, the same principles will apply in this context (see Acquiring rights above). However, you have a distinct advantage when you are commissioning original music because you have the opportunity to acquire 'all rights' with no caveats.

The most straightforward way is to adopt a catch-all phrase, for example, the exclusive right to reproduce the music on the soundtrack of the film for the purpose of exploiting the film in all media and in any manner whether now or hereafter known. Care should be taken to include the right to use the music in trailers, sequels and re-makes if these are envisaged.

The composer may only be prepared to grant limited synchronization rights for the original commissioning fee, but you should try wherever possible to acquire 'all rights'. You may find, for example, that composers will seek a royalty payment based on the standard rate fixed by the Mechanical Rights Society in conjunction with the MCPS. If you agree to make further payments for video use, try to negotiate a flat fee; you will find accounting to the composer on a regular basis for every video manufactured and sold throughout the world extremely difficult. Distributors can be very bad indeed about supplying these details to you.

Included in the contract should be a number of general provisions to cover the following:

- Termination and suspension of contract: you will need to provide for the situation where, for example, the composer falls ill and is unable to render his services.
- Originality of music: there should be a warranty from the composer to you that the music is original and has not been previously used, and that the music is not defamatory or obscene and does not infringe the copyright or other rights of any third party.
- Right to make adaptations: you will want to make sure that you

have the right to make adaptations of the music and to employ other composers and arrangers, if necessary, in connection with the film.
- Restrictions on the right of others to use the music: in this example the copyright in the music is owned by the composer. You want to limit the composer's right to grant synchronization licences to other film producers for inclusion of the music in their films. It is quite usual to have an absolute restriction of this kind for a period of five years or more.

There are a number of points that have not been touched upon above, therefore the list should not be treated as exhaustive.

Soundtrack albums

The release of soundtrack albums involves some difficult legal problems which are the result of the interrelationship between copyright and contract laws and the trade practices of the music publishers and record companies. For example, it may be impossible for you to acquire the right from the composer for the release of the soundtrack on record if the composer performs on the soundtrack, because the composer's performing services are under exclusive contract to a record company as an artist. Therefore if you wish to issue a soundtrack album you will have to reach a commercial agreement with the record company. This should be done at the earliest possible stage before recording takes place, otherwise they will be in a position to hold you to ransom over royalties. Similar restrictions may be imposed by music publishers who negotiate exclusive contracts with composers.

At the time you commission the composer it is important to check the existence of these types of exclusive contract. You must be sure that you have obtained all relevant releases and contracted to pay to the appropriate party the royalty payments due for the use of the music. It is normal practice to agree to pay the customary royalty or statutory royalty prevailing at the time the record is released. See under Music publishing below.

The musicians, including a composer/conductor, will be due further performance fees in accordance with the applicable union agreement. These may vary depending on whether the record is released from the original soundtrack or re-recorded especially. The composer as a conductor, performer or record producer may negotiate additional royalties for these services based on, for example, the retail selling price of each record sold.

Music publishing

The music composed for the film is a valuable work in its own right. It may be used in a variety of ways, for example, on record, synchronized with other films, or published in the form of sheet music. The owner of the music copyright collects licence fees and royalties from the users, the licensees. The collection of performing rights royalties from the PRS has already been dealt with briefly at the beginning of this section.

It is common for a commercial publisher to be appointed to promote the use of music in these different ways. The division of royalties between you, the composer and the publisher will be subject to negotiation. If you own the copyright and agree to pay to the composer a proportion of the royalties received by you from the music publisher, the accounting provisions should be included in the commissioning agreement. Similarly, if the composer retains the copyright and subsequently assigns the rights to a publisher, you should incorporate a clause in the commissioning agreement placing an obligation on the composer to procure payment to you by the publisher of an agreed share of the publisher's royalties. In these circumstances, 50 per cent of the publisher's share of royalties would not be unreasonable.

It is beyond the scope of this book to describe publishing agreements in great detail, but to complete this section, a reference should be made to the 'statutory recording right', which is an expression you may hear from time to time. Contained within the Copyright Act is an exception to the rule that copyright owners cannot be forced to license the reproduction of their work. If permission has been given already for use of the musical work on record, subsequent recording of the work can automatically be made by anyone provided:

- the person intending to make the recording of the work first gives notice of this intention to the copyright owner, and
- the recording is for the purpose of the manufacture and sale by retail of records of the work, and

– there is to be paid to the copyright owner the prescribed statutory royalty on the sale of the records of the work: i.e. $6\frac{1}{4}$ per cent of the retail selling price less VAT.

Effectively, therefore, the levels of mechanical licence fees are fixed by statute and are not negotiable.

3
THE BUDGET

The budget means different things to the different people involved in the film. To you, as the producer, it is the administrative and financial fulcrum; to investors, co-producers and insurance underwriters, it is a measure of risk and liability. Adequate preparation and presentation of the budget is a vital part of the process of getting the right kind of funding, establishes a method of controlling costs, which can escalate wildly without constant supervision, and is generally essential for the information and peace of mind of all concerned.

3.1 Preparation of the budget

The Channel 4 standard forms of budget and cost proposal which you will find in Appendix One, show the kind of detail in which costs should be broken down. Although a budget can never be totally exact because it is an estimate of future expenditure, you should aim to be as accurate as possible. This involves the painstaking analysis of every element in the film. Everything has to be taken into account, not only the obvious major items but also an infinite number of smaller ones where the cumulative cost can be great. Particular attention should be given to the logistics of your film such as how many people are to be used, for what, where and when, and what the travel, hotel and subsistence arrangements are for each person involved. The use of even small pieces of a copyright work, such as a few seconds of music, will have to be paid for.

Often the most important calculations in your budget are the application of the various union agreements under which most of the personnel on your film will be contracted. You must read them thoroughly and conduct the appropriate negotiations before committing yourself to the production. All union agreements contain very detailed provisions for the payment of their members. On top of the basic minimum payments, additional payments may be attracted for overtime, work on public holidays, night work, transport outside a certain area, subsistence, porterage for certain instruments, holiday credits (in which a pro-rated payment is made to guarantee a minimum holiday in any given year), dubbing, costume fitting, etc. Agreed breaks during work periods must also be allowed for and minimum staffing levels must be maintained. You should also bear in mind that union agreements only specify minimum terms and that in many instances, particularly for higher grade personnel, payments will be significantly higher than the stated minimum.

As an employer you will also be responsible for administering PAYE and National Insurance contributions on behalf of your employees. Remember that while PAYE and employees' National Insurance contributions come out of the employee's payment, employers' National Insurance contributions are an additional burden on you. Also remember that if any of your contracted personnel are registered for VAT this will be payable in addition to their fee and they must give you an invoice so that you can reclaim it.

As can be seen from the above, an accurate budget is dependent to a large extent on accurate production scheduling. Overtime, for instance, is a significant element that can never be wholly predictable, but adequate allowance for it, organization of personnel and the realization that it is highly unlikely that every minute of allocated time will be used to its best advantage will allow you to assess it usefully.

A budget should not be prepared passively. Although it is inevitably a reflection of the agreements that you have reached or will enter into, it is in itself a determining factor in your negotiations. A good budget will tell you what you can allow for negotiable elements and enable you to set limits on what you spend. Unless you have an inexhaustible supply of money, you may at some point have to compromise for reasons of expense. Obviously, you will want your film to be of the highest possible quality, and so to safeguard its integrity as well as its completion, the following should be considered at the budget stage.

Do not under budget

It is easy to allow yourself to be pressured into this by co-producers or investors who are understandably more enthusiastic about a producer if it appears that he or she can bring a film in cheaper than anyone else. Do not allow this to influence your estimation of costs.

At the earliest possible stage in your preparation of the film you should investigate all negotiable costs and if, in spite of negotiation, they are still higher than you think your finances can bear, you should find either additional finances or alternatives to those things that you cannot afford. There are no rules on this, but you, as producer, must decide which compromises you can live with and which are unacceptable. You should bear in mind that some economies have a knock-on effect. There is no point, for instance, in spending money on the best photography if cut-price and less than satisfactory editing does not do it justice.

Use a contingency fund

This is essential. Apart from the fact that you will need it, co-producers and financiers will not accept a budget without one. Completion guarantors, for instance, demand a contingency buffer of 10 per cent on top of direct costs and this must be used before the completion guarantee is payable. Channel 4 insists on contingencies related to specified items rather than a blanket percentage. It is possible, in addition, to build in a hidden contingency by deliberately over budgeting unpredictable elements. It goes without saying that you should never use money allocated for future specified payments as a contingency fund.

Pay attention to cash flow

A budget should not only show how much is payable but also indicate when all payments are due. The Channel 4 budget requires this to be calculated on a weekly basis. You will see that certain payments must be made prior to production. Under the British Film and Television Producers Association (BFTPA)/ Independent Programme Producers Association (IPPA) arrangement with the Federation of Film Unions, a proportion of payments under certain BFTPA/IPPA Union agreements including up to two weeks' salary and return air fares must be paid into a separate account as assurance of the producer's intentions. For insurance purposes among other things you should distinguish between those payments that will have to be made whether or not the film is completed (such as the time and commitment of personnel, facilities, materials, etc.) and those things that need only to be paid for as and when the film is completed and exploitable. Once you have established your cash flow demands, you should make sure that they are compatible with your incoming funds. Make sure that the money from co-producers, pre-purchasers and financiers is available when you need it.

Finally, the discrepancy between your original budget and the amount actually spent should be constantly checked throughout production and your budget updated accordingly. Channel 4 provides forms for this analysis at various stages throughout production.

3.2 Buyouts, royalties and residuals

3.2.1 Buyouts

As we have just seen, certain costs must be met during production or shortly after completion of the film. Others, however, may be deferred and met out of income from its eventual exploitation. This applies particularly to payments for overseas rights and consents in both copyright and performances. It is not always possible to weight payments entirely on one side or the other, but where there is flexibility it is worth considering whether you wish to pay for as much as possible up front ('buy out') or stagger a large number of payments during the commercial life of your film, in the form of deferred payments, royalties or residuals. What you decide will depend largely on the commercial context of your film.

The advantage of buying out as much as possible is that the relevant income from the film can be applied to its investors or whoever else is entitled to it and the film is generally easier to exploit. The disadvantages are that the risks are more likely to be yours and that your up-front costs are considerably higher than if you make some payments out of future income. It is generally true, however, that buyouts are cheaper in the long run if the film is exploited to any significant extent.

The advantage of making certain payments out of income from the film is that your up-front costs are reduced and your risks are, to some extent, spread among the contributors to the film. In the same way, if the film is successful, these contributors will benefit from its success.

3.2.2 Royalties

Royalties are expressed as a percentage of income from the film and may be payable from any or all sources of income, i.e.

theatrical, videogram or television. When negotiating royalties you should keep in mind a total cost of making these payments, which the income of your film will have to bear. The total royalties must not approach the actual amount of money out of which they are to be paid, otherwise, after administration expenses, there will be nothing over for you.

Advances are often payable against royalties to various contributors. They are non-returnable, so if you make no sales you can never claim them back, but they are recoupable against receipts. For instance, if you pay an advance of £1,000 against a royalty of 1 per cent of producer's gross receipts, then nothing further will be payable until income from the film reaches £1,000,000 after which you must pay out 1 per cent of the relevant income.

The advantage to the recipient of royalties payable with an advance is that the risk involved in participation in the future success of the film is balanced by the guarantee of a certain amount of money when the work is done.

3.2.3 Residuals

Various standard union and other agreements use this system for paying artists and others, such as copyright owners, mostly for overseas rights. They work like this. In many agreements a payment is built in that is the benchmark for the calculation of the residual. When the film is sold to overseas television a different percentage of that basic fee is paid for each territory in which the film is sold. The standard agreements list the fixed percentages for each territory, which vary enormously. It is important to note that these payments relate to the basic fee paid at the time the film is produced and *not* to the income you receive. It is therefore essential to make sure that you are not actually losing money by making the sale. This can happen if what you receive does not cover the total residual. Residuals are also obviously complicated to administer as the applicable percentages vary from territory to territory. Again, as with royalties, it is important to be aware of the total residuals payable from exploitation of your film, and to take into account the cost of administering them.

Deferred payments

These are simply agreed lump sum payments which the recipients have agreed to defer until money is received from the exploitation of the film. (See Co-production.)

3.2.4 Definition of gross and net receipts/income

A payment made from the income of a film must come out of receipts at a certain stage. Receipts pass first to the distributor who takes a commission and expenses and then to the producer who has to pay off debts in a certain order. Definitions of each stage are made in a number of different ways, and it is important to qualify your use of commonly used expressions (such as producer's gross) by a detailed definition. The following are some of those terms with their usual meanings.

Distributor's gross

Distributor's actual receipts from which customs duties, VAT and withheld foreign tax may be deducted.

Distributor's net

This is distributor's gross less distribution commission and sales expenses.

Producer's gross

This is distributor's net as received by the producer.

Producer's net

This is producer's gross less various costs which the producer pays off first. These must always be specified and may include production costs and interest and overhead charges, all of which may have to be certified by an accountant.

3.2.5 Cross-collateralization

Cross-collateralization is the combination of different sources of income in the recoupment of total costs. If the sources of income and related costs and expenses are separated in the definition of recoupable net, you may find costs from one area are recovered and royalties become payable on *that* source of income before other income meets defined recoupable net from another source. This means that you are paying out royalties before the full recoupment of your total costs. This can work both for and against you. It is therefore very important to make sure that all your specified costs are recoupable before any royalties are paid.

3.2.6 Accounting provisions

Accounting to those who are paid royalties or residuals is usually done half-yearly at specified times. A statement should be sent to each individual setting out income from each sale with any net deductions, recoupment of advances, if any, and payments if those advances and net deductions have been recovered.

Your accounting practices are subject to various professional rules and your books must be kept in an orderly and systematic way. Some creditors insist on the right to inspect them.

Bad debts

Payments from income should ideally be made only out of money actually received by you and not money owing to you or 'credited to your account'. In the latter cases, if you sell your film to a distributor or television service which goes into liquidation, you will be liable to pay out royalties and residuals even though it is highly unlikely that you will receive payment for your sale. The consequences of this can be devastating and it is, therefore, worth insisting where possible that payments be made only out of money which you have actually received.

3.3 Insurance

Adequate insurance protection is essential and its value is often overlooked or forgotten until the financially disastrous claim occurs.

Professional advice is a vital part of your insurance planning and you are advised to contact one of a number of brokers specializing in film insurance.

It is helpful to the broker if you approach him as early as possible in pre-production. He will have to present your case to an underwriter, obtain a quotation and negotiate on your behalf. He will have to approach several markets on your behalf and present your case. The broker has a professional duty to *you*. Give the broker as much information as you can about your film: a copy of the budget, the shooting schedule, details of locations. The script is important as the broker will read it and can build a picture of the risks for which you will need insurance.

Insurers can avoid their obligations under the contract if they can prove that you did not disclose all material facts or misrepresented the situation, i.e. that you failed to tell the broker of circumstances that would affect the assessment of the risk. This duty of disclosure continues through the entire period of cover.

It is important that you maintain a relationship with your broker throughout production, perhaps by sending progress reports. You may need to contact him in an emergency. Be sure to keep your broker informed of any changes in direction in the production, even after cover has been set, as these may affect your right to claim.

If you suffer loss or damage, notify your broker *at once*. Bear in mind that you have a duty to do all that is reasonably practicable to reduce or mitigate any loss or damage.

Set out below are the main areas that can be covered by film insurance. In any claim there will be a 'deductible', which is the amount of the claim that you will be required to pay before the insurers pay out. This deductible is your risk and is negotiable, though reducing the amount of the deductible may increase the premium. Discuss this with your broker. Each policy has exclusions; these vary and so are not dealt with in any detail.

CAST

This is cover for the additional costs over and above what would have been spent, or abandonment involving costs already incurred, as a result of an insured person being unable to complete their duties owing to death, sickness or an accident. A medical examination is normally required. It is important to advise the broker of any insured person taking part in a hazardous situation. You can insure any animals involved in your film under a separate policy.

NEGATIVE, FILM AND VIDEO TAPE

The policy is written on an all risks basis and pays either the additional expenses to complete the production or the costs incurred as a result of the production being abandoned, or caused by damage or destruction to the film or video tape.

It is advisable to extend the cover to include faulty developing and processing as the laboratories and post-production facility houses do not accept responsibility for your material. This extension normally includes cover for faulty camera or sound equipment and faulty film or tape stock. It will not cover mistakes made by your technical personnel. Do not destroy any unused footage or back-up tapes until after the post-production has been completely finished.

Ensure also that the equipment you use is in perfect working order before you begin work. If you are filming abroad and shooting on film try and ensure that you send the film back to the laboratory as regularly as you can. This will minimize the extent of the loss and reduce the premium.

TECHNICAL EQUIPMENT (INCLUDING CAMERA, LIGHTS AND SOUND EQUIPMENT)

Cover is usually all risks of loss or damage from external causes and normally excludes electrical and mechanical breakdown claims. If you are hiring equipment the insurance can be built into the hire agreement, at a charge, but it may be more economical for you to insure it as part of your production insurance package.

PROPS, SETS AND WARDROBE

Again this is normally all risks or loss or damage. Motorized vehicles, watercraft and aircraft used stationary as props are usually included, but if they are used under their own power they must be insured under a separate policy for motor, marine or aviation insurance.

EMPLOYERS' LIABILITY INSURANCE

This is compulsory to comply with statute in the UK, to protect both your employees and the production company in respect of death, injury or disease to employees arising out of their work.

Cover should be effected at the earliest possible time in tandem with public liability insurance, to protect your activities in research, development or very early stages of pre-production.

PUBLIC LIABILITY INSURANCE

This covers your legal liability at law for death or injury to third parties, and loss or damage to third party property arising out of your production.

If you are filming in a studio or on location, you should consider the value of the studio, surrounding property and the maximum amount of compensation that may need to be paid, including your legal costs, if negligence is proved and you are held responsible. It is wise to limit your liability where possible by issuing a location release form.

PROPERTY DAMAGE LIABILITY

This is cover for what you are legally obliged to pay as damages as a result of loss or damage to the property of others while it is in your care.

EXTRA EXPENSE

Cover is normally all risks and pays the costs resulting from the production being held up or postponed due to damage occurring to the studios, equipment and sets or whatever facilities are used.

PRODUCERS' INDEMNITY – ERRORS AND OMISSIONS

This is extremely important, particularly if you plan to distribute your film in North America as litigation costs there are high. Distributors will normally require that you indemnify them against any claims arising from breach of copyright or underlying rights (see pp. 110 and 216). It also covers you for the costs of defending a claim or damages that you are required to pay for legal actions arising from:

- Infringement of rights of privacy (see Chapter 6, Trespass and Nuisance).
- Infringement of copyright or trademarks.
- Breach of contract as a result of your use of music, literary or programme material.
- Action over unauthorized use of 'titles, formats, ideas, characters, plots, performances'.
- Libel or slander (see Chapter 7, Defamation).

Cover will not be provided until you have satisfied the Insurers that you have cleared all the necessary rights. You are advised to take legal advice over the need for this insurance.

FILM UNION INSURANCE

This is compulsory when using union personnel outside the United Kingdom. The levels of cover in respect of personal accident, sickness, death, medical expenses, personal baggage and money, repatriation, etc., are laid down by the unions.

PERSONAL ACCIDENT

Cover will be required to comply with union requirements for personal accident benefits of £100,000 for union members working in hazardous situations, e.g. in a helicopter or high tower crane.

This section on insurance has been designed as an introduction to a complicated subject and it is advisable for all film production companies to be fully conversant with insurance requirements.

4
FUNDING

4.1 Government support
4.1.1 The Arts Council of Great Britain
4.1.2 Regional Arts Associations
4.1.3 The Scottish Arts Council
4.1.4 The Scottish Film Council
4.1.5 The Welsh Arts Council
4.1.6 Welsh Films Board
4.1.7 The British Screen Finance Consortium Limited
4.1.8 The National Film Development Fund
4.1.9 The British Film Institute Production Board

4.2 Sponsorship
4.2.1 Sponsorship of film and video
4.2.2 Independent Broadcasting Authority *Guidelines on Sponsorship*

4.3 The Channel 4 commissioning process

4.4 Bank finance
4.4.1 Discounting pre-sales agreements
4.4.2 The completion guarantee

4.5 Co-production
4.5.1 Principles of co-production
4.5.2 Co-production agreements: financial arrangements
4.5.3 Co-production agreements: other provisions
4.5.4 Co-production partners

Finding the money is perhaps the most difficult part of the pre-production process but this can also be the time when imagination and conviction stand you in good stead. However, being in love with your project is not enough. Film investment is a high risk business and no financier will be wooed by enthusiasm alone. Financiers make money, *you* make movies.

Aim to eat. Research the market. Do your homework and make the package pithy. Learn to speak the language of the money men. A potential backer will appreciate that you understand a little of their financial constraints, motives for investment and the way in which they operate. Remember you are dealing with a relatively small circuit and those you approach are more than likely to be in touch with others you have already seen. One merchant banker sends out a plea to the independent sector not to return to a backer after the initial approach until you are ready. Repeated phone calls with largely irrelevant progress reports are 'very boring'.

Despite the success of British Film Year, at the time of writing 'bleak' is a word being regularly applied to the future of film finance in this country. The British Film and Television Industry earned £285 million in income from abroad in 1983. You are working in an industry that is a net exporter. It deserves support. Maintaining the level of growth in the independent sector is the independents' responsibility.

This chapter sets out the existing financing structures available to you. Knowing the rules should enable you to break them and invent new ones.

4.1 Government support

4.1.1 The Arts Council of Great Britain

The 1984/5 budget for the Arts Council of Great Britain was £2 million, of which £360,250 was allocated to the production of films. Broadly speaking, two types of production come from the Arts Council stable:

- Films on art and artists, in particular those areas of the arts already funded by the Council, such as dance, painting, music, sculpture and drama. Usually these films are professionally made documentaries, with an innovative approach to the material. The Arts Council commissions the film and copyright is vested in the Arts Council. British residency and experience in film-making are prerequisites for a grant for this sort of film.

– Films *by* artists: grants for films of this kind are also subject to a prerequisite of British residency, but copyright remains with the film-maker. Full-time students are not eligible for such a grant.

In both cases, in applying for a grant, you should submit a detailed budget, treatment of the script/story, and give an idea of the structure or 'look' of the finished film. Some information about your past experience in film-making is also important. Guidelines for application are available from the Arts Council of Great Britain.

In addition to the above grants, the Arts Council will consider applications for bursaries for work in progress, and awards on a materials-only basis. These awards are granted either for a specific project, or for completion of work. Bursaries for work in progress contain no provision for wages for the film-maker.

4.1.2 Regional Arts Associations

England has twelve Regional Arts Associations (RAAs), jointly funded by the Arts Council and the British Film Institute, with additional funding from the local authorities in each area. The abolition of the Metropolitan Councils has meant that those Associations receiving extra funding from the Metropolitan Councils are having to seek other ways of supplementing their already meagre budgets. Each RAA has a film officer, and they maintain close contact with Channel 4 commissioning editors and the BFI, as well as co-ordinating bodies interested in the support and promotion of the arts and the RAA's activities.

Primarily concerned with funding independent film and video, the RAAs place no restriction on subject matter, format or style when considering an application. Though a grant for the use of 35 mm film is unlikely they will view your project in terms of whether it is likely to be regarded as unsuitable for conventional production, financing or distribution. The emphasis is on projects of an innovative or experimental nature, unlikely to find support within the commercial sectors of the film and television industry.

In seeking grant aid from your RAA, you should first contact the appropriate film officers. Sound them out about your idea and build with them a picture of what is on offer from their film budget, and what you may need. If the film officer thinks your idea merits a formal application, you will be asked to complete an application form. Any application for grant aid will involve a degree of bureaucracy, but try to make your application as full as possible, including treatment and supporting material. Give some thought to the envisaged exhibition and distribution of your film. RAAs are public bodies, serving the needs and interests of the local community, and your application should indicate your intended audience. Your application will go before a film and television panel – a group sitting as individuals, not as representatives of organizations, and drawn from a cross-section of backgrounds and areas within your region. You will not normally be present at the discussion of your application, though in some cases you will have the opportunity to meet with more than one panel member prior to your application being considered. On occasions your application may be discussed with one of the Independent Broadcasting Authority companies, Channel 4 or the BFI, if the film officer thinks it possible that it may be of interest to them directly.

If you are offered grant aid, the film officer will act as executive producer, advising you and overseeing production. You will, however, maintain full creative control, and copyright in the completed work remains with you. The RAA will require a credit. Depending on local policy, the RAA may take responsibility for distribution. If your work is picked up by a major distributor and enjoys some commercial success, you will probably be required to return some or all of your original grant to the RAA's production budget.

You will find there is a residential qualification for grant aid from a Regional Arts Association. Grants are not available to students to help with course work, nor to fund profit-distributing companies. (See Workshops in Chapters 1 and 5.)

A condition of grant-aid funding for film or video is consultation with the ACTT under their Code of Practice for grant-aided productions. While funding *is* available for one-off projects, most film and television budgets are spent on establishing and supporting community-based workshops and services, providing capital to purchase equipment or paying overheads on establishments while other funding is drawn from – possibly – the private sector. (See also the ACTT Code of Practice and the ACTT Workshop Declaration.) Some RAAs provide production equipment at reasonable rates for both funded and unfunded groups and individuals within the area.

4.1.3 The Scottish Arts Council

The Scottish Arts Council has provision for independent film and video makers under its Award to Artists Scheme. You must have been out of full-time education for two years, and have been resident in Scotland for one year. Also available are bursaries in recognition of particular achievement which can run from three months to twelve months. For those of you under thirty, you may be eligible for a Young Artist's Bursary, again available for periods between three and twelve months. Awards are also made to contribute towards the cost of a specific project.

4.1.4 The Scottish Film Council

Awards are available for exhibition, study and production, and are intended to foster Scottish film culture. Within the Scottish Film Council is the Scottish Film Production Fund, providing partial production funding and an allocation for script development, pre-production and post-production. Training and work experience is available through the Scottish Film Training Trust. Some assistance with film school costs for students is also offered.

4.1.5 The Welsh Arts Council (Cyngor Celfyddydau Cymru)

The Welsh Arts Council makes awards for both group and individual projects. There is a one-year residency qualification, and no grants are awarded to full-time students, although applications for postgraduate work are considered. Awards for group projects are made to existing production facilities, or to help develop such facilities, but individual projects intended to provoke discussion will be considered. Individual awards are made for pilots, script development or video, 8 mm and 16 mm.

4.1.6 The Welsh Films Board (Bwrdd Ffilmiau Cymraeg)

The Welsh Films Board was established to promote the making of films in the Welsh language. It commissions scripts and employs personnel for individual film projects. A charity, it is funded by the Welsh Arts Council, the North Wales Arts Association and the Welsh Office.

4.1.7 The British Screen Finance Consortium Limited

The British Screen Finance Consortium Limited (BSFC), the successor body to the National Film Finance Corporation, is a limited liability company whose shareholders are Channel 4 Television, the Rank Organization, Thorn–EMI Screen Entertainment and the British Videogram Association, an umbrella body representing the video distribution companies. The annual funds are made up of the following:

- £1,500,000 direct grant from the government (for a period of five years)
- £1,100,000 from the shareholders named above (for a period of three years)
- £500,000 from the loan of the National Film Finance Corporation's portfolio of rights. (This £500,000 value is based on an estimate made by an independent survey.)

The BSFC is run by a chief executive who is responsible for making investment decisions within broad guidelines laid down by the board. This board consists of the following directors: the chief executive, a government-nominated director, four directors – one from each of the investing companies – and an independent chairman. The statutory provisions for the dissolution of the National Film Finance Corporation and the setting-up of the BSFC are contained within the Films Act 1985. This statute enables the Secretary of State to attach conditions to the grant of the government's money and to the loan of the NFFC's portfolio of rights. These are that the BSFC will use its best endeavours to encourage the production of relevant films on a commercially successful basis. (For relevant films see below.) In addition to these statutory conditions, the board has given the chief executive powers to invest up to £500,000 in any one production. All investments in excess of £500,000 can be made only with the full approval of the board.

The projects that are most likely to receive finance from the BSFC will fall into the medium–low budget range of £1–2 million with the BSFC's contribution representing 25–33⅓ per cent of the total budget. If you are seeking finance for your project it should be fully developed when it is submitted for consideration, with a finished script, a preliminary budget and perhaps a director already attached. Ideally you should have some idea of where the rest of the finance will come from.

4.1.8 The National Film Development Fund

The National Film Development Fund (NFDF) receives £500,000 direct funding from the government for the specific purpose of project development *and* the production of short films. A short film is defined in the Films Act 1985 as a film with a total playing time of less than thirty-five minutes. The NFDF will continue to operate in much the same way as it did before the Films Act 1985. The administrator is responsible for making preliminary assessments about which projects should receive development finance. In assessing projects the Fund pays particular attention to the originality of the subject, the likely extent of British involvement, in both development and the production process, and the likelihood of the film receiving production finance as a cinema film. All its decisions will be subject to a series of ratification procedures, including the government's own, via the office of the Secretary of State for Trade and Industry. At the time of writing it is unclear how these funds will be allocated, particularly in view of the government's declared intention to advance only two-thirds of any development budget. It remains to be seen how this rule will be applied. If the condition is automatically satisfied by including in the budget preparatory work already done on the project, monies expended on securing options to published works and the producer's fee, then it may be relatively easy to satisfy the requirement that one-third of the budget must come from independent sources.

The average loan will be in two stages amounting to £24,000 and includes, for example, screenwriting fees, legal costs, producer's and/or director's retainer, an option on a published work. If the Fund enters into a loan agreement it takes a charge on the copyright of the subject as security. The loan bears an interest rate of 1 per cent above bank base rate and there is also a

20 per cent premium on repayment. The loan must be repaid on the first day of principal photography.

Relevant films

Whether you are seeking finance from the NFDF or the BSFC, the Films Act 1985 makes it clear that all monies must be applied with a view to the production of relevant films or to relevant films themselves. 'Relevant films' are defined as those films which satisfy wholly or to a substantial extent the conditions set out in the Films Act 1985 Schedule 1. The purpose of these conditions is to ensure that all films qualifying for benefits, whether in the form of BSFC, NFDF funds or special tax advantages, are 'British'. The first year capital allowance provisions contained within the Financial Act 1982 s. 72 no longer apply. Thus these conditions are applicable to now redundant tax provisions, with deviations from this standard permitted in the case of films receiving BSFC or NFDF funds. Hence the requirement that they must 'wholly or to a substantial extent' satisfy the Schedule 1 conditions. Further deviations are permitted under the official co-production treaties, for example the Franco-British Co-Production Treaty which allows in exceptional circumstances for each co-producer to contribute 20 per cent of the total production costs of a co-production film without the film losing its Franco-British nationality and hence the benefits flowing from that status. (See Co-production agreements below.)

These conditions are difficult to summarize and express in non-legal terms because they include references to certain legal concepts. These are, for example, 'nationality' and 'citizenship' in relation to individuals employed on the film, and 'management and control' and 'registration' in relation to production companies. These conditions also incorporate references to member states of the European Economic Community (EEC) and Commonwealth countries as qualifying for these purposes as British. However, the intention of the schedule is clear: for a film to qualify as a British production the following must apply:

- it should be made by a British producer *and*
- if a studio is used it should be in the UK, or other Commonwealth country or the Republic of Ireland *and*

– a substantial 'proportion', in the region of 75 per cent, of total labour costs should be paid to British persons employed on the film. The formula that is applied to establish this relevant 'proportion' is complex and guidance should be sought from the Films Branch at the Department of Trade and Industry on how it will apply to your film.

Even if you satisfy these conditions, however, the film will fail to qualify if 20 per cent of the total playing time of the film is shot outside the UK unless:

– all the preparatory work, as far as practicable, was carried out in the UK *and*
– the normal laboratory processing work incidental to the making of the film was carried out in the UK *and*
– at least 50 per cent in terms of value of the technical equipment used in making the film was provided from sources in the UK.

What constitutes 'substantially' fulfilling the conditions is anyone's guess at the moment.

4.1.9 The British Film Institute Production Board

The British Film Institute Production Board's activities include production funding and distribution. Its distribution work involves both theatric and non-theatric releases, video cassette sales and rentals, television and an international profile through film festivals and foreign sales. Its productions lie outside the mainstream of commercial film and tend to be experimental in style and subject matter.

The Board's budget is not large, and while 100 per cent finance is provided, co-production monies help to stretch its resources. Projects funded are usually low-budget features coming in at around £300,000, and short films. In the past, directors whose work has been funded by the Board include Peter Greenaway, Derek Jarman, Chris Petit and Hugh Brody. Finance is available for script development, production, and in certain circumstances, completion.

Although it is a part of a statutory body, the Production Board operates in a similar way as a production company, the head of production acting as executive producer. The on-line producer, if there is one, and the director receive a fee. In addition, the director receives a percentage of net income. Net revenue is returned to the Board's production budget. The film-maker retains the copyright in the completed work.

It is possible to keep production costs well below those in the commercial sector for a number of reasons:

- Full-time production, technical and accounting staff at the BFI mean that these costs and overheads do not have to be built into individual budgets.
- The BFI will pay for rights clearances.
- Personnel are employed on a freelance basis and are employed under the terms of the ACTT/BFTPA/IPPA Specialized Production Agreement (also known as the Shorts and Documentaries Agreement). There is provision, however, for topping-up payments to the level of the ACTT/BFTPA/IPPA Film Production Agreement in the event of commercial success theatrically.
- While production equipment is hired in, editing done in-house keeps post-production costs down.

Your application for funding should be made in writing. Forms are available from the Board's production offices. If you are applying for development finance you should include a treatment, an estimate of the amount of money you will need, and some supporting biographical information. Applications for production finance should be accompanied by a full script, an estimated budget and details of your experience. Should your proposal be considered suitable it will go before the Board. At this stage there is only the opportunity for provisional approval as the full package must be properly budgeted before being returned to the Production Board for voting.

4.2 Sponsorship

4.2.1 Sponsorship of film and video

Sponsorship, broadly speaking, is where a company or organization donates finance, goods or services with no financial return or profit participation in your film. Many companies or organizations will sponsor films as part of a campaign to increase public awareness of an issue or service related to their own activities. However, in addition, many companies wish to take advantage of the promotional benefits that come from being associated with or credited in a production.

Short sponsored films for non-theatric release are a valuable area in which to gain experience. It is an 'investor's' market, so presentation is vital. To a large extent the subject matter of your film will determine where you seek sponsorship, whether from local companies, multinationals, charities or international bodies. Many organizations may require more editorial control than a statutory body giving grant aid. It is important to establish at the outset the extent of this control.

The film officer at the RAA may help with contacting potential sponsors in the commercial sector for the purchase of equipment, or capital to establish a workshop or group project. It is also worth exploring the possibility of support from a local education authority, social services department, economic and community development budgets, trade unions or the use of equipment belonging to schools, colleges, polytechnics or universities.

While a direct approach can be fruitful when you seek sponsorship, there are a number of sources that may help to speed up the process. The *British National Film and Video Catalogue* lists most of the short films and videos released non-theatrically and it contains a list of corporate sponsors. The *Charities Digest* may also be of use.

The Association for Business Sponsorship of the Arts (ABSA)

This is the national trade association for the businesses sponsoring the arts. Its primary function is the representation of the businesses who are its members, and it does not fund the arts directly. However, advice about seeking sponsorship is available and it administers two schemes that may be of use to you.

- *Register of Sponsorship Opportunities*: this is a register of projects that are seeking funding from the private sector. Your project's details will be kept on file at ABSA and may be submitted to a potential sponsor who has some idea in mind about the kind of event or project with which they want to become involved. A prospective sponsor will contact you direct. There are no restrictions for entry to the Register and details can be obtained from ABSA's offices. Bear in mind that businesses, particularly larger companies, will be committing funds well in advance, thus you would be wise to register early.

- *Business Sponsorship Incentive Scheme*: launched in May 1984, ABSA administers this scheme on behalf of the Minister for the Arts. The scheme provides for first-time sponsors contributing between £1,000 and £25,000 to have their contribution matched pound for pound by the government. Existing arts sponsors contributing between £3,000 and £75,000 will have their payments topped up by government award equal to one-third of their contribution.

While neither of these services will give you access to funding directly, a link with ABSA can present considerable advantages to corporate sponsors that you approach yourself.

4.2.2 The Independent Broadcasting Authority *Guidelines on Sponsorship*

While sponsorship of theatric films is unrestricted, you should consider the possibility that your film may be released through other media. Sponsorship can be a valuable source of support, but there are strict limits to its use on independent television. To maintain the editorial independence of programmes, and to curb free advertising by companies through television programme sponsorship, the Independent Broadcasting Authority publishes *Guidelines on Sponsorship*. They are, however, both flexible and discretionary in their application. Section 8 (6) of the Broadcasting Act 1981 prohibits any programme other than an advertisement which might be taken to suggest that the programme was suggested, supplied or paid for in whole or in part by an advertiser. Sponsorship is restricted to 'factual' programmes (see below).

Responsibility is placed firmly on the broadcaster. Consultation with your broadcaster in the initial stages of your discussions with a prospective sponsor is essential. Both the independent television companies and the Independent Broadcasting Authority reserve the right to refuse a sponsorship deal made without their approval. Written agreements will be required.

Approach with caution the offer of free use of services and facilities from an organization, commercial or otherwise. They cannot be acknowledged, nor can the supplier advertise his products or services in conjunction with your proposed programme. However, organizations and institutions providing you with free access to, for example, a unique location or material central to the programme, may be permitted a screen credit.

Avoid the use of brand names or readily identifiable products in your programme. While this is not always possible, try to steer clear of anything that may be seen as undue advertising. An exception to this is the legitimate reference to venues, or reviews of 'literary, artistic or other publications or productions . . . interviews with the writers or artists concerned, and excerpts from the work . . .' Prizes or gifts offered in your production should not be identified by their brand names and must be purchased out of your budget 'at not less than wholesale prices'.

In the USA product placement agencies provide a service to programme makers by producing for them props and sets to a general specification, for which they are paid by the manufacturers of the goods. The use of such agencies for programmes to be broadcast in the UK may conflict with the IBA *Guidelines* and is not generally approved by commissioning companies.

If you are making a programme dealing with consumer advice, take care that you check the advertising commitments of any personality, presenter or expert before you use them. The IBA will not permit the use of someone who takes part in advertisements, in any medium, for goods or services that you may wish to examine in your production.

Ideally, funding should be of mutual benefit to both you and the organization wishing to enhance its image through involvement with the production. There are restrictions on what you can and cannot offer a sponsor willing to contribute to your programme budget. It is important to make these very clear at the outset of your discussions.

You will not be permitted to receive funding from a commercial organization whose business is directly related to your programme content. Nor will you be permitted to include advertising, or elements that could be seen to be advertising, for the products, services or facilities of the company from whom you are receiving funds. For example, A. C. Delco sponsored a Channel 4 motor show series which was withdrawn by the IBA because the sponsor's business and the subject of the programme were too closely allied. Your sponsor must not have editorial control over your programme, nor control over scheduling for broadcast. In circumstances where your programme cannot be broadcast or is judged unfit for broadcasting, you cannot undertake to return monies to your sponsor. Equity investors cannot be sponsors and will not be acknowledged as such (see Co-production below). Some independent television companies restrict screen credits to those sponsors contributing a certain percentage of the total programme budget. If there are or will be advertising boards belonging to your sponsor in view at your coverage of a live event or performance, you cannot offer a screen credit.

And now the good news. Your sponsor will be permitted to advertise his goods and services in conjunction with advertisements for your forthcoming programme in other media – known as 'tune-in' advertising – but the format of his advertising may be subject to the approval of the broadcaster. Also, what your sponsor spends on 'tune-in' advertising must not exceed the amount contributed to your budget. Your sponsor may advertise in and around the programme, but the advertisement must not relate in content or style to your production. You can offer a written screen credit at the end of the programme and in some circumstances at the beginning. This credit can refer to both company names and brand names, provided they are not cigarette brand names or products banned by the IBA Code. Wording of the screen credit must be agreed with the IBA in advance. While trade advertisements are not permitted, your sponsor can join with you and/or the broadcaster for a launch or preview to which the sponsor's clients and trade press can be invited. Your sponsor may have the opportunity to enhance his overseas image as some ancillary and television rights in overseas territories may be offered to him by the broadcaster/distributor. There is always the possibility of altering credits for sales in overseas territories.

Off-air educational material or services provided by your sponsor in conjunction with your programme (for example books) can enable you to make a reference to the sponsor on-air. Normally this should be done at the end of the programme, but if reference is seen by the IBA as 'clearly essential in the context of the programme' you may be able to refer to your sponsor within the production. Such a reference must, however, be flatly informative and relate only to the off-air material or services. Clear them in advance with the IBA.

Acknowledgement of funding, other than from independent television companies and independent production houses, is restricted by the IBA *Television Programme Guidelines* to programmes dealing with 'a factual portrayal of doings, happenings, places or things . . . which have an existence independent of the television broadcast itself'. While this possibly includes documentaries, the concession does *not* apply to news or programmes covering 'political or industrial controversy' or 'current public policy'.

The IBA *Guidelines* set out comprehensively the restrictions surrounding sponsored events, competitive sports and tobacco sponsorship. They cover rulings on display advertising, on-screen verbal credits and the frequency with which hoardings or banners can be presented within coverage. You are advised to check these restrictions as set out in the *Guidelines*. They are quite specific, and can be obtained by application to the IBA.

Coverage of sponsored events is not allowed to be sponsored.

4.3 The Channel 4 commissioning process

In 1981 the Broadcasting Act passed on to the statute books, and included among its provisions the legal framework for the establishment of the fourth channel. Channel 4 started transmitting from its Charlotte Street headquarters on 2 November 1982 and since that date has developed steadily, capturing an ever-increasing share of the audience. Channel 4 receives its funds from the ITV companies which in turn sell the advertising space on the Channel to advertisers. The contribution made by each of the regional companies is calculated according to the relative size and wealth of each company. Apart from the way it is funded, Channel 4 is unique in other ways.

Firstly, it is mandated to produce programmes for minority audiences, to 'contain a suitable proportion of matter calculated to appeal to tastes and interests not generally catered for by ITV' and 'to encourage innovation and experiment in the form and content of programmes' (Broadcasting Act 1981 s. 11). Secondly, it is required to commission a substantial proportion of its programmes from the independent production companies, that is, companies other than the ITV regional companies. As a consequence of this, Channel 4 has been responsible for the injection of some £40 million per annum into the independent production sector. Clearly it has a dominant position in the market place and as such will almost certainly be one of your first ports of call when you are seeking film finance.

When you submit your programme proposal to Channel 4, remember that your script or proposal is one of many. For example, the Drama Department receives approximately fifty scripts and treatments each week. Your presentation should be short, to the point and incorporate a draft budget for preliminary assessment. If you are not sure which of the commissioning editors is most appropriate, or indeed which department, send your proposal to two editors. However, make sure all those involved are aware that it is a dual submission, otherwise confusion will reign. The individual commissioning editor will assess your programme proposal in the light of current commissioning criteria, as well as in relation to the intrinsic merit of the programme idea. The Channel endeavours to respond within seven days to acknowledge at the very least that the proposal has been received. A substantial proportion of proposals are indeed rejected even at this early stage – but at least you will know right away. Commissioning policy is formulated by the Commissioning Department at programme planning meetings held ten times a year. The policy is designed to ensure that all commissioned programmes fit into Channel 4's overall objectives. As a national network, Channel 4 must take account of and constantly monitor audience reaction, trends and the competition from the three networks, ITV, BBC 1 and BBC 2. It must also have clear ideas about its future programme needs. The Commissioning Department is headed by Channel 4's chief executive, and consists of the controller of programmes and commissioning editors with responsibilities in the following areas:

– Drama:
 Senior Commissioning Editor, Drama
 Commissioning Editor, Drama Series and Serials

Assistant Editor, Fiction
Light Entertainment:
Senior Commissioning Editor, Light Entertainment
Commissioning Editor, Youth
Assistant Editor, Light Entertainment

- Education and Documentaries:
Senior Commissioning Editor, Education
Commissioning Editor, Education
Assistant Editor, Education
Commissioning Editor, Documentaries
Assistant Editor, Documentaries
- Multicultural Programmes:
Commissioning Editor
- Religious Programmes:
Commissioning Editor
- Arts and Music:
Commissioning Editor, Arts
Editor, Comment and Classical Music Consultant
- Independent Film and Video:
Commissioning Editor
Assistant Editor
- News and Current Affairs/Finance and Industry:
Senior Commissioning Editor, News and Current Affairs
Assistant Editor, Actuality
Commissioning Editor, Finance and Industry
- Sport:
Commissioning Editor

Every two weeks each commissioning editor has a commissioning meeting with either the chief executive or the controller of programmes, where the editor can discuss the proposals received that are thought to be suitable. If the commissioning form is signed at the commissioning meeting you will be notified in the form of a pre-contractual memorandum, but do not assume that the Channel is committed at this stage. There are further ratification procedures that must take place. For example, the Channel's full board must approve all productions with budgets in excess of £500,000 or programmes dealing with, say, politically sensitive subjects. You must be prepared for delays and a series of meetings with editors and cost controllers, and you may be asked to revise the proposal in the light of the reactions from both the business and editorial sides of the company. The assigned acquisition executive will complete an internal document, the Deal Memorandum, for consideration by the fortnightly Programme Finance Committee meeting, when the senior executives from the business side of the Channel headed by the chief executive or the managing director sit to approve all projects. You will receive a deal letter from the acquisition executive as a preliminary to the issuing of the contract.

The relationship between you, the producer and Channel 4 is governed by terms of trade negotiated between the Independent Programme Producers' Association (IPPA) and Channel 4. They relate only to 100 per cent financed productions. Co-financed programmes will be governed by their own unique terms. A copy of these terms of trade can be obtained from Channel 4.

Your contract will be negotiated in the light of the standard terms and you should read them extremely carefully in conjunction with the contract. The contract places the responsibility firmly on your shoulders to deliver the film in accordance with defined specifications. These include editorial, technical, financial and legal criteria. You are asked to indemnify Channel 4 'against all claims, costs, proceedings, demands, issues, damages, expenses or liabilities whatsoever arising directly or reasonably foreseeably as a result of any breach' by you 'of any representation warranties or other terms' contained or implied by law in the production agreement. This is an all-embracing clause and you should be very careful to ensure that you have complied with all the legal obligations you are expected to fulfil.

For those of you who already have financial backing, the Channel may also buy complete programmes made by independent producers and may, occasionally, agree to pre-purchase the UK rights of such programmes.

4.4 Bank finance

4.4.1 Discounting pre-sales agreements

Pre-selling your film to one or several distributors, where the bulk of the money will be paid on delivery of the completed production, enables you to approach one or other of the city banks who engage in film finance. Such banks can provide a secured cash-flow facility to cover production costs, subject to certain conditions. Your film is a high-risk, short-term venture, and as such you will be required to provide the bank with a guaranteed source of repayment. The bank will almost never lend unsecured. It is highly unlikely that the bank will take an equity position in your film sharing the risks and the profits, but you may find a bank with access to clients' funds that will recommend equity involvement to a client. The conditions laid down by the banks are very clear and they will not hesitate to withdraw their offer if the conditions are not satisfied. It is important that you have some idea of what the bank is going to ask of you, and that you do not approach a bank before you have prepared a basic package that goes some way towards satisfying these criteria. However, it is advisable to approach a bank in the early stages of your negotiations with your distributors or sales agents.

In assessing you as a potential borrower, the bank will want professional references from you and will look at your 'track record'. While banks prefer to lend to an experienced producer, there is some evidence that completion guarantors – with whom the banks are in close contact – view the first-time producer more favourably. This is possibly because the 'first-timer' has more riding on the success or failure of his or her film. Even if you do not have a reputation you may still be able to get bank finance.

Assuming that the banks are happy with your character and standing, they will concentrate on the two principal risks in providing a loan to cover production costs. These are:

– A risk that you will not deliver the film on time and within budget (the delivery risk).
– A risk that the distributor will be unable for financial reasons to pay up on delivery (the credit risk).

The delivery risk can be secured through a completion guarantee. The bank loan will not be available until you have the completion guarantee which itself will not come into effect until 100 per cent of production finance has been committed. (See the completion guarantee below.) This means that all the bank's requirements except the completion guarantee must have been met before the loan can be drawn.

With regard to the credit risk, the loan facility is secured by the selection of documents that the bank will hold while the production goes ahead, and until repayment occurs. You will be required to provide the bank with a package that is sufficiently secure to assure them of this repayment.

Securing the loan

In order to be assured of repayment the bank will require as security:
- The completion guarantee (see below).
- A first legal charge over one or several distribution agreements under which payments are guaranteed to be made on specified dates sufficient to cover your costs of production including the cost of the money. It is essential to obtain the bank's approval of the form of the distribution agreement, as the bank will be the last to sign the package of agreements necessary for production to begin. Normally the bank's lawyer will be involved in the drafting of all major documents. The bank will look closely at who is contracting to pay, and will want to be satisfied that the distributor is able to do so. Checking the credit position of an American major is reasonably simple for the officers of the bank, but a deal with a smaller distributor can mean the bank has difficulty gaining access to that company's balance sheets, and making a proper credit assessment. Thus you may be asked for what is called a bank letter of credit. This takes the form of a letter from the distributor's bank to the effect that, on satisfying the conditions in the distribution contract, the distributor's bank will guarantee to pay. Both distribution agreements and letter of credit should specify the amount and dates of repayment. Payment will have to be made direct to the bank providing the loan facility to avoid the risk of default on the loan should the production company or producer go into liquidation. Throughout the process the bank will ensure that it is first in line for payment from income from the film. The banks will wish to ensure that the delivery risk is fully secured and as such the delivery requirements in the distribution agreement should be mirrored in the completion guarantee; for example, a *force majeure* clause in the distribution agreement

should be reflected by one in the completion guarantee. If you are discounting more than one distribution agreement, you should ensure that the rights granted under the agreements do not conflict or overlap. For example, if guaranteed payments for exploitation in one medium (say, videotape and disc) are to be 'triggered' by your film's success in, say, theatrical release, the bank will want a commitment from the theatrical distributor that is sufficient to 'trigger' payment for video rights. Or, for example, your theatrical distribution agreement may contain a 'holdback' clause, specifying the period of time to elapse before, say, video release. When negotiating the guarantee in the video distribution agreement, you should take account of the fact that interest will have to be paid on the loan during the period the holdback clause is in effect.

- The bank will want a first legal charge over the copyright, underlying rights and master negative of the film and an undertaking from the laboratory to hold the master negative to the bank's order.
- All the appropriate insurances will have to be in place and the policies lodged with the bank. (See Insurance above.)
- The bank will want documentation that assures them that you have the rights to exploit your story, and that you have cleared all the necessary rights, including music.
- The bank will want to examine and approve your budget and cash-flow projection and to have from you an undertaking that the loan will be used solely to finance your film. Generally speaking, however, the bank will rely on the completion guarantee in these matters.
- Approval of the script will be required. It is rare for the bank to take issue with content, but it will check that your film is one with which it is willing to be associated. Certification is guaranteed by the completion guarantor but not the actual rating. You will be required to undertake that you will not change the script over and above the demands of shooting. Your shooting schedule will also be approved.
- The contracts with all your major personnel may be examined and discussed, possibly between the bank and the completion guarantor. These contracts will also be held by the bank.

You will now have to negotiate the interest rate and the rate at which you will draw down on the facility you have been offered. You will be required to lodge with the bank the documents set out above and be required to guarantee that the terms of any of your agreements will not be altered and that there are no third parties with rights that would impose upon the rights you are granting to the bank. Try to incorporate a clause that states requirements of future distribution agreements that will be seen by the bank to be approved if these requirements are met. This will save you time and administrative problems. Try to avoid undertaking a personal guarantee in addition to the security provided by what the bank already holds. If the bank is satisfied that the package is sufficient security, you will be sent a conditional offer letter that states the bank's willingness to advance funds provided that certain conditions are fulfilled.

The cost of the money

The money will cost you the following:

- An arrangement fee, payable on acceptance of the conditional offer letter or perhaps partially on first draw down. This arrangement fee covers the bank's costs for meetings and documentation. It is calculated as a percentage of the total facility, normally between 1 and 3 per cent, and is payable in cash or deducted from the account. The amount depends on the complexity of the proposition (i.e. time spent) and the overall remuneration required by the bank since the actual interest return to the bank may be inadequate in view of the short term involved.
- Legal fees. These are the costs of drawing up agreements, checking the documentation of title. The amount varies and some banks with in-house lawyers thus build the legal fees into the arrangement fee. You may be asked to provide funds on account in advance to cover these costs.
- Commitment fee. This is usually around ½ per cent per annum on the amount of the facility undrawn. It is charged quarterly on the account, and the percentage is calculated on the basis of the total amount less the amount used to date. This is for the bank's commitment to hold the total amount of the facility in reserve for you. Some banks combine arrangement fees and commitment fees in a single up-front payment.

- Interest. The bank has funded its loan on the London Inter Bank Market and will charge you a margin of interest over the London Inter Bank Offered Rate, or LIBOR, usually 2 to 3 per cent. You should negotiate for the actual interest rate to be fixed. A fixed rate enables you to establish the maximum cost of your money in your budget. Moreover, a completion guarantor is unlikely to accept a loan tied to a floating interest rate. Equally the bank would not wish to see itself exposed to the possibility that a rise in interest rates would push up its total exposure above the amounts guaranteed under the distribution contracts.

Finally, it is worth bearing in mind that many banks do not have experience of film finance. Do not be afraid to ask (politely, of course) about *their* track record. Have they approved this type of loan before? Did they complete the deal? After all, you do not want them to pull out at the last minute when you think they are about to make an offer. As always, it pays to shop around.

4.4.2 The completion guaranteee

The completion guarantee is a special form of insurance given by a completion guarantee company to those investing in the film, to cover the risk that the film will not be completed. The completion guarantor contracts with the bank or financier that the film will be completed and delivered by a set date, or that it will repay the loan with interest if the film is not completed and fund any overspends. The companies offering completion guarantees require a special combination of skills and expertise including a comprehensive knowledge of the film production process and the different financing structures. The bank from whom you are seeking a loan must be confident that the completion guarantor has the financial resources to put in additional funds to complete the film, if required. For all these reasons there are few completion guarantors in the business.

The fee which will be charged by the completion guarantor will be about 6 per cent of the approved budget. This figure does not include the contingency element which is never less than 10 per cent of the above and below line costs, or the completion guarantor's fees themselves. The fee is subject to a 'no claims bonus' of anything between 25 and 50 per cent, dependent upon your previous record as a producer.

The completion guarantee consists of two parts:

- The guarantee from the completion guarantor to the bank.
- The mutual obligations between you and the completion guarantor.

The bank and the guarantor

The guarantee may be given to any financier involved in the production, although in most cases this will be a bank. The contract between them will contain an undertaking by the completion guarantor to fund any overspend so that the film can be completed and delivered, and a guarantee that if the producer is unable to complete the production within the agreed budget and schedule the guarantor will take over the production. The completion guarantor will have an option not to complete and deliver the film but, instead, to repay the loan, plus interest, to the bank. The first undertaking is most important when the financier has an equity investment in the film. The completion guarantor will rank low in the list of creditors, after the bank and other financiers, so that if there is a failure to complete, the completion guarantor may recover very little. The completion guarantor is vulnerable, and therefore very careful.

However, the liability of the completion guarantor is not absolute. For example:

- The completion guarantor will not be liable for costs caused by a defect in the copyright title in the story and script. The bank will get its own lawyers to investigate the adequacy of the rights you have acquired but will also seek warranties and undertakings from both of you in a corporate and personal capacity in this regard.
- In the UK a completion guarantor will guarantee a British Board of Film Certification Certificate, though not in any particular category. Foreign certificates are virtually never guaranteed and the bank will be unwilling to accept the distributor's guarantees or advances from territories whose censors are particularly sensitive on certain subjects if the distributor's payment is conditional upon a certificate being obtained.

- The completion guarantor will only guarantee the film when 100 per cent of the budget is available. This pre-condition can be difficult to satisfy because the bank's loan is usually only for a part of the budget and only payable when the completion guarantee is in place. To break this cycle, the completion guarantor will issue a letter of intent stating in principle that it will be prepared to offer the guarantee, subject to certain conditions.

If a completion guarantee is required, you should approach the completion guarantors at the earliest stage of production. They will expect to see the same documents as the bank, for example, your distribution agreements, the script and shooting schedule including details of location and budget. If they are satisfied at this stage that the project is feasible, then a series of meetings will take place between you, the director, the production accountant, the line producer and other relevant personnel and the completion guarantor to discuss features of the production, such as the use of particular locations and special effects which may inflate the budget if not carefully controlled. If they are satisfied with the explanations they are given they will issue a letter of intent.

The letter of intent

This confirms that the completion guarantor is prepared to go forward with the giving of the completion guarantee, subject to the fulfilment of certain conditions. These might include that specified personnel, artistic or technical, will be available for the making and completion of the film and specific confirmation on other matters such as studio, insurance and locations agreements. It will list a number of budget items which are outside the orbit of the completion guarantor's responsibility. These can be covered under a security agreement which is described below.

As soon as the bank has accepted the terms of the letter of intent, the completion guarantor will then wish to see all the legal documentation relating to the film. In particular, the completion guarantor will want to see that you have acquired sufficient underlying rights to deliver the film to the distributors in accordance with the approved distribution agreements. They will also examine the contract with main personnel including the director and principal artists to check start and stop dates and remuneration and to ensure that the director and artists have not been granted editing and approval rights which might interfere with the delivery of the film in accordance with the distribution agreements.

The security agreement and personal guarantees

Before executing the completion guarantee in favour of the bank, the completion guarantor will expect you to enter into the security agreement, the second part of the completion guarantee. This contract performs two functions. Firstly, it contains warranties from you and from your production company that you own the rights and will make the film in accordance with all contractual commitments, and secondly, it gives the completion guarantor certain rights to enable it to comply with its guarantee of completion. For example, the completion guarantor will have rights to daily progress reports of shooting and weekly cost statements including forecasts of production costs and statements of any other expenditure. The completion guarantor will have the right to call for explanation from any personnel involved with the production of the film. Most importantly, it can decide to take over the production if there is a real danger that the film will not be completed on time and within budget. The completion guarantor will expect its delivery commitment under the guarantee to last for a fixed period from the start of principal photography and therefore must have the right throughout to oversee the production. It should be stressed that this extreme action is only taken as a last resort and occurs on fewer than 5 per cent of films guaranteed.

This security agreement will also incorporate a charge on the film in favour of the guarantor for any sums advanced by it under the guarantee, plus interest. This 'mortgage' on the film will be subject to the security of the other financiers under the financing agreements, so the completion guarantor will not recover any money until after the financiers have been paid in full. The director will also sign a contract confirming that the film can be shot within the agreed period and budget.

You will also be expected to enter into agreement to accept

responsibility for any costs in excess of the budget which are outside the range of the completion guarantor's responsibilities. These will include publicity, music and sometimes legal and finance charges if these are not included in the budget. There are exclusions that you are not responsible for legitimate excess costs on artists' remuneration and expenses, such as those payable because of an extended shooting schedule. An example of illegitimate expenses would be if you contracted to pay the artists fees in excess of those agreed in your budget. Even though the completion guarantor's liability is reduced in this way, these terms between you and the completion guarantor do not affect the validity of the guarantee.

A completion guarantee will not be issued until the completion guarantor is satisfied that all the documentation is in order.

4.5 Co-production

4.5.1 Principles of co-production

The term 'co-production' is widely used as part of the producer's vocabulary to describe a number of different types of collaboration in which you work with other people who contribute something to the production in return for some share in its income or for specified rights. The most common form involves the contribution of facilities and/or personnel by the co-producer in exchange for rights in a particular territory. There are variations, with the co-producer providing cash as well as non-cash contributions, and others where the contribution is totally financial. These include the different types of co-financing arrangements in the form of pre-sales/pre-purchases and co-financing ventures.

A pre-sale/pre-purchase is distinguishable from a co-production; a co-producer contributes to the creative fabric of the production by providing personnel, performers, facilities, etc., whereas a pre-sale/purchase is an agreement by a broadcaster or distributor to purchase a film for agreed rights in the territory concerned when it is completed and delivered. A pre-sale/purchase is distinguishable from a co-financing venture in which the co-financier contributes his cash input during the course of the production according to an agreed cash-flow. This avoids the need to use a bank discounting facility. The co-financier may be a straight equity investor seeking a return on his investment from sales of the film and/or acquiring certain rights plus an interest in the equity in the film.

As financing structures for films become increasingly complex there must be a parallel development within the financing institutions, particularly in relation to discounting techniques, if funds are to be available during production.

All the above distinctions can be blurred in practice, as they are in the case of Channel 4, for example, and every deal will include a different combination of the elements discussed above.

What is important to you are the practical implications of each arrangement: what creative involvement the co-producer will demand, how much money and/or what facilities it will contribute and at what point during the production the contribution will be made.

4.5.2 Co-production agreements: financial arrangements

You must make sure that the co-producer does not cost you more than it brings to the production. Remember that all the contributors to a film, whether actors, musicians, composers, writers, etc., expect compensation for their services and contributions related to the rights you acquire. If you are granting the co-producer rights in a territory the co-producer should be responsible for clearing those rights itself or the money provided by it should cover the necessary clearances. This means careful budgeting. You gain nothing if you pre-sell the rights to a video distributor for worldwide distribution on video for £100,000 and have to pay out £110,000 to clear the underlying rights. This may seem ridiculous, but it *does* happen. Remember, too, that distributors and broadcasters will expect certain specified delivery items under the terms of their contracts. You must ensure that the budget is sufficient to cover all these items, otherwise you will be forced to pay these costs out of your own pocket to comply with these contractual obligations.

If the co-producer is contributing money during the production this should be payable within a specified time. To be of any use to you this money must be available when you need it in accordance with a defined payment schedule. It goes without saying that any delays in these payments will cause great difficulties for you during production.

The recoupment by investors and profit by investors and contributors, the director, artists, etc., is always a matter for negotiation. The greater the number of parties involved, the more complex will be these negotiations and the chain of contracts that reflect the final agreement. If you offer to the contributors percentages of 'net' or 'gross' profits, it is crucial during negotiations that all these terms are clearly defined and incorporated in all relevant contracts. At the outset it must be stressed that all definitions in this section are open to interpretation and none is carved in tablets of stone.

As we have seen, there can be a variety of investors in a film. The following is an example of the way the whole thing can work.

A film has total budgeted costs of £1 million with three co-producers investing: A and B investing £300,000 each and C investing £400,000. The certified or negative costs of the production up to the delivery of the film amount to the budgeted £1 million.

These costs include:

- 'Below the line' costs, such as production costs, facilities, materials, equipment and personnel.
- 'Above the line' costs, such as services of performers, writers, directors, producers, and the cost of acquiring rights.
- Indirect costs, such as legal, accountancy and financial fees.
- Completion guarantor's fee, say 6 per cent of the above and below the line costs.
- A production fee, paid to the production company.
- The built-in contingency element of between 5 and 10 per cent of the budget and used to cover unforeseen costs. For the purposes of this example we will assume that the contingency element is used during production.

You should assume here that there are no copyright or residuals payable on the exercise of the distributor's rights, and all initial delivery items have been covered in the budget. Distribution expenses are advanced by the distributor and recovered out of distribution revenues before remitting the balance to the producer. This will be the 'distributor's net' or the 'producers' gross'.

The producers' gross will now have to be distributed. The investors A, B and C may share on a *pari passu* basis, that is, on equal terms pro rata to their respective investments. This means that from the first £1 in, C receives 40p, A 30p and B 30p until each has recovered its original investment plus interest. Alternatively, investor C may negotiate to recover part of its investment from the producers' gross, say £100,000, before any division of the producers' net, at which point the investors will share *pari passu*, in this case, 33½p in the £ as C's exposure has now been reduced to the same level as A's and B's. Another variation might be that C may be a broadcaster who will offset half of its investment for the broadcasting rights, and will therefore only take a share in the distributor's gross on the basis of a contribution of £200,000. Clearly there is scope for imaginative variations on the recoupment of investments. It is only once the financial contributors have recovered their investment and agreed interest that the film is said to break even, and after that is in net profit. As the producer your agreement with the financiers will specify the proportions in which profits will be shared. Usually 50/50 is the starting point for negotiations.

You may have agreed to pay artists or writers a share in net profits. If possible, this should come out of net profits before division between you and the financiers. However, they may insist that it comes from your share. It is vital that you ensure your agreements with artists and distributors and financiers all connect. If they don't, it may make the difference between a profit and a loss.

This may appear to be fairly straightforward. Unfortunately in practice matters will be complicated by the introduction of various other payments which may be paid from either producers' gross or producers' net, subject to negotiation. Payments from producers' gross are more secure, and are known in the industry as recoupment in the first position. Whether payments are made from producers' gross or producers' net depends on the negotiating power of the party wanting payment.

The following are some of the things that may be deducted from producers' gross or producers' net receipts:

Overcost

These are costs not covered in the original budget, or included in the contingency provision and *not* advanced by the completion guarantor. These costs may be advanced by one of the financiers or by the producer. There may be provision in the financing agreement for the advancement and recovery of overcost or it may be the subject of a supplementary agreement negotiated in the context of the particular circumstances that led to the overspend. The financier of the overspend will almost invariably seek to recover these funds in first position. If you have contracted to advance these costs, make sure you recover them before any income is distributed.

The contingency: if this is used it may be treated as overcost and recoverable by the financier of the overspend from the first receipts before recoupment of the negative cost. In this case the negative cost should be defined to exclude the contingency element.

Deferred payments and royalties

It is not unusual for writers, producers and artists, and in some cases other personnel, to receive royalties calculated as a proportion of net profits or producers' net. These may be paid before division between the producer and the financier, or from the producers' share of the net profits. Producers, artists and technical personnel may also receive deferred payments out of producers' gross. There may also be deferred payments to facilities houses. In theory, deferred payments fall into two categories: they may be fees due for work done, the payment of which is deferred until after the production is over in order to keep down the budgeted costs, or they may be regarded as an investment in the production, with payments being recognition of the participation in the risk. In practice the distinction is blurred, and is subject to negotiation. Where you or anyone else is accepting a lower fee than normal, then the deferred payments should be paid out of producers' gross, so that they are made before any profits are distributed.

The calculation of the amount payable may be either that of a fixed total or an amount calculated by reference to receipts, on a fixed or sliding scale. Whether deferred payments, including royalties, are calculated by reference to producers' gross, producers' net or net profits is entirely a matter for negotiation. Whatever agreement you reach with artists, distributors and co-producers, all agreements must be mutually compatible. Some bankable artists want to receive a proportion of income received from the film on a gross basis. The sums due to them will be deducted before producers' gross is arrived at, and are *not* royalties. Provision must be made in all the distribution contracts to ensure these deductions occur at the appropriate point and are accounted for correctly to the beneficiaries. In the same way the production agreements must specify that these deductions are to be made before the investors participate in producers' gross.

Distribution expenses

In the example it was assumed that all copyright clearance fees and residuals had been paid as part of the negative costs of the film. This may not always be the case and therefore provision must be made in all financing agreements for the advancement and deduction of these payments. Make sure wherever possible that you are not responsible for making these payments. If, however, you are responsible for them, you should ensure that you receive the first income in the form of distributor's net or producers' gross from which you can advance these payments. In addition, these payments should be treated as distribution expenses and as such should be deducted from producers' gross before arriving at net profit. You should not fund these costs out of your share of net profits.

The same principles apply in relation to delivery requirements, i.e. the production of publicity materials, colour reversal inter-negatives, prints, music and effects tracks, or all items not covered in the original budget. The cost of manufacturing these items should be:

- borne by the distributor and recovered out of distributor's gross before remitting the distributor's net/producers' gross to the financiers, *or*
- advanced by one of the financiers and recovered as distribution expenses as a first charge on the producers' gross or as part of the financier's investment to be recovered in accordance with the recoupment schedule.

Producers' credit from completion guarantee fee

If there is a credit of no claims bonus this will reduce the negative cost of the film. The amount of the credit may be treated as part of the producers' gross receipts to be applied in accordance with the production agreement.

Completion guarantor

If the completion guarantor advances money in order to complete the delivery of the film, then these sums, together with interest, will be recoverable out of producers' gross. The completion guarantor will take a low recoupment position. Usually this is after the financiers/investors have recouped their investment and before the deferees. If the original guarantor's fees have been charged on a budget including deferments it may even recoup after the deferees.

4.5.3 Co-production agreements: other provisions

The advantages of co-production are obviously financial ones. Films are expensive to make and this is an efficient way of financing them. The disadvantages are significant, but less obvious. They can be mitigated by understanding and pre-empting the more common problems.

Copyright

Copyright in a film is automatically vested in the person or company who is responsible for making the arrangements for its production. If your co-producer has played a significant part in making the arrangements, then it may be in a position to claim that the copyright should be owned jointly or solely owned by it in specified territories. This means that neither party can use the film without the consent of the other, so the contract should specify exactly how each co-producer may use the film. This should not only include territorial and media uses but also establish whether each party can use the film freely within its territory. If you do agree to joint ownership of the copyright, then you should ensure that you are entitled to make unrestricted use of it in your territories without further reference to the other joint owner.

Editorial control

Unless you are going to the expense of making two different versions of the same film it is important to establish editorial policy very clearly from the start. The editorial problems increase where the project is complex or innovative, and every effort must be made throughout the production to try to recognize and reconcile the interests of the various parties involved. The facts of life are that the requirements of two or more broadcasters and the requirements of a broadcaster and a distributor are different. For example, when Channel 4 commissions a programme for a one-hour slot length it expects a programme of between fifty-one and fifty-two minutes, whereas on TV-PBS in the USA they are looking for a fifty-eight-minute programme.

Areas of responsibility

The co-producers must put together a team that can produce the film effectively. Problems arising with the allocation of editorial control and other authority will manifest themselves in an accumulation of personnel with conflicting responsibilities. Everyone's role must be defined from the start in order to avoid this. It is particularly important that the director should not be caught between incompatible demands.

Insurance

Establish who is responsible for what and make sure that all your production risks are covered. In law a co-producer is liable for any loss or damage while holding the film or tapes. Although materials in the possession of the co-producer are its responsibility it may not take out insurance itself. Large organizations, particularly, tend to regard themselves as their own insurance. It is therefore very important that provision for insurance is included in your contracts with your co-producer/s.

Communications

The difficulties of producing a film are exacerbated by sharing the responsibility with another unfamiliar organization whose responses to particular problems are unpredictable. Regular discussions and meetings are essential as well as generally friendly relations so that these inevitable difficulties do not make the project unworkable.

General note

All the above points, except the last, can and should be dealt with in your co-production contract. This should be in place before shooting.

4.5.4 Co-production partners

Equity investment or risk finance

An equity co-producer/financier invests for profit on a strictly commercial basis, taking account of the likely returns from sales of the film and the risks of non-completion or poor sales. Straight equity investors are very rare indeed, not surprisingly given the special nature of the film and television industry. It is difficult to assess accurately the risks involved. They can write off part of their contribution against the rights they acquire in their accounts and for taxation purposes. The broadcasters and distributors are the most likely investors because they employ personnel who are in a better position to assess the commercial viability of a project than someone outside the industry. In order to make film investment attractive to the corporate and private investor, there must be the opportunity for tax write-offs to reduce their financial exposure.

The BBC

The BBC tends to operate in the same way as foreign broadcasters, using co-production as a way of attracting cash for productions for which they do not have all the necessary cash elements. However, in recent years the co-production finance injected into production through the BBC's co-production department has grown substantially from £5 million in 1981/2 to £15 million in 1984/5, the latter made up of £12 million in cash and £3 million in non-cash elements such as scripts, performances and facilities. This seems like good news for the independent producer, but unfortunately the BBC generally collaborates with other broadcasters and distributors including its own Enterprises Division. For example, it has a guaranteed co-production partner in the US Arts and Entertainment Network for certain programmes. This basic cable operation reaches 13 million homes in North America and has first options on all music, arts, light entertainment and dramatized documentary projects. The BBC has long-standing arrangements with Australia, Japan and other European broadcasters, all of which combine to make a fixed structure which can be difficult to penetrate.

The increasing political and financial pressures experienced by the BBC may force it to open its doors further to the independent sector. You can approach the BBC through a number of different routes. The general manager of the Co-Production Department itself will refer you to the appropriate individual with editorial decision-making powers. The most common route is through the heads of the production departments, in either London or the major production centres. Once the project has been evaluated according to editorial criteria it will be passed to the Co-Production Department for financial assessment and the commencement of contractual negotiations. An alternative approach is through a larger production company or distributor with an established track record of working with the BBC who will umbrella your project and get it off the ground. Finally, you can approach the BBC's Acquisitions Department to pre-purchase rights to your film. If you pursue this route you will have to be involved in some kind of co-production arrangement with a third party financier or producer, as the sums paid by the BBC are unlikely to cover the full production costs.

Although the BBC is a non-profit-making organization, this does not mean it ignores the ratio between your co-producer's contribution and the rights you retain. Any profit share will be payable to BBC Enterprises and will be negotiated in the light of the respective financial exposure of the BBC, yourself and other investors in the film.

Channel 4

Channel 4 is a cash business. It does not make or produce programmes, therefore it does not, strictly speaking, co-produce them; rather, it 100 per cent finances them or co-finances them. As already explained, co-financing may take the form of a pre-sale/pre-purchase or a co-financing venture. In the case of Channel 4 the distinction between the two has become blurred. On the financial side Channel 4 requires approval of the budget whatever the nature of its involvement with an uncompleted film. Channel 4 is prepared to inject cash during production to bridge the gap left by unaccommodating city institutions. Hence the Channel will pre-purchase the rights to a film for a set number of transmissions in the UK and will also inject cash at the outset of the production provided it has approved the budget and the other financiers. It will negotiate an equity position plus a profit participation in the net profits from the film and write off part of its contribution against what it would have paid for a licence for a UK transmission. This sum will be the value it places on the UK television rights. On the creative side, too, the distinction is blurred because the Channel wishes to have editorial involvement in programmes whether they are pre-purchased or co-financed. The film, once delivered, must meet with the requirements of a particular commissioning editor. Through its commissioning department, Channel 4 seeks to show to its UK audience the best of film and television from throughout the world. It is more interested in collaborating with partners with similar programme objectives than in obtaining programmes of an 'international' style. Your initial approach to the Channel will be through one of its commissioning departments. You may be looking for 100 per cent of the finance initially, but the project can become a co-production if Channel 4 is only putting up part of the financing. This will happen when a particular commissioning editor wishes to commission a project but does not have sufficient funds available within their budget. In these circumstances Channel 4 will issue a letter of intent to you stating that, subject to your raising the rest of the budget within a specified time, the Channel will commit a particular sum to the project. This letter can be very useful when you are approaching other financiers who will almost invariably want to see some evidence of such a prior commitment before committing themselves.

Channel 4 has established links with a number of broadcasters, particularly within Europe. Because of their bureaucratic nature, the broadcasters have developed a style of collaboration that requires contact to be made on the broadcaster to broadcaster level. They will negotiate complex agreements based on long-term commitment to commission jointly and exchange a portfolio of films and programmes over a number of years. These arrangements can extend the range of contacts you are in a position to initiate yourself. One of the most elaborate and high-profile schemes has been the coming together of six television companies – Channel 4, Antenne 2 (France), ORF (Austria), RAI (Italy), SRG/SSR (Switzerland), and ZDF (The Federal Republic of Germany) – to establish a European programme group principally for the production of single dramas and drama series.

Whatever the nature of the final co-financing agreements with Channel 4, you will find yourself liaising between the business side of the Channel, the acquisitions and financial departments, and the commissioning editors before a contract is signed. Channel 4 is an obvious choice as a co-financing partner, but you must be prepared for long delays.

Foreign broadcasters

It may sound rather perverse, but foreign broadcasters will invest more substantial sums in films which are not completed and they have not seen than they will for completed films that they have seen. They are prepared to pre-purchase the rights to films for up to ten times what they will pay once the film is finished. Thus there are potentially great rewards for you if you succeed in co-producing with a broadcaster (see the discussion of working with TV-PBS in the USA pp. 223–7). Broadcasters tend to choose projects which have a particular connection with or relevance to their audience profile. In the case of a foreign broadcaster this will include subject matter relevant to or associated with their own country. The production itself must meet the broadcasting standards, both legal and technical, laid down for domestic productions, and fulfil the editorial requirements of the contracting broadcaster. For you, caught in the middle, the areas of compromise can prove to be most uncomfortable.

On the whole broadcasters, because of the number of personnel they employ and facilities they control, prefer their contributions to be in non-cash elements. Thus they will turn to you to provide a substantial amount of the cash resources together with the rights to a published work, for example.

Foreign production companies and International Co-production Treaties

You may collaborate with an overseas-based producer who contributes its share of the budget in a variety of different ways, for example facilities, services, personnel or perhaps an option on a published work. Most significantly a foreign-based producer may have access to funds from local broadcasters and distributors based on an established track record with them. The co-producer may also be eligible for public funds in the form of subsidies and grants, or private investment because of tax-based incentives which encourage investment in national films.

Various schemes are used throughout the world to encourage or sustain indigenous film production. There are several ways in which governments intervene to assist their film industries and these measures are used individually or in combination:

– Direct investment in production.

- Subsidies to film producers for films on release.
- Tax concessions on certain production costs.
- Tax concessions on different revenues which usually permit an amount to be recovered free of tax.
- Preferential treatment for indigenous productions on theatrical release either by support to exhibitors and distributors in the form of tax rebates *or*
- Quotas restricting the number of foreign films that can be imported and exhibited.
- Fiscal measures, tax incentives encouraging investment in films by allowing investors, corporate or individual, to write off the investment against their tax liabilities.

The key to all of the available benefits is whether the film qualifies according to the appropriate legislation as a certified French/Norwegian/Canadian production. (See BSFC for British certification, p. 98.) One way for you to take advantage of these measures would be to set up, for example, a French or Norwegian company to produce the film. An alternative route would be to utilize one of the five official Co-production Treaties existing between the UK and the following countries: Canada, Norway, France, Italy and Germany. The purpose of the treaties is to enable the producer to obtain finance from the BSFC and collaborate with, say, a French producer who has received funds from the Centre National de la Cinématographie Française (CNC), or perhaps via a tax shelter company, thereby raising sufficient funds to cover the budget. It must be emphasized that the applicable rules in each country are complex and subject to frequent changes. Sometimes government officials are given discretionary powers to decide in individual cases whether there is sufficient national content for a particular film to qualify for grants and relief.

It should be noted that in the five years 1980–5 there have been only five films made under the official Co-production Treaties: France – *Tess*, registered 1981, and *Lady Chatterley's Lover*, registered 1980; Germany – *Radio On*, registered 1980; Canada – *Murder By Decree*, registered 1980, and *Death Ship*, registered 1981. This is a reflection of two problems. Firstly, the legal and administrative difficulties of satisfying the provisions of the Treaties, and secondly, and perhaps more significantly, the lack of incentives in this country present few financial attractions to foreign producers wishing to collaborate with their UK counterparts.

Deferred production and facilities fees

If you cannot raise enough finance to cover all production costs, you may be forced to defer the fees due to you or your production company, that is, the profit element in the budget representing, in part, the business overheads incurred by your company during production. If you defer all or part of these fees you should try to negotiate a first recoupment position together with a fixed percentage of interest.

Some facilities companies, laboratories, sound studios and dubbing theatres may be prepared to contribute their services at favourable rates or even free in return for a deferment, a share of the net profit. However, this is very rare indeed. It will be easier to obtain such facilities from the broadcaster, who may make their contribution to the budget in the form of non-cash elements.

The distributors

Pre-sales to theatrical and video distributors are important sources of co-finance monies for feature films. (See Bank finance and Distribution, p. 110 and pp. 207–23.) As partners they may be easier to deal with than the broadcasters as they are not tied to annual budgets and can, at least in theory, make decisions faster. The extent of their editorial involvement will vary depending on a number of factors, not least their contribution to the budget relative to the other financiers. Their contribution may be contingent upon particular star names playing lead roles.

It remains to be seen whether, with increased competition from the different media such as cable and satellite, they will be more inclined to pre-purchase rights to secure them in a particular territory at the earliest stages of production.

5
EMPLOYMENT

5.1 General employment law

In most circumstances your relationship with the people whom you pay to work on your production will be determined by the various union agreements which apply in the film industry. However, there are general principles which apply whether you are using a union agreement or are negotiating individual contracts. These will affect the legal nature of your contracts by inserting implied terms and granting statutory rights which cannot be overridden by agreement between you and your employees.

5.1.1 Employees and independent contractors

If you pay a person to do something for you, that person may be either an employee or an independent contractor. The difference is difficult to define but important, as different laws apply. Employees have additional rights granted to them by law, and greater obligations are imposed on their employers.

An independent contractor makes a contract to carry out a particular task, and can do so in any way, provided that the task is completed in accordance with the terms of the contract. An employee makes a contract to serve the employer personally and to carry out any jobs which the employer directs, provided that they are within any limitations contained in the contract. Because contracts with employees or independent contractors can impose precise limitations on what they are to do and how they are to do it, the difference between them may not be immediately obvious. For example, if you want some publicity material produced you may contract with a public relations consultant to produce it, specifying what types of material you want, when you want it, and how much you will pay. The consultant will be an independent contractor. Alternatively you may employ someone for a fixed period and also tell them what material to produce, when and how much they will be paid. They will be your employees. If the material is not delivered you will have different remedies. You can refuse to pay independent contractors, or sue them to recover anything you have already paid, but your remedy against your employees will be to sack or demote them. Independent contractors are in business on their own account and are expected to bear the loss if anything goes wrong. Employees, even if they participate in a profit-sharing agreement or receive royalties, are part of their employer's business and take no risks except as part of that business.

If it is not absolutely clear whether the relationship is one of an employer and employee or an independent contractor these are some of the factors which would suggest that the relationship was that of an employer and employee:

- A high degree of control exercised over what work is done, when and how, and working for one individual at a time.
- The regular arrangement, including any unwritten understanding that work will be provided.
- Equipment is provided by the employer.
- The employer takes all the financial risks and arranges all insurance against other risks.

You will recall that copyright in an artistic work is obtained by the first owner. This is normally the creator, but where that creator is an employee of another individual, the copyright will be owned by the employer. Although some of your personnel may be employed, it is likely that much of the creative input will be from independent contractors, such as writers, art directors and performers, commissioned to make specific contributions. Copyright in those contributions will remain with them unless you contract to obtain it. To avoid any possible doubt, all your contracts with personnel should include a provision that the copyright in any creative contribution to the production will be owned by you. Even technical personnel may make an artistic contribution, capable of being copyright. Many contributors, such as composers or writers, will not grant you the copyright, but may license you to use specific aspects of it. It is then for you to negotiate with them to obtain the rights you require.

5.1.2 Taxation

The most immediate reason why you must know the difference between employees and independent contractors is because different rules apply to each of them for the payment of income tax and National Insurance contributions. Employers act as tax collectors from their employees. They must deduct income tax in accordance with the PAYE scheme, and also retain their employees' National Insurance contributions from their gross pay. The employee only receives net pay from the employer. The amounts deducted must be paid periodically by the employer to the Inland Revenue and Department of Health and Social Security (DHSS).

Independent contractors have a significant advantage over employers in that they are entitled to be taxed as self-employed under Schedule D. This means that they are paid gross, without tax or National Insurance contributions being deducted from their income. They pay their own National Insurance contributions and are assessed for income tax on their income, less expenses, over the financial year. Not only does this allow them to use the money which will become due as tax until they have to pay it, but it also allows the opportunity for 'creative accounting' and straightforward tax evasion.

For many years large numbers of people in the film industry have enjoyed the advantage of being treated by the Inland Revenue as independent contractors entitled to pay income tax under Schedule D. This is now changing, and the Inland Revenue have issued a new list of personnel whom it will now regard as legitimately self-employed and entitled to be taxed under Schedule D. As an employer you must adhere to this list. If you pay someone gross pay in the expectation that they will make their own Schedule D tax return but are wrong, the Inland Revenue can still seek to recover from you the amount of tax which should have been paid under the PAYE scheme.

5.1.3 Employers' duties

The law imposes on employers duties towards their employees. Some of these reflect good industrial relations practice, others are intended to protect employees from unscrupulous exploitation and abuse.

You must always act reasonably towards your employees. This does not prohibit you from criticizing them, but this must be in proportion. You should not indulge in Cecil B. de Mille acts of egocentric rage and hurl abuse at someone over the temperature of your tea. Even without your having used the magic words, 'You're fired', someone may be entitled to treat themselves as constructively dismissed, and may legally decide to, just when it does not suit you.

A more important duty is to ensure the safety of your employees, by providing adequate equipment and a safe system of working, including competent colleagues. Film sets, studios and locations can be dangerous places with heavy equipment, dark areas, cables across the ground and constant movement. It is your duty to ensure that they are no more dangerous than they need to be. It is also in your interests to do so, because if as a consequence an employee is injured you will have to pay compensation. Employers' liability insurance may also be void if conditions are unsafe.

Employees are entitled to be paid for any expenses which they incur in the course of their employment. They cannot deduct expenses from their tax liability like independent contractors. You should ensure that any contract explicitly states those items which you will regard as legitimate expenses and reimburse.

Employers are also obliged to administer the government's Statutory Sick Pay (SSP) scheme. This requires them to pay SSP to employees, and to apply to the DHSS for reimbursement of the amount of SSP which they are obliged by law to pay. If they pay more than this they must cover the cost of the balance.

5.1.4 Employees' duties

Employees' duties are mainly implied by law as necessary to ensure that the employee carries out the contract properly and in person. They include a duty to carry out reasonable and lawful instructions and to take reasonable care in doing so. By entering into the contract of employment the employees imply that they are personally competent to carry out the work. Incompetence is grounds for dismissal, subject to appropriate warnings and notice periods. Dangerous incompetence may also result in your being liable for damage or injuries caused by your employee to other employees or third parties. Employers are vicariously liable for damage or injuries caused by their employees in the course of their employment, even if they are caused by an employee doing the work in a way which was expressly forbidden. Once again, insurance is absolutely essential.

Employees owe a duty of honesty and confidentiality to their employers. The duty of confidentiality prohibits the revelation of information obtained during the course of their employment, not only during that employment, but after it has come to an end. The circumstances in which confidentiality may exist and be enforced are discussed in detail in the section dealing with restrictions on programme content (see p. 190).

5.1.5 Employees' rights and protection

Employment rights

Under the Employment Protection (Consolidation) Act, as much amended, employees can acquire various rights after specified periods of employment. The nature of these rights and the qualifying periods are complex. Most of them will only affect you if you will have an employee working for you continuously for a period of two years, including any time in a business you have acquired. These include rights to maternity pay and leave, and protection from dismissal for other than specified reasons, such as unavoidable redundancy.

Employees all quickly acquire rights to a minimum period of notice, which is one week after four weeks' employment and one extra week per additional year after the first, up to a maximum of 12 weeks. They also acquire a right after twelve weeks to a statement of written terms and conditions of employment.

Discrimination on grounds of sex and race

One of the duties which Parliament has taken upon itself in recent decades is the reduction of discrimination against particular sections of the population. This is a reaction to the existence of discrimination and also a response to EEC directives. The main Acts aimed against discrimination against women in employment on the grounds of their sex are the Equal Pay Act 1970 and the Sex Discrimination Act 1975. Discrimination in employment on the grounds of race is covered by the Race Relations Act 1976.

The Sex Discrimination Act and the Race Relations Act contain similar provisions and it is possible to deal with them together, although the Sex Discrimination Act does not apply to employers with five employees or less. It is unlawful for an employer to discriminate on the grounds of race, gender or marital status when:

- advertising a job, considering applications, or offering the job to the applicant
- promoting or transferring employees or offering them training
- dismissing employees or making them redundant.

The discrimination need not be direct. It includes putting a condition on employment which it would be more difficult for a particular racial or gender group to fulfil. If a significantly smaller proportion of one group could fulfil the condition, the condition would constitute unlawful discrimination. The limitations imposed by the Acts appear to be a problem when you are casting. However, there are exceptions to the Acts. Discrimination is not unlawful where the condition required is a 'genuine occupational qualification'. It is important to note that reverse discrimination is not lawful in Britain, and policies which are intended to maintain for example ethnic minority groups may also be unlawful.

Discrimination by employers on grounds of sexual orientation or physical disability is not unlawful. However, there have been successful cases for unfair dismissal, where people have been dismissed on the grounds of sexual orientation or physical disability when this did not in fact affect their ability to do their job.

The Equal Pay Act enables employees to take action against employers if the terms of their employment are not as good as those of another employee whose work is:

- equivalent
- rated as equivalent
- of equal value.

It covers not only the amount of pay but also the conditions of employment, and to an extent overlaps with the Sex Discrimination Act. The only grounds on which inequality is justifiable are:

– to comply with the law.
– conditions which favour women in relation to pregnancy and childbirth.

An employee who considers that he/she is being unfairly treated can take a case to an employment tribunal. The tribunal will decide whether there is unfairness by comparing the treatment of the person applying to the tribunal with the treatment of another employee. There must be an actual person actually or recently employed with whom the applicant can be compared. They need not do an identical job but it must be similar enough to allow comparison.

Performers' Protection Acts 1958–72

Under these Acts it is a criminal offence to make an audio and/or visual record or broadcast or transmission of an artist's performance without their written consent, or to sell, hire or otherwise exploit these recordings or broadcasts. It is therefore essential that all performers are contracted in writing before production of the film. Normally a performer's contract will refer to these Acts very briefly, saying that the performer gives the producer all the consents required by the Performers' Protection Acts 1958–72. Infringement of these Acts is, for instance, the making of an unauthorized recording of a live performance, commonly known as bootlegging. There is no civil remedy for this offence and it is often felt that penalties are too low to make private criminal prosecution for bootlegging worthwhile.

Children

For the purposes of the law a child is any person who has not completed compulsory full-time education. This means anyone below the age of sixteen, or anyone who has not completed the appropriate school term following their sixteenth birthday. Children are protected by various statutes, including the Children and Young Persons Act 1933, the Children and Young Persons Act 1963, and the Children (Performances) Regulations 1965. Licences are required for the employment of children under sixteen, and there are also specific restrictions applicable to children under fourteen. Under the Children and Young Persons

Act 1963, a licence must be granted by a local authority for a child to take part in:

- any performance in connection with which a charge is made (whether for admission or otherwise)
- any performance in premises licensed under the Licensing Acts 1953 and 1961 and the Licensing (Scotland) Act 1959
- in any broadcast performance
- any performance included in a cable programme service
- in any performance recorded (by whatever means) with a view to its use in a broadcast or a film intended for public exhibition.

A child is considered to be taking part in a performance if it takes the part of a performer for a rehearsal or for preparation for a recording of a performance. Penalties for major infringements of the Act and Regulations, such as failure to procure a licence or to observe its conditions or failure to produce relevant records and take statements made in application for a licence, can be fines or imprisonment.

Licences are not granted to a child under fourteen unless:

- the licence is for acting and the application for the licence is accompanied by a statement that the part to be performed cannot be performed except by a child of its age.
- the licence is for dancing in a ballet which does not form part of anything other than a ballet or opera and the application for the licence is accompanied by a declaration that the part to be danced can only be taken by a child of about its age.

A licence is not needed if:

- the arrangements for the performance are made by a school or other organization approved by the Home Office and no payment is made to the child or anyone on its behalf except for expenses.
- the child does not take part in performances for more than three days in any six month period.

The local authority will not grant a licence unless it is satisfied that the child is fit to perform and that proper provision has been made to secure its health and kind treatment, that both its education will not suffer and any money earned is protected.

A licence may be granted only in accordance with the rules contained within the Children (Performances) Regulations. The Regulations contain detailed rules concerning the welfare of children for whose services a licence has been granted. They include place and hours of work, rehearsal accommodation, chaperoning, medical examination and protection of earnings.

As producer, you would be responsible for applying for a licence from the local education authority covering the area in which the child lives. Application for a child who lives abroad should be made to the local authority in which you are located. Applications should be made at least twenty-one days before the date of the child's first performance. Application forms require comprehensive details of the child's services. It must be signed by the applicant and also by the child's parent or guardian on its behalf. The licence will also require the applicant to maintain certain records of the child's employment which must be kept for six months after the last relevant performance for inspection by an official on demand. A licence can be granted for a maximum of three months and can be renewed, revoked or varied at the authority's discretion.

Responsibility for compliance with the licence rests with the applicant and its enforcement can be carried out by officials from the local authority and the police, both of whom have powers of entry to pursue inquiries.

A licence for a young person over fourteen but under the age of eighteen to perform abroad must be obtained with at least seven days' notice from the police court magistrate and not from the local authority.

Under the Children and Young Persons Act 1933, training a child under twelve for a dangerous performance is prohibited. Training is restricted to young people under the age of sixteen, subject to a licence from the local authority. Dangerous performances are not defined but they include acrobatics and contortions.

Although a contract for a child's services is usually binding if it is generally beneficial to the child, the parent or guardian should always be a signatory to the contract. This will lessen the risk that unfair advantage is taken of the child, help ensure compliance with the arrangements you may have made, and, as the signature of a parent or guardian must be added to any application for a licence, be consistent with the requirements of the Acts and Regulations.

Animals

The training and use of animals in performances is governed by the Performing Animals (Regulations) Act 1925. This provides that any animal trained and exhibited to the public, which includes any entertainment to which the public is admitted whether by payment or otherwise, must be registered. Registration and enforcement is administered by the local authority. The Protection of Animals Act 1911 includes comprehensive provisions making almost any form of cruelty to an animal a criminal offence. You should also be aware of the provisions of the Cinematograph Films (Animals) Act 1937, which are discussed below.

5.2 Provisions in employment contracts

5.2.1 The contracts

Most members of trade unions will be contracted under the standard terms and conditions set out in the applicable trade union agreement. These agreements are discussed below.

The services of certain individuals, however, such as principal artists, directors and senior personnel, may be negotiated and contracted for separately, although always subject to the conditions set by the relevant union. In these cases you will have to provide separate contracts. You should take advice from a film industry lawyer or use the legal services offered by your trade association. The following should be considered when drawing up contracts for any individual contributor to the film. Remember that contracts for the use of copyright material are separate from employment contracts.

Personal or company contracts An individual can be contracted either as a person directly or through a company which provides its services. The latter is used primarily for tax purposes and will compose a main contract for services that will be between the producer and the company on behalf of the individual. The company grants the individual's services for the film and the producer agrees to pay the company. In addition there is an 'inducement letter' in which the individual writes to the producer undertaking personally to honour the main contract.

Agency A contract can, with the individual's consent, be made with an authorized agent on his behalf. Payment is often made through the agent.

Payment The amount and times of payment should be clearly set out. If the work is to be carried out over a certain period then payment is often made in instalments, for instance, part on signature and part on completion of the work with possibly an intermediate payment which allows the person concerned to commit their time with confidence. If the production is cancelled then payments due up to the cancellation must be made and this will be insurable. It is important that people who commit time and work to a production are properly paid, whatever the outcome of the film, unless they have agreed to defer payments. If the person is registered for VAT this should be noted in the contract. If payment is to be made in a foreign currency this should be specified, and also a date for any rate of exchange should be fixed as this will fluctuate.

Any expenses to be paid should be set out in detail in the contract so that there is no possibility of an argument with the performers.

Description of services You must set out in detail what the contracted individual is required to do. This will include the following:
- job description, for example dancer;
- dates on which services are required subject to the producer's right to alter them, if necessary;
- description of duties including attendances at camera rehearsals and during editing or for post-production publicity;
- the title of the person to whom the individual is responsible, for example director or executive producer.

Performers' Protection Acts If the individual is a performer, then written consent under the Performers' Protection Act 1958–72 is required. The contract need only say that 'the artist gives all consents under the Performers' Protection Act 1958–72'.

Copyright Certain people may contribute a copyright element to the film, e.g. there is copyright in a director's camera script, and for these you should require that the copyright in the product of their services belongs to you as producer.

The grant of rights and consents Media, use, territories and period covered by the contract should be set out and any limitations should be clearly stated.

Special conditions Sometimes a producer may wish to impose special conditions to ensure the availability and value of the performers' contributions. Sometimes a limited exclusivity is justifiable, but this must never be prejudicial to the individuals' livelihood or career. If an individual is prominent and central to the film it is important that the film is not unnecessarily put at risk by that individual during the contractual term. Leading artists are therefore sometimes forbidden to indulge in dangerous sports or fly private aircraft. Whether it is necessary to include such a provision depends on the reputation of the artist. Financiers and completion guarantors may require such a provision to protect themselves.

Credits Very often this will be obvious, but sometimes special credits are justified. These should be specified in the contract. The variations and problems with credits are dealt with in Chapter 8.

Termination The contract should indicate what will happen if it were to be terminated. A contract could be terminated or suspended and this can happen if the producer is forced to abandon or suspend the production for instance as a result of a *force majeure* event. In this case the person concerned should be paid for his commitment of time and work. The contract could also indicate that it may also be terminated at no obligation to the producer if the person is in breach of their obligations in the contract, but this is contractually implied anyway.

5.2.2 Negotiation

In many cases you will have to negotiate with an agent acting for an artist. Whether you are negotiating with an agent or directly with an individual, an understanding of that person's point of view is essential. When you are negotiating you should do the following:

- Explain as much as possible about your production, and the role of the individual whose services you are seeking to use. The more the other person understands what you are trying to do, the more sympathetic the response is likely to be. Negotiation is really all about communication. Keep the lines open.

- While negotiating, put as much as possible in writing, by taking notes. Keep an accurate dated record of telephone conversations.
- Start negotiating in good time. Aim to have the contract signed before that person does any work, and before you use any copyright material otherwise you may be in breach of the Performers' Protection Acts or copyright legislation.
- People without agents should be treated fairly and as if they were represented.
- People who fulfil similar functions in your film should be paid similar amounts. They will get together during the shoot and make comparisons. Blatant unfairness will cause problems on the set and is a false economy.

5.3 Trade unions and collective agreements

5.3.1 The use of agreements

Most people who are contracted to work on a film are members of a trade union or trade association and sometimes both. In the case of trade unions an agreement must exist between the producer and the relevant union in respect of the film for the work of its members. This does not preclude the use of separately negotiated contracts for certain individuals of which the union will be aware, but most people will be contracted and paid on the terms set out in the applicable collective agreement.

5.3.2 The unions

The following are the trade unions whose members are most commonly employed in the production of film and video.

- Association of Cinematograph Television and Allied Technicians (ACTT)
- The British Actors' Equity Association (Equity)
- Broadcasting and Entertainment Trades Alliance (BETA)
- Electrical, Electronic, Telecommunications and Plumbing Union (EETPU)
- Film Artistes Association (FAA)
- The Musicians' Union (MU)
- The Writers' Guild of Great Britain

5.3.3 The applicable agreements and the negotiating bodies

Independent producers contract union members in accordance with existing current agreements between the unions and the following bodies:

- The British Film and Television Producers Association (BFTPA) and the Independent Programme Producers Association (IPPA) – jointly, *or*
- The Independent Television Companies – jointly, or
- The BBC

Which agreements are applicable depend in each case on the nature and context of your film or programme including, amongst other things, medium, budget, co-producer and source of finance. As the circumstances of each film vary so widely it is not possible to explain here which agreement will apply in any particular instance. You may find, for example, that if you are co-producing within the structure of the BBC or the Independent Television Companies that the agreements to which these bodies are party apply automatically. However, very often the best approach for your film or programme, whether co-produced, made for Channel 4 or independently financed, will be through the BFTPA/IPPA Joint Industrial Relations Service.

BFTPA/IPPA Joint Industrial Relations Service

The BFTPA and IPPA are joint parties to several trade union agreements which are made specifically for independent films and television programmes in certain contexts. Membership of either IPPA or the BFTPA gives an independent producer access to the Joint Industrial Relations Service (JIRS). The application of BFTPA/IPPA agreements and others as appropriate must be negotiated by an authorized negotiator from JIRS. If you are producing for Channel 4 you should be aware that you and not the Channel are responsible for reaching agreement with the unions. Channel 4 will not become directly involved with your negotiations, although JIRS does liaise with Channel 4.

It is essential that you start negotiations as soon as possible. If you wish to use agreements negotiated through JIRS you must join the BFTPA or IPPA at the earliest opportunity, and consult JIRS which will then be in a position to advise you, and may carry out negotiations on your behalf. Although linked by JIRS, IPPA and the BFTPA are separate and distinct employers' organizations which offer other facilities to their members. BFTPA is a very long-standing association which was established to represent producers of films primarily intended for theatrical release, with television exhibition as an ancillary concern. IPPA was established in the context of Channel 4 although it does represent other producers. Its primary concern is the production of programmes for television on film or tape. Your choice of BFTPA or IPPA depends therefore on the nature of your production and you should make enquiries of both organizations before deciding which is more suitable.

5.3.4 Application of the agreements

No attempt has been made here to give details of current available agreements as most of them are re-negotiated regularly and therefore change frequently. It is essential that you acquire the latest applicable agreement and read in full any agreement that you intend to use. The following, however, are some points which you should bear in mind:

- *Negotiation*: The application of any standard union agreement is not automatic, and its terms are negotiable. Negotiations should therefore take place in good time with the relevant unions or through JIRS if you are using its services.
- *Minimum terms*: The agreements specify minimum terms only and certain circumstances may justify the negotiation of higher payments. Personnel contracted on higher grades and principal artists may also be contracted at a higher rate than the minimum stated for the appropriate grade.
- *Payment*: Most union agreements have a complex payment structure in which a basic payment for a defined period or session of work is supplemented by payments for overtime, work on stated holidays, additional obligations and allowances, etc. These have to be calculated very carefully. Basic payment will often give the right to use the product of an individual's work in a specified way, i.e. to use the individual's work for a specified period and to exploit the film for two UK television transmissions. Additional exploitation will then attract additional payments which are often expressed as a percentage of a specified original payment. This is known as a residual payment. The specific original payment acts as a baseline for all future payments and should be identified as early as possible. Sometimes it is possible to buy out a number of different methods of exploitation.
- *Foreign personnel and work permits*: Nationals of non-EEC states can only be used if they are granted a work permit. This will only be given if the function fulfilled by the person in question cannot be performed by a UK national. Application forms are obtainable from IPPA, the BFTPA offices or the Department of Employment. Applications are sent as a matter of course to the appropriate union which may object and make

representations to the Department of Employment. Applications should be made at least one month before the person concerned is intended to be used for the film. UK union dues are payable by all foreign nationals in this context for the period of their involvement in the film. Proposed use of foreign nationals of both EEC and non-EEC states should be declared to JIRS as early as possible if you are using its services.

- *Restrictions on use*: Certain union agreements do not include the use of a film in a particular way, leaving a particular use entirely open to negotiation or establishing other restrictions. You should be aware of these and establish exactly how you wish to exploit your film before completing your negotiations. In this context it is important to note that many agreements do not allow the exploitation of a film in South Africa.
- *Other conditions*: Union agreements provide not only for terms of payment but also for conditions of work, which must be closely observed. These include hours worked, minimum staffing levels, specified breaks, limitation on dangerous performances, living and travelling conditions, etc.
- *Communication and information*: The observation and enforcement of union agreements are crucial to the successful production of a film. You must read and understand the relevant agreements before making a commitment to a production. Do not hesitate to make enquiries about their terms to the relevant negotiating body and/or trade union. Establish contact as early as possible and maintain communication throughout production. In this way everyone involved will have a better idea of what to expect and any problems can be anticipated in good time.

5.3.5 ACTT Code of Practice and the Workshop Declaration

The ACTT Code of Practice was drawn up in consultation with the RAAs, the Welsh Arts Council and the Distribution Division of the BFI, and the Workshop Declaration in consultation with the BFI, Channel 4, the RAAs and the Independent Film and Video Makers' Association (IFVA). These agreements recognize the cultural, educational and social contribution of grant-aided film and video, and take into account the fact that those working in this sector tend *not* to work as specialist technicians. The agreements build a wage element into work in this sector, and have helped to establish a solid base from which the non-commercial grant-aided sector can grow. The main advantage to you in using the Code of Practice and Workshop Declaration is access to network broadcasting time on Channel 4 and funding from Channel 4, without having to operate under the restrictions on the use of technical personnel imposed by other broadcasting agreements.

ACTT Code of Practice for grant-aided productions

This agreement covers grant-aided productions that are non-commercial, and relates to both individuals and groups and workshops not enfranchised by the ACTT. The RAAs keep ACTT informed of grant-aided projects, and a pre-condition of such aid is consultation with ACTT prior to production. This requirement is also set out in the Code of Practice.

The Code specifically applies to:

- 'experimental productions', providing for payment for personnel at what is called the 'newcomer rate'.
- 'short documentary films' that are intended for limited regional theatric exhibition. On consultation with the union some non-union crew may be permitted.
- 'grant-aided feature films' with only non-commercial distribution. You may be able to use some non-union crew, subject to consultation.

The Code of Practice provides for payment, waiving of overtime rates (subject to certain conditions), monitoring by the union and 'topping-up' payments should your film be exploited commercially. Working under the Code of Practice also entitles those working to apply to ACTT for membership in certain circumstances as 'grant-aided technicians'. The ACTT Code of Practice is available from the union's head office.

ACTT Workshop Declaration

This agreement applies to grant-aided workshops, predominantly engaged in production, that are enfranchised by the ACTT. It is applicable to workshops funded by public bodies and charities, and to those that operate on a strictly 'non-commercial, non-profit-distributing basis', i.e. any income generated is reinvested in the workshop and its activities. While the Declaration stresses the co-operative non-commercial nature of an accredited workshop, the productions are eligible for Channel 4 screening under the Channel 4 quota agreement, which sets out the number of hours of workshop material which can be screened annually.

The Declaration covers what the ACTT requires of the workshop, for example an annually revised salary scale, and the terms and conditions of employment of workshop personnel (i.e. sick pay, holidays, maternity leave, etc.). Regular members of staff can apply for union membership. A copy of the Declaration can be obtained from the ACTT head office.

In the case of both the Code of Practice and the Workshop Declaration, as with the other union agreements set out above, it is recommended that you get hold of them and familiarize yourself with them before attempting to negotiate or work under them.

6

WORKING WITH THE REST OF THE WORLD

6.1 Facilities and equipment
6.1.1 Borrowing to buy
6.1.2 Sale of goods and hire purchase
6.1.3 Hire companies and facilities houses

6.2 Private locations
6.2.1 Trespass
6.2.2 Nuisance

6.3 Public locations
6.3.1 Obstructing the highway
6.3.2 Obstructing a police officer
6.3.3 Conduct likely to cause a breach of the peace
6.3.4 Criminal damage
6.3.5 The Wildlife and Countryside Act 1981
6.3.6 Military bases
6.3.7 The courts
6.3.8 Parks, railways and motorways

6.4 Filming from the air

6.1 Facilities and equipment

So far we have been looking at the software that film and video production involves. Let's turn briefly to the hardware. It would be impertinent to recommend which camera, lighting gear or tape/film stock you should be using, but a brief guide to your rights when buying or hiring production equipment may prevent you coming unstuck just when things appear to be running smoothly.

6.1.1 Borrowing to buy

If you are buying as an individual you may be able to arrange a loan through your bank or a finance company. The latter will be more expensive but may be prepared to lend at a greater risk than your high street bank.

There is a limit to a personal loan through a bank and the bank will need an assurance of repayment over a three to five year period. If, however, you have established a good relationship with your bank in your previous dealings this is something that is up to you and your bank manager. Any credit arrangement will be drawn up as a Consumer Credit Agreement regulated by the Consumer Credit Act of 1974. This Act regulates loans made to individuals and unincorporated bodies, such as workshops, partnerships and charities, for sums up to £15,000. The Act is intended to protect the consumer, and applies also to hire purchase agreements which are briefly dealt with below.

The agreement will specify the purpose for which the loan is intended, the amount you are borrowing, the annual rate of interest, the dates and rates of repayment, and the security you are putting up for the loan.

If you are taking out the loan for a business where you intend to make a profit the bank may require copies of your balance sheets and profit and loss accounts.

The bank will seldom make unsecured loans. The life of the equipment you are purchasing, and its earning potential, will be taken into account, but a Sony 330 camera is of little use to a high street bank. If you are a house-owner you may be required to take out a second mortgage on your house as security. It is worth noting that once the bank has security in this form, the mortgage will not automatically be lifted upon repayment of the loan. It will be necessary specifically to instruct the bank to lift the charge on the house. In addition to any interest payable, you will be charged an arrangement fee, and the legal costs and/or valuation fees incurred in organizing the loan and security.

Borrowing as a limited company may still require the provision of personal security in the form of a guarantee or mortgage. However, the background of your company and the financial structure of your film deal will be examined and may be regarded as sufficient collateral for a business loan.

Small Business Loan Guarantee Scheme

Established in June 1981, the Small Business Loan Guarantee Scheme is administered by the Department of Trade and Industry. Although the conditions for borrowing under the Scheme are strict it may be worth your considering it. The basic requirement is no capital of your own and the absence of security will not prevent your company taking advantage of what the Scheme offers. In certain circumstances the Department of Trade and Industry will guarantee the repayment of 70 per cent of a loan of up to £75,000 over a period of two to seven years. In addition to the interest your company or business will pay, you will be charged a 5 per cent premium on the outstanding balance. The Department of Trade and Industry produces a leaflet about the Scheme entitled 'Loan Guarantees for Small Businesses'.

6.1.2 Sale of goods and hire purchase

Sale of goods

Your rights when purchasing are governed by the Sale of Goods Act 1979, which consolidates the previous legislation in this area.

Contracts for work and materials are not covered by the Act.

A contract of sale can be written or oral, but the essential ingredients of a contract still apply. (See Chapter 1, Legal basics.) A sale of goods as covered by the Act is when a seller during the course of its business transfers or agrees to transfer property in goods in exchange for a money consideration, the price. Thus the Act does not apply to a private sale.

There are a number of terms implied in a contract for sale of goods:

- That the seller has the right to sell at the time the property passes to the buyer, and that the buyer will be able to have uninterrupted enjoyment of the goods. Any defect in the title must be communicated to the buyer at the time of sale. For example, if you buy a second-hand blonde from a trader and there are unpaid repair charges on that light, the trader must make this known to you at the time of sale.
- The goods must be of merchantable quality. Any defects must be communicated to the buyer at the time of purchase. As the purchaser you must take reasonable steps to make sure the goods are what you could reasonably expect them to be. If at the time of purchase you examine the goods, any defect subsequently discovered will not necessarily be the liability of the seller if your examination could reasonably have revealed the defect.
- The goods must be fit for the purpose for which they are sold. It is advisable to make known to the seller anything unusual that you intend to do with the thing you are buying. If you are advised by the seller that the goods will be fit for that purpose and the goods prove unsuitable, then you will have recourse against the seller for any loss or damage that you suffer as a result.
- If the goods are being sold by description they must correspond with the description. 'Description' includes quality, content, dimensions and quantity.
- If the goods are being sold by sample the bulk must tally with the sample. You are entitled to a reasonable opportunity to examine the bulk of the goods to identify any defect that would not be apparent by examination of the sample.

It is useful to understand at what point ownership passes from seller to buyer, in order to establish, for example, who must bear the cost for accidental damage to the goods. If the seller becomes bankrupt, where ownership lies may make the difference between your having production gear and not having it. The seller can only sue you for the price once ownership has passed. Ownership does not require actual delivery, it passes when the parties intend it to pass. If this is not clear from the contract of sale it will be said to pass when the contract is formed, whether delivery or payment has occurred or not. If work has to be done to put the goods in a deliverable state, then ownership does not pass until that work is done. If you take something on sale or return ownership does not pass until you communicate your acceptance of the goods to the seller.

Delivery is the handing over of the goods *or* making them available for collection.

If the contract does not specify a delivery date, delivery should take place within a reasonable time. If the time of the delivery is specified then the seller's failure to deliver on time gives you the right to reject the goods, even if they are undamaged. (See *Time is of the essence*, p. 23.)

Failure to agree on the price does not mean there is no contract of sale. The price may be specified in the contract or left to be determined by a method specified in the contract, or determined as a result of previous dealings between the buyer and the seller. The Act provides that if there is no fixed price the buyer will pay a reasonable price for the goods.

Payment is usually stipulated in the contract, but failure to pay on time does not entitle the seller to take action against you for breach of the contract of sale. But the seller can sue for damages.

The Unfair Contract Terms Act

The Unfair Contract Terms Act of 1977 was enacted to protect the consumer from clauses in a contract that unfairly limit a seller or hirer, or perhaps a finance company's liability for loss or damage under that contract. However, to be protected by the Act you must be purchasing as a consumer at a place of business or in the course of, for example, the seller's business or under written standard terms of trade.

Simply because you are purchasing on behalf of a company does not mean you are not a consumer. You may be buying something that is ordinarily used for private consumption, for example a prop, and using it for the purpose for which it is intended. The burden of proving you are not a consumer lies with the seller.

When you are dealing as a consumer the seller cannot:

- Restrict or exclude its liability for death or personal injury caused by its negligence. This also applies to a manufacturer or distributor.
- Restrict its liability for loss or damage caused by a breach of the implied terms as to quality, fitness for purpose, etc. set out above.
- Exclude itself from liability through an exclusion clause except where that clause is reasonable.

When you purchase as otherwise than as a consumer, the seller cannot exclude liability for loss or damage as a result of the goods failing to meet with the requirements of merchantable quality, purpose, etc. unless the goods' failure to meet these requirements is reasonable. What is reasonable is determined by the circumstances of the contract in question. The courts will look at:

- The relative bargaining power of the two parties to the contract and whether there was an alternative available to you where the goods could have been obtained without the exclusion clauses being part of the contract of sale or hire.
- Whether the customer knew, or ought to have known, of the exclusions from liability, for example as a result of previous dealings. If you sign a contract of hire and when you go into the warehouse to collect there is a large notice excluding the hire company's liability for loss or damage, you may not be bound by this notice if you did not see it at the time of forming the contract. However, if you have been dealing with the particular hire company on previous productions, the court may take the view that you have accepted the exclusion from liability as a result of continuing to deal with the company over the years, and have had opportunity before to see and accept the restriction imposed by the notice in the warehouse.
- Whether the exclusion from liability only comes into effect when you breach a condition of the contract. The court will ask

whether it was reasonable to assume you could comply with that condition at the time you formed the contract.
- Whether the goods had been adapted to your specifications, or tailored to your particular requirements.

Where the goods are those ordinarily used for private consumption the seller cannot exclude its liability for loss or damage if the loss or damage arises from:
- The goods proving defective whilst in consumer use, being used for the purpose for which they were intended.
- The negligence of the manufacturer or distributor of those goods.

The Act does *not* apply to contracts of insurance, *nor* to contracts involving the creation, transfer or termination of intellectual property, i.e. copyright, trademarks, patents or designs.

Hire purchase

If you obtain equipment through hire purchase you are not protected by the Sale of Goods Act. A hire purchase agreement is a hire agreement with an option to buy. The supplier sells the goods to a bank or to a finance company (the creditor), who hires the goods to you (the debtor) with payment of the purchase price plus interest being made in instalments. Ownership in the goods does not pass until you exercise your option to purchase. This can be done at any time throughout the period of hire simply by completing the payments due on the goods. A hire purchase or consumer credit agreement is regulated by the Consumer Credit Act 1974. The same requirements that govern the sale of goods, i.e. title, quality, fitness for purpose, etc., apply. The Act regulates agreements for the purchase of goods up to £15,000.

Unlike contracts for the sale of goods, consumer credit agreements must be in writing. You may give notice to terminate the agreement at any time before the final payment is due. If you give notice to the creditor to terminate you must pay any sums due at the date of termination, plus a further sum to bring the payments up to half the total price or up to a sum that covers the creditor's loss on termination. What this might be will be determined by a court in the event of a dispute.

You have an obligation to take reasonable care of the goods, and on termination you may be required to compensate the creditor if you have failed to keep the goods in good condition.

If you default on your instalments the creditor is required by the Act to serve you with a default notice and entitled to demand payment in full, *or* terminate the agreement, *or* claim any security you have pledged. If you receive a default notice and comply with its conditions the consumer credit agreement will be treated as if you had not in fact committed a breach of its terms.

As the discussion here of consumer credit is brief it is appropriate to end with one final exhortation – if you are about to sign a hire purchase agreement *read the small print.*

6.1.3 Hire companies and facilities houses

It is a commercial decision on your part whether you hire or buy your equipment. Establishments that hire have standard terms of trade under which they operate. You are less likely to run into difficulties if you read the company's conditions of hire before committing yourself. These conditions will set out not just rates of hire and your liability for damage to the equipment, but also the company's restrictions on its liability for loss or damage caused by its actions or equipment. Any terms of business will seek to limit the company's liability as much as possible. What is reasonable is determined by the Unfair Contract Terms Act, and the tests of reasonableness set out above. Under the Act the hire company cannot restrict its liability for loss or damage as a result of its negligence or the negligence of its servants or agents, unless that restriction is reasonable. Nor can a company limit liability for death or personal injury arising from negligence. If the terms of trade contain a notice of restriction of liability for negligence, your agreement to the term will not necessarily be held to be acceptance of the risk.

Variations on the standard terms of trade are, of course, negotiable, but should be in writing. For example, if you wish to take the gear abroad or use it in a hazardous situation you should notify the hire company.

Insurance is vital. It may be built into hire or post-production charges, but check with your broker. It may be cheaper to include it in your own insurance package. When hiring you will be required to undertake not to sell, loan or hire the equipment to a third party, to use the equipment with reasonable skill and care, and protect it from the elements. You may have to bear the cost of damage to the equipment while it is in your care. You may also be required to compensate the hire company for any loss of revenue that it suffers as a result of damage, or of your failure to return the equipment when agreed. Collection and storage charges are likely to be your responsibility.

When using a facilities house for post-production, whether editing or processing, bear in mind that *you* bear the risk for loss or damage to your materials. Companies limit their liability for damage to the replacement of raw stock, some set a financial limit to any compensation. Facilities houses and laboratories will want to be assured that nothing in your film or tape is defamatory or obscene and that you have cleared all the relevant rights to the material. You may be required to indemnify them against any action brought against them as a result of incomplete title.

Check when the post-production companies will require payment. You may be able to negotiate a deferred payment. Some companies will hold a charge on your material until it is paid for. (See also Laboratory access letter, p. 213.) In some circumstances a contractual credit may be part of the contract.

6.2 Private locations

Finding the location

It is quite possible to seek out your own locations, negotiate a fee with the location owner, and shoot, but it can be time-consuming. Property owners are becoming increasingly aware of the cash advantages and risks to their properties that come with the film crew. There are companies that specialize in the finding and management of locations that can save you a lot of time and trouble. They offer a repository of information which may enable you to find what you want more quickly. They also act as a buffer between you and the location owners as they have their reputation and a relationship with a location owner to preserve. There are two forms in which they operate:

- The company that represents the owners of the locations, and takes its fee as a percentage of the location fee. While it may be willing to adjust its fee according to your budget, it is in its interest that the location fee is as high as possible.
- The company that will negotiate on your behalf. It offers a complete package; finding and negotiating the fee. The production company pays the location owner from the production budget, and a flat fee to the location finder. This kind of operation will work within your budget, often negotiating a special deal that is within your means.

Both kinds of location finders will want a brief as to what you are looking for, but in the case of the latter type of finder you will be quoted a price for their services. Be clear as to what your budget is as this will affect the finder's negotiations with the location owner, and may even affect what he charges you for his services.

If the services of a location finder are not within your budget, begin with libraries, guidebooks, maps and shoe leather. The more experienced you are the easier the process. Be honest with the owner of a location that you would like to use, making it clear just what will be involved. Remember, if the owner has never had a crew on his property before, he may be appalled at just what is required. It would be a shame if you spoilt it for another crew on another occasion, or for yourself if you find you need to reshoot. Negotiate a fee. You and the owner should sign an agreement.

Whether you are using a location finding service or negotiating your own contract you must have specific agreement on:

- Dates and hours of access and the area within which you will be working.
- The fee.
- The level of insurance that you have (usually £½ million to £2 million) against damage to the property. This is imperative.
- Be prepared to sign a letter of indemnity with the owner. A small or first-time location owner may not require this, but all public corporations will. This protects the owner from you or your servants suing for loss or damage to equipment, or injury to personnel while on the property. However, this indemnity would exclude damage to production equipment or injury or death caused by the negligence of the property owner, for example, where the owner ought to have warned of the danger.

Confirm that nobody is going to do anything to muck up your location between the time when you agree to use it and the time you will actually shoot. Ask yourself the question: 'If I wanted to mess this area up, what would *I* do?' For example, check with the local council and the gas board that no one is coming to dig the place up. Check that any features that make the location particularly desirable aren't going to be pulled down, painted or ploughed. And not just vision, but sound. Is the location on a holding pattern for a nearby airport for use in certain weather conditions, or on an alternative flight path? Everyone on or near the location should be informed. It may be useful to leaflet the area so that residents know what is going on. Your location manager should be the last to leave.

If you have found a location but cannot find the owner, try the local council rates office, who may pass on a letter, even if they will not tell you the name of the owner. If you cannot locate the owner but still want to go ahead you should be aware of the law of trespass.

6.2.1 Trespass

With some exceptions trespass is a tort and not a crime. Thus you cannot, despite what the signs always say, be prosecuted for trespass, you can only be sued in the civil courts.

Unless you have permission to be on land which is owned by someone else you are trespassing on it. This does not only include cases where you have entered the land without permission. If you have limited permission to use the land and you use it for something outside that permission you no longer have lawful permission to be on that land. In law, you are then regarded as having been a trespasser from the moment you first entered on to that land. You should be aware of this if you want to film at a place to which you have to gain entrance by ticket or if you have a limited agreement to use a location.

If you are a trespasser you can be asked to leave by the person who owns the land or by anyone on their behalf. If you do not leave, that person is entitled to use reasonable force to remove you. If in fact you did have permission to be there or the force which was used to eject you was more than was reasonable you can sue for assault, and for any damage to your equipment and financial loss. A person ejecting you has no right to demand your unexposed film or video cassette from you.

You can be sued in trespass even though the person bringing the action has suffered no physical or financial loss. In such a case the damages that the court might order against you would be very small. However, an injunction could be obtained against you to prevent you trespassing again, or from making use of the material which you have illegally obtained.

The ownership of the land can also include the ownership of the land on which an adjacent highway is built, even though the surface of the road may be owned by the local authority. When someone owns the land on both sides of the highway he also owns the land on which the highway is built. If someone owns the land on one side of the highway he will sometimes own that half of the land on which the highway is built which is closest to his land. In the 1890s the then Duke of Rutland owned some moors on which he enjoyed shooting grouse. One Harrison had a grievance against the Duke and while the Duke and his guests were shooting he would stand on a road which ran between the beaters and the guns and scare the grouse off. The Duke sued him in trespass and succeeded. It was held by the court that it was not a trespass to use the road for normal purposes but that it was a trespass to use it for an unusual and unreasonable purpose. It might be held to be a trespass if from the adjacent highway you filmed someone on his own land who did not want to be filmed. In a case in 1900 a landowner successfully sued in trespass a man who walked up and down on the highway making notes of racehorse trials which were being held on his land. You should also be aware of the criminal offence of obstructing the highway.

6.2.2 Nuisance

Your filming may cause a great deal of disturbance, and whether or not you have permission to film you should be aware of the law of nuisance. There is no simple definition of the law of nuisance. It includes anything which interferes with a landowner's 'use and enjoyment' of land. Use and enjoyment covers any legitimate use of the land. Only people who own the freehold or a lease of the land can take action in nuisance. They must also show that they have suffered damage different from that suffered by the rest of the public. A court will only grant an injunction to restrain a nuisance if it is continuous or repeated, or if it is deliberate. However, an order for damages may still be made against you.

It is likely that an action in nuisance would only succeed against you if you did something such as setting up camp outside someone's house to photograph them, or if your continuous filming at night kept someone awake. It is also possible that someone would succeed against you if your shooting outside his shop prevented or discouraged his customers from entering, and as a result he suffered loss of trade. It is also likely that in such circumstances you could be charged with obstructing the highway.

6.3 Public locations

One obvious but vital point to remember when filming in a public place is that you are not filming in a vacuum. The responses of the public will be affected by your presence just as much as your behaviour will be affected by members of the public strolling into shot at an inopportune moment. An extreme example of this is an incident that took place some years ago. A small crew was shooting above a river. The cameraman located, through the viewfinder, a person in the water. It was only when the head disappeared under water for the third time and did not come up again that the cameraman realized that he was filming a suicide. The crew was too far away to have reached the victim, but members of the public who witnessed the incident from the river bank, from where they could perhaps have intervened, may well have been influenced by the presence of the camera. What may have looked like a stunt was in fact reality.

Britain is a free country. This doesn't mean that you can do anything that you want. It means that you cannot be punished for anything that is not a breach of the law, and that you must be able to find out what the law says. As a film-maker you don't have any special privileges. In America, for example, you can obtain filming permits, which serve to help the film-maker avoid problems when filming in public. Filming on location entails not only the filming but the backup, including generators, catering and Portaloos. In urban areas these can take up a lot of space and even in the country can cause considerable disruption. Knowing the letter of the British law will not only help you to obtain assistance from the police but also help you enforce your rights if they are obstructive. As with everything, preparation is the key. It can help you to avoid problems in the first place and to present yourself to the police as a sensible professional, which will be more likely to secure their co-operation.

If you are going to film in a public place there are numerous offences that you may commit, and the most common of these are discussed below. For more detailed discussion of these and other offences, and of your rights if you are arrested, you should consult an up-to-date civil rights handbook, or get legal advice. As this is an area of the law where your liberty is at risk you must get advice from a lawyer as soon as you run into trouble. Legal aid may be available if you cannot afford to pay for your own lawyer.

It is advisable to inform the local police of your presence. Let them know even if you will be on private property, even if only to tell them you have permission. The police in this country have no powers to grant permission to film. Also inform the local council, particularly if you wish to divert or restrict traffic. Road closure is very difficult to obtain, but if you want to try to get permission apply for it yourself through both the police and the local council. The police have no power to grant you the right to obstruct the Queen's highway, and may in fact prevent your filming on the grounds of obstruction. Most forces are flexible, but it is unlikely that you will be permitted to film if, for example, your presence is seen as a security risk, such as filming close to royalty, or you are seen to be likely to cause riot or commotion. An example of the latter would be filming in a sensitive area of the community where the intrusion of film cameras might incite the locals to riot. Obtain parking dispensation through the traffic wardens' office, via the police duty desk. You may be permitted to cone areas for parking prior to the shoot. Inform the authorities of the number and the size of the vehicles and where they need to be parked for access to, say, power.

While you are on the street you will find it difficult to avoid committing a technical breach of one of the offences mentioned below, and will be technically liable to arrest. Whether or not you are arrested is at the discretion of the police and in most instances you will not be.

If you are arrested you are entitled to contact a lawyer from the police station, and you should do this. Legal aid will be available without a means test while you are at the station. If you are charged you will appear first in a magistrates' court, before one stipendiary magistrate or three lay magistrates. You may choose to be tried in the magistrates' court, called 'summary trial', or, for more serious offences, elect to be tried in the Crown Court by a jury, called 'trial on indictment'. Trial in the Crown Court has procedural advantage, but there is the danger of more severe penalties being imposed if you are convicted.

6.3.1 Obstructing the highway

The Highways Act 1980 makes it a criminal offence to 'wilfully obstruct the free passage along a highway without lawful authority or reasonable excuse'. The offence can only be tried in the magistrates' court and the maximum penalty is a fine of £50. The 'highway' can include the pavement, verges or anywhere used by the public to get from A to B, including pedestrian precincts. There is no need for the highway to be completely blocked, and the police do not have to show that anyone has actually been obstructed. As you can see, it would be very difficult to avoid committing this offence if you are standing still. Whether or not you are arrested will depend on the attitude of the police. The difficulty in getting a public road cleared for filming may explain why television cops and robbers car chases often end in disused scrapyards or on waste ground.

6.3.2 Obstructing a police officer

Under the Police Act 1964 it is a criminal offence to obstruct a police officer in the execution of his/her duty. It can only be tried in the magistrates' court, and is punishable by a fine of up to £400 and/or one month in prison. Almost anything which makes it more difficult for a police officer to enforce the law will be obstruction, even if your intention was actually to help. Usually the only defence is to question whether the police officer was really acting in the execution of his/her duty. There is no power to arrest for this offence, but the police will justify arrest on the grounds that a breach of the peace was anticipated. If the police ask you to move on, they may threaten you with arrest if you do not, and you may be charged with obstruction of the highway.

6.3.3 Conduct likely to cause a breach of the peace

Under the Public Order Act 1936 it is a criminal offence to use 'threatening, abusive or insulting words or behaviour' in a public place if they are likely to cause a breach of the peace. The offence can only be tried in the magistrates' court with a maximum penalty of £1,000 and/or six months in prison. It is not necessary that your conduct actually causes a breach of the peace, if it is likely to provoke anyone to use force against you or anyone else. The police almost always arrest before this happens, and it is unusual for the magistrates to disagree with their judgement. The police will often use this charge in addition to a charge of obstruction of the highway if they perceive any adverse public reaction to what you are doing.

In the area covered by the Metropolitan Police it is an offence under the Police By-Laws, Notice 833, to impersonate a police officer or to stage an incident using weapons. Without prior warning and careful handling the police are likely to take a very dim view of the situation if they come across you unexpectedly.

6.3.4 Criminal damage

Under the Criminal Damage Act 1971 it is a criminal offence to damage any property that does not belong to you. If the cost of the damage is less than £400 you can only be tried in the magistrates' court, where the maximum sentence is £2,000 and/or six months in prison. If the cost of the damage exceeds £400 you can choose to be tried in the Crown Court, where you can be sentenced to an unlimited fine and/or ten years in prison. Technically you can be guilty however minimal the damage. It need not be permanent. Leaving paint or tape marks on a wall would be enough. As before, what is important is whether the police decide to prosecute or not. Damage to derelict property is unlikely to concern them much, but even minor damage to other property may result in arrest. Use your common sense. If you are on private property you should include specific terms about the restoration or repair of any damage to the premises that you might cause. In most cases this should be covered by your insurance.

6.3.5 The Wildlife and Countryside Act 1981

This Act creates various offences intended to protect endangered species of wild plants and animals. The species which are protected are specified in the Schedules to the Act. This list can be added to by the Secretary of State for the Environment. Among other things the Act makes it an offence to intentionally:

- Pick, uproot or destroy any scheduled wild plant or uproot any wild plant.
- Damage, destroy or obstruct access to any structure or place used by a wild animal for shelter or protection.
- Disturb any scheduled wild animal while it is occupying any structure or place which that animal is using for shelter or protection.
- Disturb any scheduled wild bird while it is building a nest, or is in or near a nest containing eggs or young.
- Disturb the young of a scheduled wild bird.

It is quite possible that filming birds in their nests or animals in their shelters will disturb them, and can be an offence. The Nature Conservancy Council (NCC) will grant licences for photography which will provide immunity from prosecution. The NCC are careful about the people to whom they grant licences and may require proof of previous experience and competence. There are local offices of the NCC from which you should be able to obtain confirmation of which plants and animals are scheduled and whether what you want to do will require a licence.

6.3.6 Military bases

There are particular laws intended to protect particular locations. The most draconian are those which protect military establishments under the Official Secrets Act, although they are rarely enforced. If they were it would be impossible to approach a military establishment, let alone film one.

6.3.7 The courts

It is an offence under the Criminal Justice Act to film people involved in actual cases inside a court or in the precincts of a court. This includes filming people entering or emerging from court, even if you are outside the precincts of the court at the time. In practice action is rarely taken against people merely using the court buildings as a background. If you want to film inside court buildings using actors you will need to seek permission from the clerk of the court, who may be prepared to allow the use of the court building when the courts are not sitting. Under the Contempt of Court Act 1981 it is illegal to use a tape recorder within the court, although permission may be granted provided the recording will not be played to members of the public. If you want to make a tape recording you should contact the court clerk.

6.3.8 Parks, railways and motorways

Although they are open to the public, access is restricted to specific purposes. It is an offence to walk on the motorway or any of the grass verges, or to stop on the motorway except in an emergency. There are various offences of trespass on British Rail property created by the Railway Protection Acts 1840 and 1868 and the British Transport Commission Act 1949. In most cases it only becomes a crime after you have been asked to leave. Similar laws apply to docks, airports and parks. If you want to film at any of these locations you should treat them as private property and obtain permission from the appropriate authority.

6.4 Filming from the air

Whenever you want to film from the air you must keep within the requirements of the Civil Aviation Authority (CAA) which regulates civil aviation in Britain. You must plan any airborne shots well in advance, as not only will you have to arrange the aircraft, but approval will also have to be obtained from the CAA for any flight plan outside the normal limits. There are CAA regulations covering minimum height, flight duration, range, minimum speed and landing on airfields. These limitations are especially strict over urban areas and around major airports. There are also exclusion zones imposed on areas of this country's airspace by both British and American airforces. You must find out whether you will be allowed to do what you want before it becomes too late for you to change your plans. Operators who specialize in aerial filming will be able to advise you whether approval is likely to be granted and will obtain approvals for you from the CAA.

There are also CAA regulations which cover mountings for cameras, if, for instance, you want to remove the door of an aircraft to avoid having to film through a window. Failure to use CAA approved mountings will make your camera insurance void, as well as being potentially dangerous.

If you are filming a particular property from the air you may still be sued by a civil action in trespass or for nuisance. The ownership of land extends beyond the surface of the ground and includes anything above or below the land itself. In 1977 Lord Bernstein, the newspaper proprietor, tried to make use of this law to sue a company called Skyviews & General who had flown over his house and taken photographs of it. He failed because the court decided that the aeroplane was flying too high to interfere with any use of his land which Lord Bernstein might have had in mind. However, it is possible that his action might have succeeded if it had been based on the law of nuisance. To succeed under the law of nuisance a landowner would only have to prove that your action interfered with the 'use and enjoyment' of the land. The Civil Aviation Act 1949 provides a defence to any action in trespass or nuisance against the owner of an aircraft if flying at a reasonable height.

7

LEGAL LIMITATIONS ON CONTENT AND CERTIFICATION

7.1 Legal limitations on programme content

What your film may show is limited by various aspects of the criminal and civil law. Most of the offences are committed by those who publish or display the material, but you should bear them in mind even when you will not be showing the film yourself. A distributor will not be interested in a production that cannot be shown without the danger of a criminal prosecution or a libel action. You must also have regard to the duties and policies of bodies such as the IBA, BBC and the British Board of Film Certification (BBFC). The BBFC will not grant a certificate to a film in a form which may, in their opinion, be likely to lead to a criminal prosecution. Apart from any other consideration repeated prosecutions of films or videos granted a certificate by the BBFC would undermine its authority. The IBA has duties under the Broadcasting Act 1981 to control programme content. It publishes *Television Programme Guidelines* to assist programme makers. Nothing which might result in a criminal prosecution is likely to be suitable material for broadcasting. The BBC is not bound by the same duties as the IBA although it follows the IBA in practice.

7.1.1 Obscenity and indecency

Obscene publications

The law on obscene publications is contained in the Obscene Publications Acts 1959 and 1964, as amended by the Criminal Law Act 1977. The Cable and Broadcasting Act 1984 contains similar provisions for programmes broadcast on cable TV. The law on obscene publications does not at present affect material on broadcast television. The Obscene Publications Acts create offences of:
– having an obscene article for gain, and/or
– publishing an obscene article whether for gain or not.

These offences are punishable on conviction in the magistrates' courts with a fine of up to £1,000, or a term of up to six months' imprisonment. On conviction in the Crown Court, before a jury, the fine is unlimited and the maximum term in prison is increased to three years. Participation in the production of an obscene article can be prosecuted as aiding and abetting the offence.

What is an 'obscene article'? Although broadcasting is specifically excluded from the definition of publication, a videogram or film can be possessed and published. Not only a complete film or video but also negatives, rushes and anything else intended to be used for the production of an obscene article may also be an obscene article. There is a special provision that the approval of the Attorney General is required for prosecution of any film of a width of 16 mm or more. Thus most commercial films are exempt from prosecution under localized campaigns.

What makes an article 'obscene'? This is something that must be decided by the magistrates or the jury in each case. In deciding whether a film is obscene the court must take it as a whole. One part can make the whole film obscene, but one example of obscene conduct which the production as a whole does not glorify might not. The test is that the article taken as a whole must 'tend to deprave and corrupt'. While there is no clear definition of this vague concept, it must be something more than being indecent, shocking or disgusting. There is no limit to what may deprave and corrupt people. Violence and sexual activity can both be obscene, but in practice most prosecutions are brought against hard core commercial pornography. The decision about whether the article may deprave or corrupt must take into account the people who are likely to come into contact with it. The article must tend to deprave or corrupt 'a significant proportion' of them, though this need not be a majority. There is a difference between producing something for a group of consultant gynaecologists and producing the same thing for a rugby club. However depraved someone is, the court can always find that he can be corrupted to a lower level. Special care must be taken where, as with home format videos, the article may be seen by children, who are more likely to be depraved and corrupted than adults.

If the magistrates or the jury decide that the article is obscene, then there are a number of defences that they must consider:

- There is a general defence to a charge of publication of an obscene article that the publication was 'justified as being for the public good on the grounds that it is in the interest of science, literature, art or learning, or of other objects of general concern'. This amounts to saying that although some people may be depraved and corrupted the benefit to the public outweighs this. You may include something obscene to discuss or disapprove of it. The magistrates or jury have to balance the interests of those members of the public who may be enlightened against the interests of those who may be depraved and corrupted. To help them in this mysterious process the defence is entitled to call expert witnesses as to the benefits of the article in question. This evidence can only be on the public benefit and not on the question of whether or not the article is obscene. For instance, in the trial of Penguin Books for publishing *Lady Chatterley's Lover* evidence was given by the Bishop of Woolwich and the novelist E. M. Forster on the merits of D. H. Lawrence. This defence does not apply to a 'moving picture film' or 'moving picture soundtrack'. However, it does apply to video.

- There is a variation of this defence which applies to cable programmes and to publication of a 'moving picture film' and a 'moving picture soundtrack'. This is that its publication is, or would be, 'justified as being for the public good on the grounds that it is in the interests of drama, opera, ballet or any other art or of literature or of learning'. This is a more restricted defence than that which is available to other obscene articles, although in practice 'learning' can cover most matters. Experts may be called to give evidence to establish this defence as well.
- A person cannot be found guilty if he had not examined the article which he had, and he had no reasonable cause to suspect that it was an obscene article. It is up to the accused person to prove this defence. It is mostly of use to distributors or shopkeepers.
- If a film is produced in England but is not intended to be shown here it would be necessary for the prosecution to show that it would deprave and corrupt the people in the country in which it was intended to be shown. It is difficult to obtain such evidence. It is not uncommon in England for two versions of a film to be made, with the erotic content toned down for the domestic version.

The police may take two courses of action under the Obscene Publications Act:

- Under Section 3 of the Obscene Publications Act the police may obtain from a magistrate a warrant to search for and seize articles which they believe to be obscene and kept for publication for gain. They can then take the articles before a magistrate and a summons can be issued. It will be up to the person who owns the articles to appear in court and prove that the articles seized were not obscene or were not held for gain. The warrant will normally be issued to the person from whom the articles were seized. There is no procedure for the maker of a film seized in this way to be notified, although they would be entitled to appear to defend that person. There is no right to a trial before a jury, under Section 3, although the person from whom the articles were seized may elect to be charged under Section 2 instead, allowing trial by jury, but at the risk of a prison sentence if convicted.

- Under Section 2 the police, after consultation with the Director of Public Prosecutions, may prosecute the publisher or possessor of the obscene article. The defendant has a right to choose whether to be tried before magistrates or a jury. It is generally believed that juries are more sympathetic, and representative of actual public standards.

Because whether an article is obscene is a decision to be made in each individual case, there is little consistency between decisions in the same courts at different times, or in different courts at the same time. The same issue of *Forum* magazine was held to be obscene in Nuneaton, but not in Exmouth. In raids on the same bookshop in Leeds in 1965 and 1967 the police seized the same book, *Bawdy Setup*, on both occasions. The first time, on the advice of the Director of Public Prosecutions, they returned it as not being obscene. The second time they proceeded with charges and it was found to be obscene and the bookseller convicted.

The Director of Public Prosecutions has made public the guidelines which will be considered in deciding whether to prosecute a videogram. These include:

- The probability of a home audience consisting of children or young persons.
- The characters of the perpetrator and victim of violence and their reactions.
- How explicit, realistic and prolonged the violence is, and the weapons used, including whether they are unusual or easily copied.
- The style and general tone of the production and the relevance of the violence to the narrative.

Sending indecent material through the post

Under the Post Office Act 1983 it is an offence to send through the post material which is 'grossly offensive or of an indecent or obscene character'. It is punishable by conviction in the magistrates' court with a fine of up to £1,000, or in the Crown Court with an unlimited fine and/or a maximum of twelve months in prison. There is no simple definition of what constitutes 'grossly offensive' or 'indecent'. It clearly covers a wider range of material than the Obscene Publications Acts. It would include anything 'which an ordinary decent man or woman would find shocking, revolting or disgusting'.

The Protection of Children Act

In addition to employment legislation there are special provisions contained in the Protection of Children Act 1978 intended to prevent them being exploited as models for pornography. The Act creates the following offences:

- Taking an indecent photograph of or including a child.
- Distributing or showing an indecent photograph of a child.
- Possessing an indecent photograph of a child with the intention of distributing or showing it.
- Advertising in a way which suggests availability of such material, even if the material advertised is not in fact indecent.

For the purpose of this Act a child is any person under the age of sixteen years. It is not necessary for the child to be a party to the indecency. Therefore a scene in a film where a child is shown to be present during an indecent act would be an offence. Prosecution could be avoided by using a person aged over sixteen who looks under sixteen. The penalties are a maximum fine of £1,000 or up to six months in prison if convicted in the magistrates' court, or an unlimited fine and/or up to three years in prison if sentenced in the Crown Court. There are forfeiture provisions similar to those in the Obscene Publications Act. Prosecutions can only be brought with the consent of the Director of Public Prosecutions. Videos are specifically included under the provisions of the Act. There is no specific definition of 'indecent'; again, it clearly covers things that are immodest if not obscene.

Cruelty to animals

There is much legislation intended to protect animals from ill treatment, the most important of which are the Protection of Animals Act 1911, and the Wildlife and Countryside Act 1981.

There is also a specific offence related to films created by the Cinematograph Films (Animals) Act 1937. This makes it an offence to exhibit any film to the public if 'in connection with the production of the film any scene represented in the film was organized in such a way to involve the cruel infliction of pain or terror on any animal or the cruel goading of any animal to fury'. The offence is committed by the exhibitor, not the film-maker. However, the film-maker would almost certainly be guilty of an offence under the Protection of Animals Act which makes almost any form of cruelty to wild or captive animals a crime. The BBFC may require cuts if they consider that specific scenes show an offence under the Cinematograph Films (Animals) Act.

7.1.2 The Official Secrets Acts

The Official Secrets Acts 1911, 1920 and 1939 are probably the most consistently criticized pieces of legislation passed this century. Opposition MPs may pledge to repeal them, but as soon as they become government ministers they find more important things to occupy their time. One possible explanation for this is that the Acts provide a means whereby almost any information about government activities can be protected by the threat of prosecution. It has been calculated that the Acts create 2,324 separate offences. Prosecutions can only be brought with the approval of the Attorney General, which is discussed below.

Section 1 of the 1911 Act makes it an offence for any person for any purposes prejudicial to the safety or interest of the state:

- to approach, inspect, pass over, enter or be in the vicinity of any prohibited place, or
- to make any sketch, plan, model or note which might be or is intended to be useful to an enemy, or
- to obtain, collect, record, or communicate to any person information which might be, or is intended to be useful to an enemy.

The seemingly useful protection of the first part of the section is in practice almost valueless. Throughout this century judges have become increasingly reluctant to make their own judgments about what is in the interests of the state. The court will not question the statement of the Attorney General as to what might be prejudicial to the interest or security of the state. Thus, to be found guilty it is not necessary for the accused person to actually have any intention to prejudice the state.

As to what may be a 'prohibited place' under the Acts, the definition includes, among other things:

- any work of defence, arsenal, naval or air force establishment or station, factory, dockyard, mine, minefield, camp, ship or aircraft belonging to or occupied by or on behalf of Her Majesty, and
- any place belonging to or used for the purposes of Her Majesty which the government may declare to be a prohibited place, on the grounds that information about it may be useful to an enemy.

With such all-embracing provisions it is clear that the Acts must be broken unintentionally every day.

Section 2 of the 1911 Act makes it an offence for any person who has in their possession any information which relates to or is used in any prohibited place, or which was obtained, directly or indirectly, as a result of employment by the state:

- to communicate that information to any person to whom they are not authorized to communicate it, or
- to use the information in any manner prejudicial to the safety or interest of the state, or
- to retain the information when they have no right to retain it, or fail to deliver it to a lawful authority after being requested to do so, or
- to endanger or fail to take reasonable care of the information.

It also makes it an offence to receive any prohibited information knowing that it was communicated in contravention of the Acts, unless the person who receives it proves that it was communicated to him contrary to his desire. It is important to note that this part of the section reverses the normal presumption that a person is innocent unless proven guilty. If you are accused you must prove that you are innocent.

What is the effect of all this? The answer is that nobody really knows. As it covers not only information about, but also information used in a 'prohibited place', almost any information about government is prohibited information. It has been suggested that the number of cups of tea drunk in your local DHSS office would be prohibited information. Because of their wide scope it is not difficult to commit a breach of the Acts when dealing with government. The only thing which stands between this and a prosecution is the decision of the Attorney General whether or not to prosecute.

How do you avoid prosecution under the Official Secrets Acts? Although the courts make the final decision the application of the Acts in practice depends on the way in which the Attorney General chooses to exercise the discretion to prosecute. The Attorney General is an independent legal advisor to the government. However, the position is a political appointment, and it would be surprising if the Attorney General was not sympathetic to the government. Too often this discretion has been exercised to protect the government of the day from political embarrassment. This should not be surprising, as the first Official Secrets Act of 1889 was introduced after the Foreign Secretary, Lord Salisbury, had been embarrassed by a newspaper revelation. He had told Parliament that there was no secret treaty with Russia. With the help of a government clerk with perfect recall a newspaper was able to publish the complete text. The consequence was the first Official Secrets Act, which was extended greatly in the tense atmosphere which preceded the First World War. One Act passed through all its stages in Parliament before lunch.

Unfortunately the courts seem recently to have taken a much more serious view of offences under the Acts. In the 1970s the Acts were generally held in low regard. Two journalists, Aubrey and Campbell, were convicted in 1979 of receiving information about signals intelligence. They were conditionally discharged. In contrast when Sarah Tisdall was convicted of revealing information which did not appear to threaten national security she received an immediate prison sentence. Although revealing information is more seriously regarded than receiving it, this does seem to indicate that the courts will impose harsher sentences than in the recent past. Fortunately juries will sometimes acquit defendants in the face of the evidence and the law.

7.1.3 Defamation

The law of defamation developed to protect the reputations of people from untrue attacks. Defamation includes slander, which is the spoken word, and libel, which is the word, or picture, recorded in permanent form. In practice you will have to beware of the law of libel.

A libel is anything which is published about a person which would reduce their reputation amongst 'right-thinking' people. Except for privileged publications which are discussed below, communicating a defamatory statement to anyone other than the person the remark is about will constitute publication.

Thus even if it is published in private a libel can be actionable, if the person libelled becomes aware of it. If a person believes that they have been libelled they can take action in the courts against anyone who has published the libel for damages to compensate them, and for an injunction preventing repetition of the libel. The greatest limitation on beginning a libel action is the cost involved. Legal aid is not available. Because of this, most libel actions are taken by rich individuals or by people backed by organizations such as trade unions.

It is not possible to libel a person who is dead, nor can you libel an object, such as a machine, provided that your comments do not reflect libellously upon any person associated with it. It is possible for an action for 'injurious falsehood' to be taken over comment on a product, but it would only succeed if it could be shown that the comment was not merely untrue but also malicious.

What sort of comment could be a libel? Abuse and ridicule are not sufficient unless they actually affect the reputation of the person at whom they are directed. However, the comment need not be direct. Innuendo can be enough. Putting a star singer only third on the billing for a concert has been held to be a libel because it suggested that the singer was not worthy of top billing. A libel need not suggest morally reprehensible behaviour, if it would still cause someone to be shunned by 'right-thinking' people. In 1934 MGM produced a film which suggested that a Russian princess had been seduced or raped by Rasputin. Because it resulted in social embarrassment for the princess it was held to be a libel, even though there was no suggestion that she was at fault. A decision in a libel case must take into account present social standards, and it is unlikely that the same decision would be reached today. If a person is in fact shunned by their friends as a result of a revelation about them that will not in itself make it a libel. In one case a man was avoided by his fellow members at a golf club after it was revealed that he had told the police about an illegal fruit machine. The court held that this could not be a libel because 'right-thinking' people would have approved of his action.

There are various defences to an action for defamation:

- That what was published was true, or that those parts which were defamatory were substantially true, even if other parts were not. It is not enough that you believe that it was true. You must be able to prove in court that it is true. There are rules of evidence which may prevent you from presenting to the court some of the information which you yourself relied upon. For instance, you cannot prove that something happened by calling a witness who can only say that someone else told them about it. There is an exception to this defence. It would be a libel to reveal a criminal conviction which has become 'spent' under the Rehabilitation of Offenders Act 1974, if it was motivated by malice. This Act is intended to prevent minor criminal convictions from haunting a person for the rest of his life. The period of time after which a conviction becomes spent depends upon the sentence. If you intend to reveal a conviction for which a person was sentenced to less than two and a half years in prison you should take advice on whether this would be in breach of the Act.
- That it was in the public interest to publish the libel, or in the particular interest of the person to whom it was published. This defence will apply even if the statement was untrue, provided that the person publishing it was not motivated by malice and believed at the time that it was true. This belief must not be the result of ignoring evidence to the contrary. The defence assists investigative reporting of individuals and organizations in the public eye.
- That it was fair comment on a matter of public interest. The comment must be an opinion and not a statement of fact. This defence applies mainly to comments about artistic productions and the activities of people in the public eye.
- That the publication was 'privileged' because it was a fair and accurate report of proceedings in court or in Parliament.

The person who will be sued is the publisher of the libel. Thus a distributor and exhibitor will also be liable, as well as the producer. The aggrieved person will sue the individual with the most money, usually the distributor. Libel actions can be heard by juries and the amounts awarded can be substantial. If there is any fear of libel the distributor may want you to obtain legal advice that the production is not defamatory or that there is a good defence to any libel action.

Criminal and blasphemous libel

Normally libel can only give rise to a civil claim for damages. There are two exceptions, both of which arise from the rule that in English law a criminal offence does not disappear merely because it has not been used for many years. Although the higher courts have disapproved of the use of criminal libel prosecutions, except where the Crown or the courts are involved, a private prosecution was commenced by Sir James Goldsmith against *Private Eye* in 1976 although it was dropped after a settlement was reached in a parallel libel action in the civil courts. Similarly it was a private individual, Mrs Mary Whitehouse of the National Viewers' and Listeners' Association, who resurrected the offence of blasphemous libel. The conviction of Denis Lemon, the editor of *Gay News*, for publishing a poem about homosexual love for Jesus Christ was upheld by the House of Lords. To be convicted it is not necessary to intend to blaspheme if what is published actually does insult, vilify or offend the Christian religion. It is not possible to blaspheme any other religion, and the Law Commission has recommended the abolition of the offence. It is difficult to predict whether any further prosecutions are likely to be made, as the prosecution of *Gay News* brought far more publicity to the poem than it would otherwise have received.

7.1.4 Breach of confidence

The law about breach of confidence is discussed in detail earlier in the book (see pp. 40–2). It can protect you but it can also work against you if you want to base a production on information which was first obtained in confidential circumstances. Confidential circumstances may arise from a contractual relationship between employer and employee, or from the circumstances in which the information became available to you or your source. Employees owe a duty of confidentiality to their employers. If information is revealed in circumstances which make it clear that it is confidential, that information can be protected by an action in the courts or an injunction can be obtained to prevent you making use of it. This is an area of law which is developing rapidly, and it is being used to restrict information where previously there were no restrictions.

An example of the use of a claim for breach of confidence is the case of *Schering Chemicals* v. *Falkman Ltd*, in 1981. Schering had been concerned about bad publicity given to their product Primodos, after claims from parents that it had caused deformities in their children. Schering sent some of their executives on a course organized by Falkman Ltd to learn how to deal with this publicity. One of the people employed by Falkman as advisors was David Elstein, a television producer. From what he had learned from the executives on the course he conceived the idea of a documentary on Primodos, which he proposed to Thames Television. Schering refused to co-operate with the production, and an independent researcher was employed. Schering applied for an injunction to prevent the programme being broadcast. They did not claim that the programme contained any information which was not publicly available before the course, but that Elstein should not be allowed to profit from an idea which he obtained in confidential circumstances. They were successful. One of the judges in the Court of Appeal, Lord Shaw, said, 'though facts might be widely known, they were not ever present in the minds of the public. To extend the knowledge or revive the recollection of matters which might be prejudicial to the interests of some person or organization was not to be condoned because the facts were already known to some and lingered in the memories of others.' He also described the programme as an 'onslaught', although Lord Denning, who did not agree that an injunction should be granted, said that he had found it 'a balanced and fair presentation'.

This case may be an aberration because of its unusual circumstances. However, it makes it clear that you must be extremely careful if you are treading on the toes of major companies, or other organizations who will not be slow to use the courts to protect their commercial interests or dignity. It is likely that the information which is most interesting is that which will be most jealously protected. However, there is a defence to an action for breach of confidence that the publication of the information is in the public interest. Such a defence is most likely to succeed where it is misconduct or hypocrisy that is revealed. However, the revelation need not be so dramatic if the public interest in publication is great and justifiable. In one case the manufacturers of the Intoximeter used by the police in drinking and driving cases failed to prevent the publication of internal memoranda on its reliability because the court held that the public interest in revealing doubts about the accuracy of the machine outweighed the issue of confidentiality.

7.1.5 Contempt of court and Parliament

Contempt of court

The origin of contempt lies in the powers acquired by both the civil and criminal courts to regulate the behaviour of people before them. These powers have been extended to protect the administration of the law as a whole and can now be used to punish actions which take place outside the precincts of the courts themselves. Much of the law was consolidated by the Contempt of Court Act 1981. Offences under the Contempt of Court Act are tried by a judge without a jury, and can be punished by a fine or up to two years' imprisonment.

What types of behaviour can be a contempt of court? There are three main categories which may affect you:

- *Comment on active cases*: under the Contempt of Court Act 1981 it is a contempt to reveal information about an 'active' case in such a way to create 'substantial risk' that the course of justice would be 'seriously impeded or prejudiced'. In civil cases a case is not 'active' until a date has been set for a trial in the High Court, or a pre-trial review in the County Court. In criminal cases a case becomes 'active' when a warrant or summons is issued or an arrest made, or a charge put. Unfortunately there is no central register where this kind of information can be checked. The warrant or summons need not have been served for the case to be 'active' although if a warrant has not been served after twelve months the proceedings will then cease to be 'active' until it is served. Discussions of the role of Lord Lucan in the death of his children's nanny were restricted because a warrant was issued for his arrest, but could not be served because he disappeared. An example of this kind of contempt was the publication in 1976 by the *Evening Standard* of a picture of Peter Hain, the anti-apartheid campaigner who had been charged with robbery. It appeared on the front page on the day that Hain was due to appear in an identity parade. It clearly prejudiced this because it might have had an influence on the person who was to make the identification. The test is not whether there is a risk that something might prejudice a case, but whether there is a 'substantial' risk and whether the prejudice would be serious. Not everything about a civil or criminal case would amount to a contempt, but you should take legal advice if you think your production might be a contempt. Action is more likely to be taken against you if the case is to be heard in the Crown Court or by a coroner, because a jury is more likely to be influenced than a judge. There is a presumption that judges will not be unduly influenced by information obtained outside court. It is probably safe to comment on cases which have been decided in the lower courts, even if they are being appealed to the higher courts. It is no defence that the matters which constitute the contempt are true, or that there was no intention to commit a contempt. Proceedings under the Contempt of Court Act must be taken by the Attorney General, and in the past a fairly liberal approach has been taken both by the Attorney General and by the courts. Criticism of the decision to prosecute and the discussion of the issues likely to be raised in court have been allowed, although interference with or interviewing of non-professional witnesses, or publishing the previous convictions of the accused, might well be a contempt.

As a film-maker, whose film may not be made public for many months, are these provisions likely to affect you? The delays of the law are legendary, and cases may take years to come to court. People concerned in cases are entitled to apply to the court for an injunction preventing the publication of information which may be a contempt. It was possible for eight Metropolitan Police officers, backed by the Police Federation, to obtain an injunction preventing a programme being shown which reconstructed various aspects of the death of a suspect in police custody. They succeeded because a coroner's inquest had not been concluded and there was a possibility that the coroner might sit with a jury who might have been influenced by the programme.

- *Reporting proceedings in courts*: the general rule is that any proceedings in open court can be reported, and any fair and accurate report will be protected from any action for libel. Because of this defence allegations made in court can be widely published. People often make use of this rule to make public allegations which would otherwise be libellous. It extends to comments made in court during proceedings, even though they are not evidence in the case. However, there are various acts which restrict the publication of information about cases which are heard in open court. It is an offence under the Contempt of Court Act 1981 to publish any information about the way in which a jury came to a decision in a particular case. Under the Magistrates' Courts Act 1980 it is an offence to publish any evidence given in committal proceedings until the trial to which it relates is over, unless this restriction is specifically lifted. There is a general prohibition on publishing the identity of the complainant in rape cases. The Contempt of Court Act also gives courts powers to order that the identity of witnesses in criminal cases should not be published, if this would be prejudicial to the interests of justice. Despite comment in the higher courts, judges in the Crown Courts continue to use this power in circumstances that do not justify it. It is not certain but it is likely that it would still be a contempt to identify a witness even if the information on which the identification was made came from outside the court and was common knowledge.

- *Comment on judges*: there is a presumption in English law that judges and others exercising a judicial function, like magistrates, are free from personal bias or prejudice. To suggest that a judge might allow such things to influence the conduct of a case, even unconsciously, may be a contempt. It may also be a libel, but the court will be likely to take its own action to protect itself against such attacks. It is not a contempt to criticize the decision a judge makes provided that the criticism does not suggest improper motives and is not motivated by malice or an intention to interfere with the administration of justice. An example of this kind of contempt is the prosecution of the *New Statesman* in 1928 when it had suggested that the judge who heard a libel action brought by Dr Marie Stopes had allowed his opposition to her birth control campaign to influence his summing up. The *New Statesman* was convicted, although in recent decades a more liberal approach has been taken by the courts taking the view that 'justice is not a cloistered virtue'.

Contempt of Parliament

Parliament is the highest legal authority in the United Kingdom, and its decisions overrule those of the highest courts. Not surprisingly it has created for itself sweeping powers to protect its own proceedings and its own dignity. The privileges of Parliament are normally enforced by the House of Commons Committee on Privileges. The Committee may empower officers of Parliament to arrest any person and bring them before the Committee to answer questions. The person under suspicion may not be told what they are suspected of having done, and have no right to speak in their own defence. If the Committee finds that a contempt has been committed and their decision is approved by the House of Commons, the guilty person may be summoned to the bar of the House of Commons to be rebuked by the Speaker, or even imprisoned.

In practice the use of contempt of Parliament is now very restricted as its exercise against people who were not MPs themselves provoked more contempt than the acts that were the subject of complaint. Its procedure also conflicts with the European Convention on Human Rights. In the 1950s a newspaper published an article suggesting that MPs sold information to journalists in return for drinks. Both the editor of the newspaper and the author were found to be in contempt of

Parliament. The author was himself an MP and was expelled from the House. It is unlikely that action would be taken against an editor in such circumstances today although similar action might still be taken against an MP.

7.1.6 Incitement to racial hatred

The Cable and Broadcasting Act 1984 created a criminal offence of incitement to racial hatred for cable TV programmes. The offence is committed by the inclusion in a cable service of a programme with threatening, abusive or insulting words in circumstances which are likely to stir up hatred against any 'racial group' in the United Kingdom. The term 'racial group' includes colour, race, nationality, ethnic and national origin, and citizenship. Prosecutions must be approved by the Attorney General. It appears that racist images are not covered.

The offence can be committed by the cable operator, the producer and director of the programme, and the person actually using the words. To be guilty there is no need for there to have been an intention to stir up racial hatred. There are defences available that you did not know of or have reasonable cause to suspect that:

- the programme would involve the use of such words, or
- the programme would be included in a cable service, or
- the circumstances of the programme would be such that the words would be likely to stir up racial hatred.

No similar law applies to film or to broadcast television and the Act specifically excludes the reception and immediate retransmission of broadcast material. There are indications that the law will be extended in the near future.

7.2 Certification and statutory bodies

7.2.1 Film certification

The present system of categorization used by the BBFC is:

Universal, suitable for all.

PG

Parental guidance, some scenes may be unsuitable for young children.

(15)	Passed only for persons of fifteen years and over.
(18)	Passed only for persons of eighteen years and over.
Restricted (18)	For restricted distribution only through specifically licensed premises.

This system is based on the BBFC's view that 'parents are generally the best judge of what their pre-teenage children are ready for'. U and PG films are open to all, but the PG rating is intended as a warning to parents who might want to (attempt to) control their children's viewing. The Restricted 18 category is intended to cover pornographic films to be shown in 'sex establishments' licensed by local authorities under the Local Government (Miscellaneous Provisions) Act 1984.

Films are normally submitted by distributors, although the cost of the certificate is usually recovered from the film-maker. The procedure of the BBFC is for a film which has been submitted for certification to be viewed by two members of the Board of Examiners. The members of the Board are chosen with the intention of reflecting a wide range of ages and views. If the original examiners cannot reach a decision the film is re-viewed by others, and in difficult cases a film may be viewed by the Secretary. Consultants from outside the BBFC may be brought in, and legal advice obtained. The President is only consulted in exceptional cases. The BBFC may make suggestions for cuts to be made, after which the film will be granted a particular certificate. In many cases distributors are prepared to make these cuts in order to get a classification certificate which they regard as commercially necessary. In a case where you anticipate problems in obtaining a certificate it is possible to submit a script for the opinion of the BBFC before shooting begins.

The criteria employed by the BBFC in granting certificates are not entirely clear. The BBFC's declared policy is 'to reflect intelligent contemporary public attitudes', including those reflected in other artistic and communications media. This means that the certification depends on more than a simple count of acres of bare flesh, or gallons of blood. In practice the BBFC is prepared to grant certificates to films of perceived or presumed artistic merit. For instance, when *The Tin Drum* directed by Volker Schlöndorff appeared at the Cannes Film Festival most British critics regretted that because of the explicitness of some of its scenes it would never be granted a certificate for public exhibition in Britain. In fact, after winning the Palme d'Or at Cannes it was granted an 18 certificate with only one brief cut.

Under the Restricted 18 category the BBFC has certificated several films of accepted artistic merit, such as Oshima's *Ai No Corrida*, which were previously refused certificates in the 18 category because of their sexual explicitness. It appears that the BBFC intends to place in this category films which are too indecent for public display but of sufficient artistic merit to avoid conviction under the Obscene Publications Act. It is doubtful if this will increase their availability to the general public, as their distribution is limited to licensed sex establishments. When a similar system was introduced in France distributors would not touch such films as they did not appeal to the dirty mac brigade who frequented what were regarded as 'porno cinemas'.

It is a common misconception that BBFC certification grants an exemption from prosecution under the Obscene Publications Act, and other legislation. This is not true. In practice the Director of Public Prosecutions will attempt to avoid initiating a prosecution against a film granted a certificate by the BBFC. However, at least one film has been the subject of a successful prosecution under the Obscene Publications Act.

7.2.2 Video certification

Video certification has its origins in campaigns in the popular media about 'video nasties'. From a general concern to prevent young children viewing scenes of explicit violence we now have the Video Recordings Act 1985, which had its origins in a Private Members' Bill promoted by Conservative MP Graham Bright. As with many pieces of legislation intended to deal with a specific problem, the effect is a great deal more extensive than is necessary. A leading legal journal described the Bill as 'all-embracing' and as a 'grossly misconceived measure which will impose the most stringent form of censorship this country has ever known'. The Video Recordings Act creates criminal offences of:

- supplying or offering to supply, and/or possessing with intent to supply, a video recording which has not been classified by the licensing authority.

There are also offences of supplying video recordings in breach of the classification given by the Licensing Authority or without the classification shown on the cassette housing and packaging. There is a maximum fine of £20,000 for supplying an unclassified video recording. The offences can only be tried in the magistrates' court.

All video recordings have to be submitted for classification before September 1986, including films that have already been certificated unless they were passed for general public exhibition before 1 January 1940. The only exemptions are 'exempted supplies' or video recordings which are:

- concerned with sport, religion or music, or
- designed to provide information, education or instruction, or
- video games.

However, there are special criteria which apply to such video recordings even if they fall within the above categories. They must still be submitted for classification if, 'to any significant extent', they show or deal with:

- human sexual activity or acts of force or restraint associated with such activity, or are designed to any significant extent to stimulate or encourage such activities, or
- mutilation, torture, or other acts of gross violence, or are designed to any extent to stimulate or encourage such actions, or
- human genital organs or human urinary or excretory functions.

A 'supply' means delivering a video recording to another individual including a firm or organization. Any supply of an unclassified video recording will be an offence unless it is an 'exempted supply' as defined in the Act. Exempted supplies include all supplies:

- for which no reward is received, *and* is not in the course of business.
- of single copies of recordings to individuals who are in the business of making or supplying video recordings.

- of multiple copies of video recordings to individuals who are in the business of making or supplying video recordings, *if* there is no intention to supply those video recordings to the public at any time in the future.
- for exhibition in public cinemas, as these would have to be certificated as films.
- for use on broadcast or licensed cable or satellite TV.
- for the training of nurses, doctors, midwives or health visitors.
- of a video recording that is a record of an event to a person who took part in it.

This exemption does not apply if the video recording deals to any significant extent with the matters discussed in the 'special criteria' referred to above. It would then have to be submitted for certification.

The licensing authority is the BBFC. The system of classification used by the BBFC for films is also used for video recordings. The Act requires the BBFC to have special regard to the likelihood of the video recordings being viewed in the home. Video differs from film in the degree of control which the viewer can exercise over the material being viewed. Video can be switched off, equally it can be re-viewed, and frozen so that what may be a flash in the cinema can be savoured with delight or disgust in the living room. The technology of video also makes it almost impossible to ensure that videos certificated 15 will not be seen by younger children. The BBFC is required to ensure that all video recordings which are certificated are 'suitable for viewing in the home'. It is quite possible that the classification given to a work in video form will be more restrictive than that given to it in film form, and this has already happened in the case of at least two films. The Act is potentially more restrictive than the law as it affects films. Uncertificated films which are available for distribution to film clubs are unlikely to be granted a certificate as video recordings, except in the Restricted 18 category. At best they may only be available in licensed sex establishments. The offence committed under the Video Recordings Act depends on the classification of the video and not the content. There is a right to appeal to an independent tribunal against the classification given by the BBFC.

In addition to the delay that will be caused, the cost of certification will be a burden to small producers. The cost for a new standard commercial film is £4.60 per minute. Charities and non-profit-making organizations 'are invited to apply for a reduced fee chargeable at the Board's discretion for works that are not distributed for private gain'.

7.2.3 Statutory bodies controlling broadcasting

Sound and vision broadcasting in the United Kingdom is controlled by two bodies, the British Broadcasting Corporation and the Independent Broadcasting Authority. The BBC directly controls broadcasts on BBC television and radio. Its powers and duties derive from its charter, and its licence agreement with Parliament, which is renewed periodically. It is funded by the TV licence fee, and any funds which it can raise itself.

The Independent Broadcasting Authority

The IBA controls commercial television and radio through its licence agreements with the broadcasting companies, and through direct control of Channel 4. Its powers and duties are set out in the Broadcasting Act 1981. The IBA has a general duty to ensure that the independent television companies provide a 'wide range' of programmes of 'high quality' and 'merit' with 'proper balance'. In addition it has a duty to ensure that Channel 4 encourages innovation and experiment. Within these duties the IBA has a duty to ensure that programmes which are broadcast on ITV and Channel 4 do not offend against public taste or decency, or offend public feeling or incite disorder or crime. The IBA must also ensure due impartiality in all news and programmes on matters of political or industrial controversy or public policy. The Board of the IBA has a duty to perform these duties, and is bound to view in advance programmes which are likely to be controversial. However, the courts will only interfere with a decision made by the IBA Board if that decision is perverse. The IBA's *Television Programme Guidelines* are issued to assist programme makers in sensitive areas. These are revised from time to time and you should be familiar with them.

The British Broadcasting Corporation

The BBC is not required to comply with the same duties as to the control of programme content as the IBA, although it undertakes to do so. Within the BBC it is the responsibility of producers to refer controversial programmes to higher management and ultimately to the Director General. The Home Secretary has a power under the BBC's licence agreement to ban any programme, without having to give a reason. Although doing so would cause a political storm the threat of its use must have some influence on the BBC, who must also be constantly aware of its dependence on the government of the day for the renewal of the licence agreement and the level of the licence fee.

The Cable Authority

The Cable Authority was created by the Cable and Broadcasting Act 1984, which sets out its powers and duties. The Cable Authority is empowered to license cable television services. The Cable Authority has duties to 'do all that they can' to ensure that programmes do not include offensive materials or material likely to incite crime or disorder. It also has a duty to ensure accuracy and impartiality in views from the United Kingdom, to prevent subliminal advertising and to provide a proper proportion of programmes from the EEC. The Act obliges the Cable Authority to produce *Guidelines* for advertisements and for programmes showing violence, and rules for appeals for donations. The Authority must prevent licensees from diffusing programmes which give undue prominence to the views or opinions of any one person or body on religion, current public policy or political or industrial controversy.

The Satellite Broadcasting Board

The Satellite Broadcasting Board was also created by the Cable and Broadcasting Act. It has statutory powers over direct broadcasting by satellite. It has a duty to control programme content limited to matters which might cause offence or incite crime or disorder.

The Broadcasting Complaints Commission

The Broadcasting Complaints Commission (BCC) was created by the Broadcasting Act 1981, following complaints from politicians of unfair treatment. Its members are appointed by the Home Secretary and are not allowed to have any connection with broadcasting while they are members. The Commission is responsible for the investigation and adjudication of complaints from individuals of:

- unjust or unfair treatment in programmes, or
- unwarranted infringement of privacy in a programme or in research for a programme.

Complaints can only be made by people with a 'direct interest' in a programme, or their close relatives. The BCC will consider the programme and a transcript of it. They will also invite submissions from the broadcasting authority responsible for transmitting the programme.

There is no legal right for film-makers to make submissions, although in practice the relevant broadcasting authority normally contacts programme makers, and you can make a submission to the BCC even if they do not request one. You can also request copies of any correspondence relating to the complaint. The BCC can require people to attend before it, and can order that its adjudication be published or broadcast.

The procedure is intended to give some redress to people who have no legal remedy. In practice its rulings have not restricted the already conservative policies of the broadcasting authorities.

8

SELLING YOUR FILM

8.1 Trading with your rights

So your film is completed and you have retained all or some of the distribution rights. How do you make international sales, enhance your reputation abroad as a film-maker and maximize your returns? Although the processes and techniques of film and television programme distribution are very different there are elements common to both. First, you must have the rights to sell. Second, you must ensure that you have the basic technical materials from which to produce publicity material and fulfil the delivery requirements set out in the sales agreements and third, you may need to employ a representative to act on your behalf.

Do you have the rights to sell?

Depending on the nature of the financing arrangements, you may only have acquired limited rights to sell. For example, an Italian broadcaster may have contributed finance in exchange for all free television rights in Italian speaking territories. Similarly, financiers, particularly the banks, will require some form of security before they are prepared to advance money. This may be achieved by the bank taking charge of the copyright or underlying rights in the film. This mortgage or charge will be released by the financier provided certain conditions have been fulfilled, and until such time, you will not be free to dispose of the rights to the film. Presupposing you own, or are free to dispose of, all the rights in the film, these cannot be exercised if sufficient underlying rights (see Chapter 2) have not also been acquired. Underlying rights, as has been explained, include both copyright material incorporated in, or 'synchronized' with, the film, and performers' rights. The nature and extent of the rights you wish to acquire and retain will depend on the market potential of the film. The market itself is divided by territory and media. Media are defined by reference to copyright law and the state of technological developments. Unfortunately there is not always a happy marriage between the two. In recent years these media have changed dramatically with the development of video cassette/disc, cable and satellite. The lawyers, legislators, copyright holders and collecting societies alike face a constant challenge to provide new legal definitions to accommodate these changes. It must be said that this is happening very slowly, and even when these definitions become part of accepted practice, it will take years for them to appear in licences issued by archive libraries, museums, galleries, individual record companies, music publishers, etc. This presents you with considerable practical difficulties if you are attempting to acquire rights now for all media worldwide in the future.

Here are some practical points:

- Where you are commissioning original material, if you are not acquiring the copyright, try to include a clause in the contract that licenses to you the right to use the material in synchronization with the film without further payment, in all media now known or hereinafter invented throughout the world for the duration of the copyright.
- Where you are using non-commissioned material, for example if you are synchronizing a record, using published music or archive footage with the film, bear in mind that you pay according to the rights you acquire. These rights will be defined in three ways: media, territory and licence period. Ask for a rate card from the library if available, discuss with the distributor the possible sales value of the film and negotiate the clearances taking into account this information. If possible acquire everything for the original fee. A music publisher may, for example, be prepared to accept a one-off payment of £500 for all rights *or* it will accept a reduced fee up-front in return for a total payment of £1,000 payable in stages if and when the rights are exercised. Clearly it is a commercial decision whether you choose to invest £500 now and take the risk that sales may never be achieved.

- Keep a look out in trade magazines for lists of prices paid for films particularly for sales to television. Remember that you must cover the following costs when making sales before you or your financier will see a return: technical costs and other distribution expenses, agent's and distributor's fees and clearance costs. The latter can sometimes be so enormous that sales are effectively 'killed'.

8.1.1 Rights definitions – media and uses

With this in mind, here are some definitions. These are the rights which can be sold according to the different distribution patterns for films and television programmes and they are here set out as media and use. The type of 'deal' agreements that can be negotiated for films are more complex than for television, although the development of the new media is slowly having an impact on the structure of these sales agreements too.

Theatrical: the exhibition of film in standard width of 35 mm and 16 mm in cinemas or other places of public viewing to which the general public is admitted and for which an admission fee is made or rental is paid for the hire of the film.

Non-theatrical: the exhibition of the film by direct projection to audiences by means of sub-standard film gauges or videograms by the following institutions or at the following places where the exhibition of films on a regular basis is not the primary purpose, and in respect of such exhibition no specific admission fee is charged in money or money's worth: educational institutions or churches, educational classes and meetings held by corporate bodies being educational institutions, clubs or other educational, cultural, charitable or social organizations including recognized film societies, hospitals, hospices, libraries, closed institutions (prisons, convents, orphanages) and similar locations where the residents have restricted access to public places.

Free television: over-the-air, cable, closed circuit, satellite as defined below, microwave or laser transmission using any format without a charge being made to the viewer for the privilege of viewing the moving picture. For purposes of this definition, the regular periodic service charge (other than a charge paid with respect to pay television) paid by a subscriber to a cable television transmission service (i.e. so-called basic cable charges) is not a charge to the viewer.

Pay television: the over-the-air, cable, closed circuit or satellite transmission where a supplemental charge is made. This charge can either be paid by the viewer for the privilege of viewing any special channel or film in a home, hotel, motel or hospital, or by the operator of the transmission service.

Satellite: the transmission of the film via low-powered communications satellite to cable head-end, for re-transmission by the cable television operators authorized by the distributor or its sub-licensees to distribute to their respective subsidiaries in the territory.

DBS: this means Direct Broadcasting by Satellite. Although the Cable and Broadcasting Act makes no attempt at a definition, the down-signal from a high-powered satellite transmitter is received directly by the individual. While it is not yet licensed in this country, a small number of people have satellite dishes in their gardens and on their roofs and can, by adjusting them, receive programmes from many different countries, including Russia. DBS has two implications for you as the film-maker.

- The inadequacy of existing definitions of DBS means that you will meet difficulties when it comes to acquiring or licensing rights for use in this medium.
- The householder with a satellite dish can receive programmes destined for cable operators who will relay to cable subscribers. The cable subscribers are paying, the householder is not; not paying the cable operator or you, the programme maker, not even indirectly.

The technological advances in satellite receivers effectively blur the distinction between DBS and pay cable delivered by low-powered satellite.

Videogram: the sale or rental of individual videotapes and videodiscs consisting of the film for the purpose only of private viewing in the home where the only money paid is for the purpose or rental of the videogram.

Merchandising: any rights in the film or any material associated with the film and to which the producer retains rights. For example, the names of characters and their characterizations, or props or logos created for the film. The rights to control merchandising will only become valuable if the film itself is successful as the film effectively creates the market for the novelizations, T-shirts and cuddly toys.

Uses describe the sort of audience to which a film may be shown. These uses are:

- Theatrical exhibition. This is exhibition to an audience which has paid to see it as in cinemas. Film shot on videotape is unlikely to achieve theatrical exhibition because the quality of the enlarged image simply is not good enough. High definition television used with a large screen may change that but it is not as yet in commercial use in this country.
- Non-theatrical exhibition. This is exhibition to an audience which has not paid to see it. There are many examples of this including various educational uses and 'captive audience' exhibition (for example, aircraft uses, etc.). Usually videograms are used non-theatrically, although they can also be combined with closed-circuit television for a limited audience, in hotels for example.
- Home use. This is the most common use for videograms. Most commercially distributed cassettes and discs carry a printed warning that they are only for private or domestic use. Although none of these terms has been defined, common sense will easily distinguish between home use and non-theatrical use. You can show your home-use-only video to friends at a party, but not to the same friends at a local club.

A licence may be restricted to specified geographical areas, called territories. Whether you acquire rights for overseas exploitation or just for the UK depends very much on the sort of film you are making as well, of course, as on your budget. Although buying only what you need immediately may seem to be all you can afford, it is worth considering that if your film has any prospect of foreign sales at all, you should acquire the foreign rights or the option to those rights. Acquiring rights after a film has been made is always more expensive than doing so before. Certain sales, such as American sales, are generally known to achieve much greater than average income. Unless you have a presale for transmissions on these markets, it may be better to acquire major elements separately by options which will protect your right to obtain the use of copyright, but will not cost too much, or you can presell your film to a broadcaster who is responsible for the acquisition of the relevant rights.

In addition to the above delivery systems and uses, the world is divided into three incompatible television systems: NTSC which has 525 lines on the screen and is used throughout North America and the Far East, SECAM which has 625 lines and is used in France and Eastern Bloc countries and PAL which also has 625 lines and is used in the UK and many other countries. Attempts to provide a worldwide compatible system have failed so far largely for reasons of expense. The advent of High Definition Television (HDTV) which has been developed in Japan may eventually change this. HDTV has 1,250 lines and has, as its name suggests, a much sharper definition than existing television. Its aspect ratio is also different. If it were used, then most existing production and delivery equipment would have to be replaced.

These then are the rights potentially available for sale to a buyer.

8.1.2 Technical materials required for distribution

In addition to the necessary clearances you will need certain technical materials for distribution. In this section it is not our intention to cover in great detail the technical aspects of film production but rather to let you know what you will need and how you can keep your out-of-pocket expenses to a minimum.

Music and effects track

This will be required to service foreign language sales where the buyer will be dubbing the film. This applies for America too. You should not be surprised if that authentic Kirby accent is unintelligible to the average American. The music and effects track is exactly that: the original triple-track with the dialogue track removed. At the sound-editing stage the extra work involved to remove the dialogue track can be done at relatively low cost, but if left until after the film is completed and the first foreign language sale made, the costs can be enormous. That presupposes that you can find the original soundtrack and the same editor!

Post-production script

Whether the film is being dubbed or sub-titled or edited you must provide the buyer with a dialogue and continuity post-production script.

Protection master

Most important of all, you must make provisions in the budget, if a major release of the work is intended, for the running-off of a protection master negative. With a modest release it is always an inherent danger that the negative will be damaged. With costs in excess of £14,000 for a duplicate negative, ultimately it is a commercial decision whether this can be justified. If only television sales are envisaged, broadcast quality videotape masters can be taken from a good quality print and used for running off further copies thereby avoiding the need to return to the original negative. Where a major cinema release is intended, the distributors may require their own master negative to run off prints in the territory. Clearly it is a matter for negotiation between you and the distributors as to who pays for this master. Ultimately you pay because the distributors will either pay a smaller advance to take account of their upfront costs, or they will deduct it from sales income before sending to you your share of the revenue. However, remember you can keep your out-of-pocket expenses to a minimum by ensuring that provision is made in the original budget for a duplicate negative, so the financiers bear the burden of the costs, or alternatively by placing the responsibility on the distributors to advance these costs and recover them from sales. Always try to ensure that the cash flow is to your advantage.

Laboratory access letter

This is a contractual document which enables the distributor to obtain prints direct from the laboratory. The letter is addressed to a specific distributor from the laboratory confirming that the laboratory holds the specified film material and that it has been authorized by you to hold the materials to the order of the distributor. This letter will usually state that the laboratory agrees to honour all orders placed by the distributor for releasing print and duplicating material and that the laboratory agrees not to exercise any right of set-off or counterclaim. Thus if one distributor orders materials and fails to pay, the laboratory will continue to honour orders from you and other distributors and will not seek to recover the money owing from anyone but the party that actually owes it. The letter should also state that the material should not be removed from the laboratory without your written consent.

8.2 Distribution

It is quite possible to arrange your own previews and viewing. Check with a local independent cinema. Many independent cinemas or arts centres will hire out a viewing room, and there is nothing to stop you simply hiring a hall in which to show your film. It would be a good idea, in the case of a hall, to check that your event complies with fire regulations.

There are a number of film and video festivals that are good showcases and they are mounted both internationally and in the UK throughout the year. Applications should be made well in advance and you will find a list of festivals in Appendix Two.

In addition, there are several film and video catalogues that advertise and distribute film and video to clubs, educational establishments and interested groups. They will want to view your material beforehand. As a rule they require three or four copies of your film and will consult with you as to hire charges, the price if you are willing to sell copies of your film, and the wording of your entry in their catalogue. They undertake to advertise and distribute on your behalf, administer income, and take between 40 and 60 per cent from total income to cover their costs.

However, if you do not want to do it yourself, you must use a representative in each territory to deal with exhibitors. Your representative may be either an agent or a distributor.

8.2.1 Sales agents

When you contract with an agent you retain all the rights and receive revenue from sales. The agent usually collects the revenue and deducts a commission and expenses before passing your share on to you. The agent acts on your behalf selling your rights to the exhibitor, although the contract may be made directly between you and the exhibitor if you want to retain a degree of direct supervision. If anything goes wrong it is you who are liable to third parties, unless the agent was acting beyond the terms of your agreement with him, or actually caused the breach. You should ensure that you retain the rights to approve any agreements before they are made to avoid this happening. To protect the money which the agent holds but which is due to you, you should insist that it is kept in a separate account from all other money held by your agent, so that if the agent goes bankrupt you can identify it and recover it.

The agent is your representative appointed to negotiate sales of your film rights to the distributor who is ultimately responsible for the exploitation of the film in the contracted territory. The agent's responsibilities are to arrange screenings for potential distributors, to send out viewing cassettes to promote the film as widely as possible by mounting a publicity campaign and attending festivals. The agent is thus the middleman between you and the exhibitor or distributor. The agent will deduct a commission from sales revenue. This commission will be in the region of 12½ to 20 per cent and should be based on actual receipts in the agent's hands. A cautionary note: agents may try to base their commission on the distributor's gross receipts. In addition to his fee, the agent will deduct expenses in the following categories:

- The cost of viewing cassettes and prints (if not already supplied by you).
- The cost of press books, artwork, advertising and stills.
- Carriage and freight, agreed telex and telephone charges.
- Costs of screenings to potential distributors.
- Sundry charges, including agreed entertaining and film festival costs.

Agents' expenses should not include any entertaining or any business overheads not agreed in advance. It is a matter for negotiation whether travel costs and attendance at film festivals can be recovered as these too can be treated as business overheads and thus be payable out of the agent's commission.

8.2.2 Distributors

You assign or license your rights to the distributor for a specific period, territory and media. The distributor usually pays you an advance for the rights plus a share of its profits. The distributor makes all the contracts and collects all the revenue. If you are getting a profit share this will be paid to you by the distributor, after the deduction of specified expenses. The distributor will be liable for any breach of contract, but may seek an indemnity from you in respect of this, so that if it is sued by a third party for failure to clear underlying rights which should have been paid, then you pay. If the distributor does not pay you, then your rights are limited to taking it to court, and if it goes bankrupt you will not be able to place yourself in a better position than all the other creditors.

The distributor is usually based in the contracted territory and once it has acquired the rights from you it negotiates the release of the film through the cinema, organizes making the necessary prints and plans the advertising and publicity campaign for the film in its territory. In addition to the theatrical/cinema rights, the distributor may also acquire from you ancillary rights which it will license according to the conditions for each prevailing territory. The number of rights the distributor acquires is a matter for negotiation and will depend on a number of factors:

- The value of the ancillary rights. A theatrical release, however modest, which generates good reviews will increase the 'perceived' value of the film and add value to the ancillary rights. However, to achieve these reviews it may be necessary to underwrite the cost of the theatrical release, so if the distributor advances all the costs it will expect to share the increased value of the ancillary rights.
- The distributor's ability to dispose of the ancillary rights. The distributor may be a video distributor with its own label, or may appoint a sub-distributor to release the film on video cassette. You may wish to avoid the use of yet another party in the distribution chain cutting into your share of income, and increasing the risk of default and delay, and prefer to license direct to the video distributor.

- The respective knowledge of your agent and local distributor; that is, who knows more about the competition between the different media? It may be sensible to grant a package of rights to the distributor in return for a defined share of income from each ancillary market. The distributor can then determine the value of each market and the best way to distribute the film. Alternatively, there may be dramatic changes in balance between the ancillary markets in different territories, as in America in recent years with the decline of pay cable and the corresponding rise in the video cassette market. It probably makes sense to appoint a local expert. The balance can become very complicated. For instance, if you retain cinema and television rights the video distributor will want a holdback clause, preventing you from selling the rights to television, which will kill its market. Similarly, you will want a clause in the contract with the video distributor specifying a date before which the video cassette cannot be released, so as not to undermine the cinema potential of the film. Already you can see how complex the chain of contracts may become and how the holdback clauses must be carefully negotiated so that the film maximizes its earning potential.

8.2.3 Deals – films, theatrical and non-theatrical

Let us assume you have appointed an agent, who negotiates on your behalf a sale of the theatrical and non-theatrical rights to a French distributor. What types of deals can be negotiated between your agent and the distributor, and between the distributor and exhibitor, the cinema owner? Box office receipts are usually the first sums to be earned by a film, so we will begin at that end.

The distributor and the exhibitor

The 'exhibitor's gross' will be 100 per cent of all sums received at the box office less only VAT or any tax replacing it. In France, for example, there is an extra tax which is deducted and paid into a film fund for the development, production and export of indigenous film productions. From the exhibitor's gross will be deducted an exhibitor's percentage, the amount of which is subject to negotiation between the exhibitor and the distributor. The exhibitor can usually retain between 30 and 60 per cent of the exhibitor's gross. The agreements normally incorporate a sliding scale, with the percentage going to the distributor increasing with the earnings. The exhibitor will also seek to retain a guaranteed amount before the division in order to cover the cinema's overheads, the so-called 'house-nut'. The sums paid by the exhibitor to the distributor will be the 'distributor's gross' or 'film rentals'. Occasionally a distributor will 'four-wall' a cinema, which means it will pay to the exhibitor a flat fee to hire the cinema and will collect all the box office receipts itself.

The agreement between agent and distributor

The division of the distributor's gross will depend on the nature of the agreement between the agent and the distributor. There are two types of agreements, so-called gross and net deals, although there can be variations which include a mixture of both. In both cases the distributor will take a commission.

Gross deal

The distributor deducts a commission based on the distributor's gross, out of which the distributor will also deduct all its expenses. These expenses include the following:

- The cost of negatives, soundtracks, prints, release prints, tapes, cassettes, etc.
- The cost of press books, artwork, advertising (probably the highest single sum) and stills.
- Carriage and freight involved in the movement and shipping of prints.
- Sundry charges for legal fees, registration, censorship and insurance.

This type of deal guarantees a flow of income from first receipts but the percentage due to you will be correspondingly low, between 25 and 40 per cent of the distributor's gross.

Net deal

In the case of the net deal the distributor either deducts its expenses from the distributor's gross and splits the net 50/50 with you, or the distributor deducts, say, a 30 per cent distribution commission based on the distributor's gross and deducts expenses from your share of the distributor's gross before sending the balance to you. If the distributor's expenses represent 40 per cent of the distributor's gross, then both types of net deal will return the same amount to you.

Outright sale

In some parts of the world distributors are not prepared – or are not trusted – to account to you for a share of income from the contracted territory. Sometimes, therefore, your film will be sold outright for a fixed fee for a limited licence period of between three and seven years.

8.2.4 Deals including ancillary rights

If in addition to theatric and non-theatric rights, your agent licenses to an American distributor a package of rights including videogram and all forms of television, the distributor's gross receipts will also include revenue flowing from these types of exploitation. The commissions payable on the distributor's gross income from these sources are usually within the range of percentages set out below:

Television:	Network television	10–25 per cent
	PBS	20–30 per cent
	Syndication	30–40 per cent
	Cable	10–35 per cent
Videogram:	Generally 20 per cent of wholesale price.	

Videogram distribution (including video-cassette and disc)

Whether the appointed distributor has its own label or not will affect the nature of the deal agreed between your agent and the distributor. If the distributor does not have a videogram distribution arm and merely licenses these rights to a third party distributor, unconnected with its company, the distributor will deduct an agreed commission based on income received from that third party distributor. In this type of arrangement the distributor will be acting more as an agent, taking an override on the videogram receipts from the territory. A typical commission would be between 15 and 25 per cent of gross videogram income collected.

If the distributor markets the videogram under its own label, then there will be a direct relationship between your sales agent and the videogram distributor. Even though the relationship is a direct one, there is still great scope by the use of 'creative accounting' by the distributor to reduce videogram gross receipts which will be the base from which *your* share of the income will be computed. If the distributor manufactures, packages and distributes to the wholesale and retail outlets, the costs at each stage can be artificially inflated, thereby reducing your income. Alternatively, the distributor may appoint a sub-distributor who is part of the same group of companies, to manufacture and/or distribute the videogram in a part of the licensed territory. For the purposes of the contract between the two companies, the commercial terms may be kept artificially low to depress the videogram gross receipts, and hence your share, yet both companies will have participated in the overall profits of the group of companies. To avoid the videogram gross receipts being whittled away in this manner, 'gross' should be defined as being equivalent to the wholesale selling price of each unit, that is the selling price charged by the distributor or the sub-distributor to the dealer less *only* any sales-related tax. This way, if your agent negotiates to receive 20 per cent of the wholesale selling price and the distributor appoints a sub-distributor, it must ensure that the sub-distributor is paid out of its share and *not* out of yours.

General points

This raises some general points about what to look out for in contracts generally.

- What access do you have to the distributor's and the agent's accounts? How detailed is the breakdown of expenditure given by the distributor? Some distributors may attempt to recover general expenses which do not relate to a specific film. Also, they may try to recover expenses from a sub-distributor or a purchasing television station and at the same time deduct the expenses from your income, thereby covering itself twice.

- If the distributor receives an advance against earnings from a sub-distributor or an exhibitor, how soon will these amounts be credited to your account? Sometimes they are deemed to have been credited only when these sums have been earned at the box office. If this is so, clearly the distributor will earn a considerable amount of interest because of this delay, yet the interest that has accrued will not feature as part of your share of income.
- How frequently are financial reports made?
- Is there an undertaking to release the film? Very often there is no such commitment in writing.

8.2.5 Television distribution

Television may be the only outlet for a large number of films and programmes. It can also be a secondary outlet for feature films, the revenue forming part of the general pot of receipts. If you want to sell to television outside the UK you will need to appoint a representative experienced in television sales.

Traditionally, sales to television, outside America, have been predictable because the market place has been relatively stable. Most countries combine public broadcast television, funded by licence fees or via direct state funding from taxation, with commercial television funded by advertisements. The broadcasters have exclusive control over their means of distribution to the consumer whether over the air or via cable. They frequently produce the majority of their programmes, but they will buy in a small percentage of programming. The amount that can be purchased is often set by government quotas. The prices paid in many instances are fixed at a set dollar per minute rate, and are not negotiable.

The role of the good television distributor is to ensure that the appropriate buyer selects your film and recommends it to the relevant film purchasing committee. The distributor will of course produce publicity and brochures to attact the attention of buyers, but these publicity materials will be modest compared with those produced for a feature film with major cinema potential. Like the film agent or distributor, the television agent/distributor should have an intimate knowledge of the market.

This, in reality, means knowing the tastes of the buyers, in liquor, food and, of course, programmes, and knowing the viewers they represent. Television sales can take months to conclude, many of the stations being large bureaucracies with committees that sit to ratify the decisions of other committees. Once the decision has been made to purchase your film, it may take six to eighteen months for the contract to be issued and months more for the licence fee to be paid. Be patient!

The scale of commissions your distributor will deduct from gross licence fees collected is a matter for negotiation. Of course, in practice, particularly if you own the rights to one film, your bargaining position will not be very strong. Most distributors work to a published scale of commissions which enables them to

Distribution fees

	% based on gross licence fees
1 *USA*	
Free TV	
Network	10–25
PBS	20–30
Syndication	30–40
Cable	
Top Cable	10–20
Secondary	20–30
Syndication	20–35
2 *Canada*	
Free TV and Cable	
Network	20–30
Syndication	35–40
3 *Rest of the world*	
Free TV and Cable	
France, Italy, Greece and Spain	25
Rest of Western Europe	20
Australia and New Zealand	20
Eastern Europe	30
Middle East	30
Africa	30
Far East	30
Latin America	30

cover the whole world, either by selling direct or through employing sub-agents in certain territories. The schedule on the previous page is by way of a guideline only and should not be taken as definitive.

8.2.6 American television market

The nature of programme production for television and the means by which the programmes are distributed to the consumer are both undergoing rapid change with the development of new technologies: cable and satellite. The extent to which these new markets, particularly within Europe, represent genuine new opportunities for the independent film-maker will not become clear for a while. There may be parallels between Europe and America, where a fully developed cable system has existed for some time. The American television market can be extremely valuable to you as a programme maker. A large English-speaking market, it has in the past proved very difficult for UK producers to penetrate. The following outline of the American television market may provide a useful background against which to examine the developments of the new media and may help you assess new commercial opportunities and locate potential buyers for your film.

The USA is overwhelmingly the most important international market for English language film of all types. The great size and population of the USA enables it to support many different television services and systems. Those factors have also resulted in the extensive use of cable and satellite as a means of transmission rather than over-the-air broadcasting. Many services are now distributed centrally by satellite to the terrestrial stations or cable operators. Only 2 per cent of American programmes are purchased from outside the USA. However, the market is huge and changing. Although at present the main market for UK-originated programmes is with cable operators and the Public Broadcasting Service (PBS), this may change, as even the networks are reconsidering the balance of their programming.

All television in the USA is governed by the Federal Communications Commission (FCC). There is no censorship, except where it is self-imposed, and so there is a significant pornographic element in cable programming, including the infamous Ugly George, who accosts women in the street of New York City and persuades them to take their clothes off for the camera. There is, however, a fairness rule under which a service presenting one political point of view must balance it with an opposing one. This is rapidly becoming unenforceable as there are so many available services. This is currently the subject of a court action in which a programme provider is arguing that television services should be like newspapers and be able to present their own point of view.

US television services fall into the following categories:

Network television: this is a national service operated by three privately owned and operated companies, ABC, NBC and CBS. Each company owns about six stations which are situated in the major cities. Network television is financed by advertising and no charge is made to the viewer. The programmes are mostly commissioned, to a maximum of 90 per cent production costs, although they have in-house news services, etc. There is little prospect of independent UK productions breaking into network television.

In addition to the 'big three', there are independent companies which are affiliated to the main network companies. They operate in the areas not covered by the 'big three', but provide exactly the same programmes and advertising and are also regulated by the FCC. Programming is provided to them free of charge by the networks; they finance themselves by carrying additional advertising. They produce their own news and buy in.

Independent stations: these are self-financing and carry advertising. Their programmes are mostly re-runs of successful network programmes which they often acquire by syndication agreements with other independent stations to cover the costs. Very few UK programmes have been successfully syndicated, with the odd exception like 'The Benny Hill Show'. However, it is a growing market, with 235 English language stations with a lot of money to spend.

Basic cable: with the development of satellite transmissions in America basic cable channels have proliferated so that now approximately 30 million cable viewers are offered between ten and twenty basic cable channels in addition to one to four optional pay cable channels. Basic cable is based on narrow-casting programmes targeted for a small audience. There is some scope for sales to cable television on a basis of payment calculated by reference to the number of subscribers and showings. There is also the possibility of co-production.

Pay cable is provided as an option in return for an additional payment by the subscriber. There are three major pay cable stations, Home Box Office, Showtime, and Cinemax, with numerous regional services, serving a total of approximately 25 million subscribers. When first launched, pay cable depended on showing major feature films in prime time. Competition from videograms and from more adventurous programming by other services has forced diversification, as the number of new subscribers has fallen off in recent years. There is a market for services and other programming which will leaven the diet of feature films and Hollywood series which they have previously provided.

There is one cable channel devoted exclusively to music, Music Television (MTV). Although MTV is free to the viewers, a charge is made to operators of the service. The Mechanical Copyright Protection Society and music publishers regard MTV and similar services as pay cable and therefore require increased royalties for sales to them.

Public Broadcasting Service: this is the non-commercial counterpart to commercial television. It has been the traditional American market for British and other foreign programming. About 10 per cent of PBS station programming is imported or is the result of co-production with a foreign company.

In contrast to most other countries, the US government neither owns nor operates the non-commercial television sector. There are nearly 300 PBS stations owned by local communities, states, colleges, schools or local authorities. They are funded, depending on their ownership, by tax receipts, voluntary subscriptions and corporate sponsorships.

The PBS itself is a national association of public stations producing no programmes but playing a representative role and acting as a link between the stations. It thus acts as the first tier of group buying for the network, screening and buying material to be distributed among the individual stations. Under this first tier lie the four regional public television networks, Central Educational Network, Pacific Mountain Network, South Educational Communications Association and Eastern Educational Network. This last one, which serves the Anglophile North-Eastern USA, is the most important for the UK producers. Each of the regional organizations screens foreign programmes to the programme managers of the individual stations who come together on a six-monthly basis. Once a programme has been selected, a price is negotiated between the distributor and the regional network on behalf of individual stations and the cost of acquisition divided between the stations in proportion to their respective budgets.

Programmes can also be sold direct to the PBS station itself, or produced for it in conjunction with a sponsorship deal. This is easiest with dramatic or educational services which will have a valuable afterlife in the lucrative educational market generally, with the circulation of literature linked with the production.

8.3 Advertising

8.3.1 Publicity

Unless you will be exhibiting to a captive audience you will need to persuade people to watch your film. If you intend to use a distributor or agent this will be part of their job, but you will have to get *them* to see it and they will want you to provide them with publicity material. No film is so good that advertisement is unnecessary. You must create an image of your film in the minds of the potential audience which will make them want to see it. If you ever want to produce anything else you must create an image of yourself and your productions which will be remembered. You are in competition for your audience. Even if you are not asking for their money you are asking for their attention. This competition is not just with other films but with reading a magazine, watching the snooker on the television or having an early night. After all, people might have to rise from their comfortable chairs and go out into the rain to get to your film. At least they will have to press the selector button on the remote control. Why should they do it?

You cannot leave the production of publicity materials as something to be cobbled together from second-hand leftovers at the end of the production process. You should have some idea of what you want before you begin and then make sure that you get it as you go along. Performers, locations and sets may not be available again, or only at a price, so make use of them while you have them. Be sure that rights to use production material in publicity are included in your contracts. An appropriate amount should be included in the production budget, although the real costs of advertising come at the distribution stage. In the case of feature films, publicity is probably the single most expensive item in your post-production package. Ensure that your distribution contracts contain some limit to this expenditure, and specify who bears the cost of it. If you can afford to employ a publicist or public relations consultant, then lucky you; if not, you will need the following.

Still photography

You cannot expect to take good-quality publicity stills off film prints or videotape. You must have colour transparencies and black and white shots taken during production. These can be done on set during the filming, or in special sessions. Make use of those inevitable periods when some of your cast is unoccupied and the set is free. You must be able to rely on the person you are using. Some shots cannot be repeated; you cannot burn down the house or drive the Rolls over a cliff again because the stills photographer was looking the other way.

Production unit publicists and unit stills photographers must be members of ACTT. If costs of film and processing are borne by you then the copyright in the stills is vested in you or your production company. This does not necessarily give you the right to reproduce the images. Write into the contract with your publicist or photographer your intended uses of the stills. You should specify:

– The method of reproduction.
– The print run.
– The purpose for which the photographs will be used.
– For how long you intend to use them.
– The territories in which they will be used.

If you wish to maintain all rights in the photographs, specify this in your contract with the unit publicist. As always, it is a matter for negotiation.

Press releases

Journalists work to deadlines and they do not have unlimited time in which to research and write their stories. You can help by providing them with materials which they can use as a basis for their story. If it comes to a choice between two equally interesting stories, a journalist will write about the one with the best background material. A good photograph will also suggest an attractive story, and may be essential for the popular press. You may get a captioned photograph without any story, but it is better than nothing.

Your press release should contain copies of any press cuttings, to show that you are established, and to suggest approaches for press coverage. It should also contain brief biographies of important personnel. Hollywood is not dead. The public are still interested in the glamorous lives of film-makers! Even if they are not glamorous, the press believes that they are and that is just as good. Even as sober an individual as Aleister Crowley, the self-styled Beast of the Apocalypse, believed in the 'cinema crowd of cocaine-crazed sexual lunatics'. If you cannot live up to this there is certain to be something about your film, personnel or the production process which can be used to give some 'colour' to a press release. It does not have to be anything to do with the film itself. One of the most widely covered film productions of the last decade concerned two people who went to an obscure island in the South Atlantic to film penguins and found themselves in the middle of a war.

Include a brief synopsis and historical or artistic background material. If your production is likely to be controversial, use the press release as your opportunity to clarify possible misunderstandings and to put your point of view. If you let the film speak for itself you risk misrepresentation which may be difficult to put right. Not that controversy is necessarily a bad thing. A public dispute, or a complaint from the National Viewers' and Listeners' Association, can produce publicity and an increased audience without much effort by you. Some people actually create controversy like this. If you want to try this, make sure that nothing in your production breaches the limitations on content.

Finally, make sure that the press release contains a contact number so that journalists can follow it up.

Previews and press showings

If you can afford it, a press showing will give journalists the chance to make their own story from your production. However, you still have to persuade them to come and you will be in competition with others who may be able to offer more comfort and convenience. If you cannot afford the best preview theatre and plenty of the best wine you must try to find an alternative attraction. Try to think of a theme that will enhance any special feature of the production. For example, preview a period film in a period house, or if your film is set in a particular place, hold your preview there, although you may have to provide transport for your audience. If you can find an organization whose interests coincide with yours, and which would also benefit from publicity, try to organize a joint venture with them.

Do not just leave the journalists to make their way home clutching a press release after the preview or press showing. Make sure that members of the cast and crew are there and that they talk to them. Be prepared to entertain them with 'colourful snippets' on which they can hang a story. Follow up any who appear to be interested with a phone call the next day. Remember, you have to distinguish your film from the dozen others they will have seen that week.

Planning a publicity campaign

Unless you have Meryl Streep as your leading actress, it will not be easy to get national press coverage without some lead-up. Just as you cannot leave the production of materials for publicity until the production is complete, you should not wait until then to publicize it. Publicity during production will whet the public's appetite. It can also keep your financial backers happy, or help you find more financial backing.

Trade papers will be interested in a production from the earliest stages, although you should not seek any publicity until you have tied up the necessary rights. Once you are under way, contact local papers who are usually delighted with any story they can find, especially if it is photogenic. If your production has any special interest to any particular group of people contact magazines, or correspondents, who cover that area of interest.

A publicity campaign will be more effective if it is concentrated on or around a particular date. Where your production has a première or a broadcast date this provides a natural point of focus, but local showings or trade fairs can also be used.

Festivals

Cannes is not the only film festival. There are numerous film festivals of different types. Some are specifically directed towards selling films to exhibitors, others give an opportunity for independent film-makers to exhibit their productions with the hope of finding distributors or exhibitors. The cost of entering a film in a festival can be anything from the cost of sending a print/cassette to the organizers to the full gin palace and bikini beauties extravaganza. Many festivals will provide board and lodging for visiting film-makers though rarely travel expenses. Keep an eye on trade papers for festivals and their entry requirements. (See Appendix Two.)

Will it work?

There is no guarantee that publicity will work. However, you are more likely to get an audience if the public have at least heard of your production. Do not be too depressed about unfavourable press comment. Adverse publicity is still publicity, and the judgement of journalists is not perfect. One reviewer of the pre-West End run of *The Mousetrap* declared: 'This company has absolutely no commercial future.' (He is now a Conservative MP.) Do not be too elated by good publicity, as it does not always guarantee an audience. On 13 August 1978 *France Soir* recommended an interview with an Armenian woman as the best programme to watch on television that night. Audience research revealed that 67 per cent of the potential viewers watched a Napoleonic costume drama, and the other 33 per cent watched 'Jeux sans Frontières'.

8.3.2 Credits

The form of the screen credits at the end of your film is often part of the consideration in your contracts with your artists. 'Star billing', for example, can be as important as the fee you have contracted to pay your leading lady. The letter size of the title of the film is defined as 100 per cent and all credits are measured in relation to this. There are no hard and fast rules. An agent may seek 'star name' or 'star billing' either above or below the title, for example. Remember to discuss the form of screen credit in your negotiations with agents prior to contract. If you use an artist by courtesy of another organization, for example a ballet or opera company, you will be obliged to acknowledge this in the credits.

Co-production can present additional headaches. If you are co-producing and have offered rights in a particular territory to your co-producer, the credits may need to be altered when it comes to distribution within the contracted territory. Try to pass on to your co-producer or distributor the contractual credit obligations that you have with your artists. In your co-production agreements include a provision that your co-producer is also bound by the terms of the artists' contracts that refer to screen credits. Disagreement between you and your co-producer as to which of you and your personnel gets what kind of credit is not so easy to settle. They are *your* negotiations!

Some artists will insist on a credit in all advertising and 'pay publicity'. This covers areas where you have no direct control, for example your distributors' publicity. If the distributor fails to acknowledge artists you have contracted to credit the artist will sue *you*. You should protect yourself by providing in your contracts with your artists that you will use your 'best endeavours' to pass on contractual credit obligations to third parties. A distributor will seek to include in the contracts a clause excluding liability for 'any inadvertent failure' to pass on contractual credit obligations to a third party. Attach a schedule to any distribution contract or publicity material setting out the various contractual credits which are in the contracts with your artists and include a provision in your contracts with distributors that they will comply with these.

Remember labels on video discs, cassette and disc sleeves and any inserts that are included in your packaging.

Even the best working relationship can be soured at the point when you try to decide on the form of a credit. When it comes to the glory, you may be surprised how even those behind the camera are quite capable of indulging in sandpit politics – the 'it's my ball and I'm not going to play any more' syndrome. Breach of contractual credit obligations has a remedy only in damages. It can also, in some circumstances, be defamatory. As ever, prevention is better than cure.

APPENDIX ONE

The Channel 4 Television Programme Budget and
The Channel 4 Television Programme Music Cue Sheet

Programme budget

Programme no. ____

Programme summary

Schedule 1

Title ____

Production company ____

____

Programme description ____

____

____

Running time ____ Video tape/film*

Schedule

Pre-production ____ to ____ (weeks)

Production ____ to ____ (weeks)

Post-production ____ to ____ (weeks)

Using: Studios at ____ for ____ weeks

Locations at ____ for ____ weeks

____ for ____ weeks

____ for ____ weeks

Finance

Source	£'000	%
Proposed cost -per schedule 2		100

Union agreements ____

Draft* no. ____ /final* budget based on script*/production schedule * dated: ____

Signed Date

* Delete as appropriate

Programme budget

Cost proposal

Schedule 2

	£'000
Budgeted direct cost - per schedule 3	

As authorised by Channel Four
(outline basis & relevant calculations)

1. Overhead £'000

2. Production fee

3. Contingency

4. Completion guarantee

.... % of £ ....

Guarantor ....

Subtotal (1 + 2 + 3 + 4)

Total proposed cost

Programme budget

Cost summary

Schedule 3

Schedule ref.		£'000
5	Story & scripts	________
6 (a & b)	Artistes	________
7	Producer & director	________
8	Salaries - production	________
9 (a to d)	- technical	________
10	- art dept.	________
11	- other depts.	________
12 (a to d)	Sets, props & lighting	________
13	Special effects	________
14	Music	________
15	Wardrobe etc.	________
16 (a to e)	Film/tape	________
17 (a & b)	Studios & other facilities	________
18	Equipment hire	________
19 (a to c)	Travel & transport	________
20 (a & b)	Hotel & living expenses	________
21	Other production expenses	________
22	Salary/wage rel. o/h	________
23	Insurance, finance & legal	________
24	Other expenses	________
	Budgeted direct cost - enter on schedule 2	

Remarks

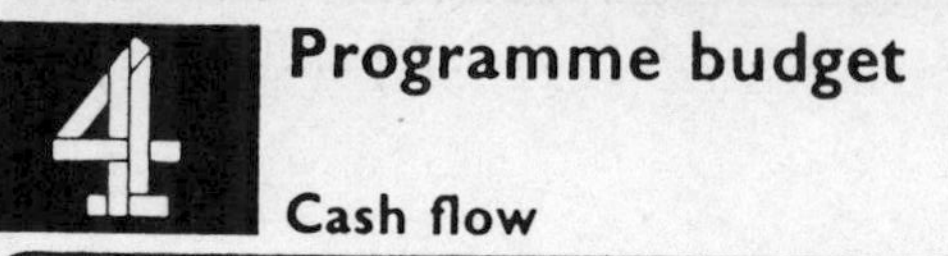

Programme budget

Cash flow

Schedule 4

Cash outflow - £'000	W/E	W/E	W/E	W/E	W/E	W/E	W/E	W/E	Total
Cost proposal									
1. Overhead									
2. Production fee									
3. Contingency									
4. Completion guarantee									
Direct production costs									
5. Story & scripts									
6. Artistes									
7. Producter & director									
8. Salaries - production									
9. - technical									
10. - art dept.									
11. - other depts.									
12. Sets, props & lighting									
13. Special effects									
14. Music									
15. Wardrobe, etc.									
16. Film/tape									
17. Studios & other facilities									
18. Equipment hire									
19. Travel & transport									
20. Hotel & living expenses									
21. Other prodn. expenses									
22. Salary & wage rel. o/h									
23. Insurance, finance & legal									
24. Other expenses									
Working capital adjustment									
Total outflow									
Channel Four contribution									

Programme budget

Story and scripts

Schedule 5

Details	Total £
1. **Story/rights**	
2. **Writers & script writers**	
3. **Preparation expenses**	
Total this section	£

Programme budget

Artistes

Schedule 6 (a)

Name	Part	Retained for weeks/days	Schedule weeks/days				Terms and Conditions	Total £
			Rehearsals	Prodn.	Post-synch	Total		
1. **Artistes** (include commentators, presenters, etc,)								
Note: Show overtime separately							Carry forward	£

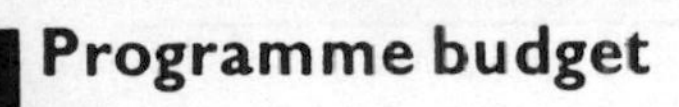

Programme budget

Artistes

Schedule 6 (b)

Details	Retained for weeks/days	Schedule - weeks/days			Rate per week/day £	Total £
		Rehearsals	Production	Total		
Brought forward **2. Extras and crowd**						
CCA fee						
3. Stuntmen, chaperones, footsteps and others						
Note: Show overtime separately.					**Total this section**	£

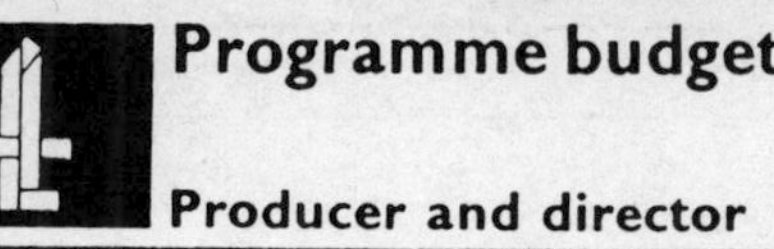

Programme budget

Producer and director

Schedule 7

Name	Schedule - weeks/days				Rate per week/day £	Total £
	Pre-production	Production	Post-production	Total		
1. **Producer**						
2. **Director**						
Note: Enter the production fee on schedule 2.					**Total this section**	£

Programme budget

Salaries - production

Schedule 8

Title	Name		Schedule - weeks/days				Rate per week/day £	Total £
			Pre-production	Production	Post-production	Total		
1. Production manager								
		O/T						
2. Location manager								
		O/T						
3. Production assistant								
		O/T						
4. Continuity								
		O/T						
5. Secretary to producer								
		O/T						
6. First assistant director /Floor manager								
		O/T						
7. Second assistant director /Floor assistant								
		O/T						
8. Casting director								
		O/T						
9. Production accountant								
		O/T						
10.								
		O/T						
							Total this section/carry forward	£

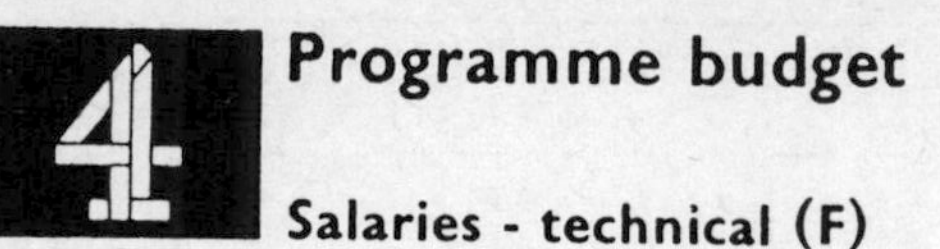

Programme budget

Salaries - technical (F)

Schedule 9 (a)

Title	Name		Schedule - weeks/days				Rate per week/day £	Total £
			Pre-production	Production	Post-production	Total		
1. Camera crew - lighting cameraman								
		O/T						
2. - operator								
		O/T						
3. - focus puller								
		O/T						
4.								
		O/T						
5.								
		O/T						
6.								
		O/T						
7. Grip/s								
		O/T						
8. Stills cameraman								
		O/T						
9. Rostrum cameraman								
		O/T						
10.								
		O/T						
							Carry forward	£

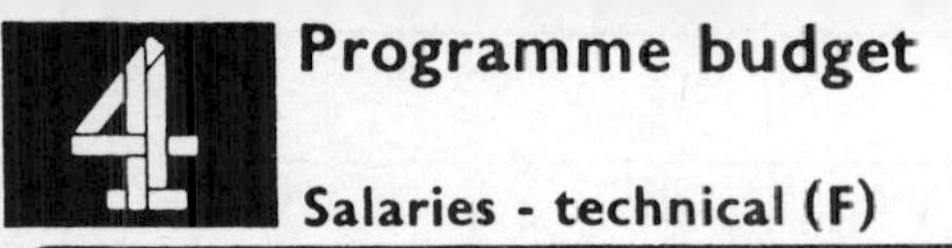

Programme budget

Salaries - technical (F)

Schedule 9 (b)

Title	Name		Schedule - weeks/days				Rate per week/day £	Total £
			Pre-production	Production	Post-production	Total		
	Brought forward							
11. **Sound crew** - mixer/recordist								
		O/T						
12. - boom operator								
		O/T						
13.								
		O/T						
14.								
		O/T						
15. **Editing** - editor/s								
		O/T						
16. - assistant/s								
		O/T						
17. - dubbing mixer								
		O/T						
18. - music								
		O/T						
19.								
		O/T						
20.								
		O/T						
							Total this section	£

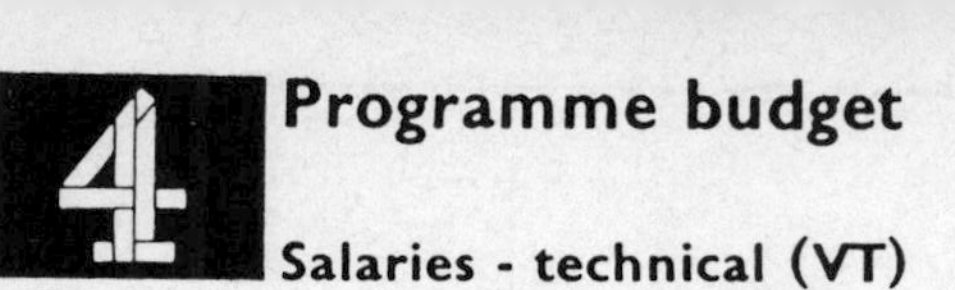

Programme budget

Salaries - technical (VT)

Schedule 9 (c)

Title	Name		Schedule - weeks/days				Rate per week/day £	Total £
			Pre-production	Production	Post-production	Total		
1. Lighting director								
		O/T						
2. Vision - supervisor								
		O/T						
3. - engineer/s								
		O/T						
4. Cameraman - senior								
		O/T						
5. - other								
		O/T						
6. Vision mixer								
		O/T						
7. VTR engineer								
		O/T						
8. Sound - supervisor								
		O/T						
9. - crew								
		O/T						
10. - engineer								
		O/T						
							Carry forward	£

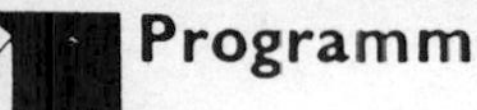

Programme budget

Salaries - technical (VT)

Schedule 9 (d)

Title	Name		Schedule - weeks/days				Rate per week/day £	Total £
			Pre-production	Production	Post-production	Total		
	Brought forward							
11. VTR - editor								
		O/T						
12. - editor's assistant								
		O/T						
13. Stills cameraman								
		O/T						
14. Rostrum cameraman								
		O/T						
15.								
		O/T						
16.								
		O/T						
17.								
		O/T						
18.								
		O/T						
19.								
		O/T						
20.								
		O/T						
							Total this section	£

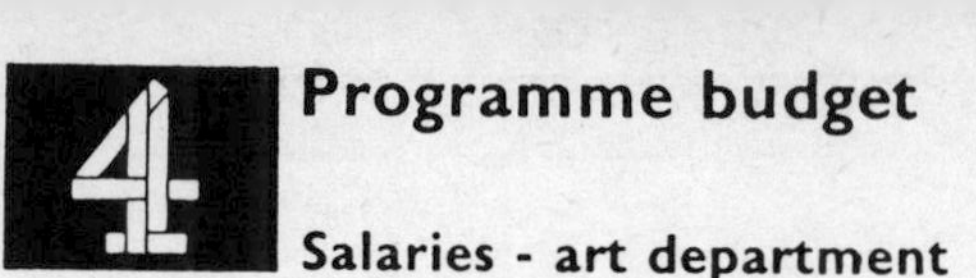

Programme budget

Salaries - art department

Schedule 10

Title	Name		Schedule - weeks/days				Rate per week/day £	Total £
			Pre-production	Production	Post-production	Total		
1. Art director/designer								
		O/T						
2. Asst. art director /designer								
		O/T						
3. Graphic designer								
		O/T						
4. Graphic artist								
		O/T						
5. Construction manager								
		O/T						
6. Scenic artist								
		O/T						
7. Property master								
		O/T						
8. Property buyer								
		O/T						
9.								
		O/T						
10.								
		O/T						
							Total this section	£

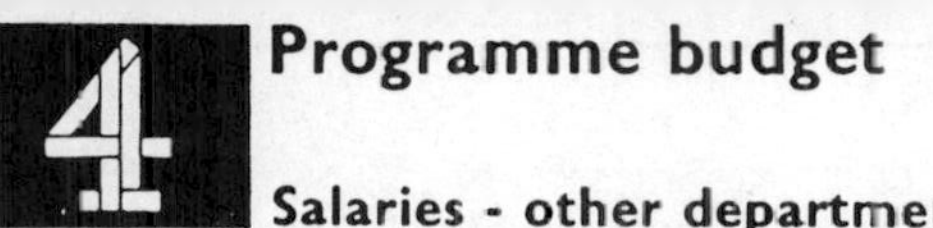

Programme budget

Salaries - other departments

Schedule 11

Title	Name		Schedule - weeks/days				Rate per week/day £	Total £
			Pre-production	Production	Post-production	Total		
1. Costume designer								
		O/T						
2. Wardrobe - master/mistress								
		O/T						
3. - assistant								
		O/T						
4. Dresser/s								
		O/T						
5. Make-up artist								
		O/T						
6. Hair dresser								
		O/T						
7.								
		O/T						
8.								
		O/T						
9.								
		O/T						
10.								
		O/T						
							Total this section	£

Programme budget

Sets, properties & lighting

Schedule 12 (a)

Title	Name		Schedule - week/days					Rate per week/day £	Total £
			Pre-production	Setting	Shooting/ recording	Striking	Total		
1. **Construction** (labour)									
		O/T							
		O/T							
		O/T							
		O/T							
		O/T							
2. **Operating** (labour) - stagehand									
		O/T							
- propman									
		O/T							
		O/T							
		O/T							
		O/T							
								Carry forward	£

Programme budget

Sets, properties & lighting

Schedule 12 (b)

Title	Name		Schedule - weeks/days					Rate per week/day £	Total £
			Pre-production	Rigging	Shooting/recording	De-rigging	Total		
	Brought forward								
3. **Lighting** (labour) - gaffer/chargehand		O/T							
- electrician/s		O/T							
		O/T							
		O/T							
4. **Other** (labour)		O/T							
		O/T							
		O/T							
		O/T							
		O/T							
		O/T							
								Carry forward	£

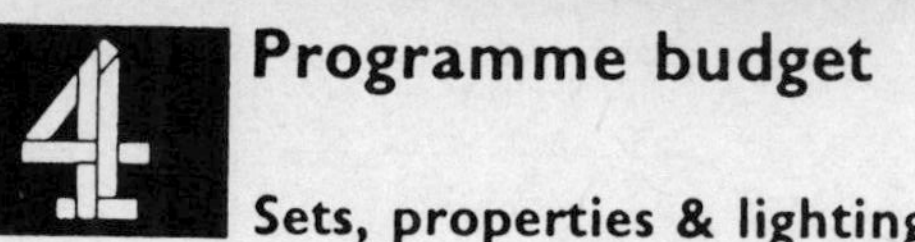

Programme budget

Sets, properties & lighting

Schedule 12 (c)

Details	Total £
5. Construction (materials) — Brought forward	
6. Sets (hired or purchased)	
Note: Details required. Use additional schedules where necessary — **Total this section** carry forward	£

Programme budget

Sets, properties & lighting

Schedule 12 (d)

Details		Total £
7. **Properties** - hired	Brought forward	
- purchased		
- action props		
- drapes		
Note: Details required. Use additional schedules where necessary	**Total this section**/carry forward	£

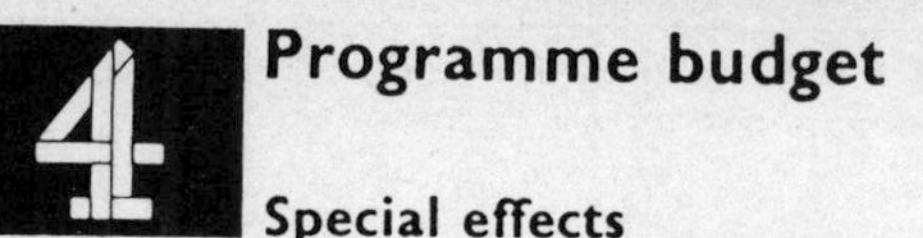

Programme budget

Special effects

Schedule 13

Details	Total £
1. **Labour**	
2. **Materials**	
Note: Details required. Use additional schedules where necessary **Total this section**	£

Programme budget

Music

Schedule 14

Details	Total £
1. Composer/s	
2. Music copyright/performing rights	
3. Musical director	
4. Musicians ________ players x ________ sessions x £ ________ per session	
5. Hire of special instruments	
6. Porterage	
7. Other	
Note: Enter details of music recording studio on Schedule 17(a) **Total this section**	£

Programme budget

Wardrobe, hairdressing, make-up & other consumables

Schedule 15

Details			Total £
1.	**Costumes**	- hired	
		- purchased	
		- materials	
2.	**Hairdressing**	- wigs hired	
		- wigs purchased	
		- materials	
3.	**Make-up**	- materials	
4.	**Other consumable materials** (specify where significant)	- art dept.	
		- lighting	
		- camera	
		- sound	
Note: Details required. Use additional schedules where necessary		**Total this section/carry forward**	£

Programme budget

Film (F)

Schedule 16 (a)

Film ______ Gauge ______ Ratio ______ Purchased from ______

Processed by ______

1. **Shooting** - stock and processing	Units	Pre-production	Production	Total	Rate (£ per unit)	Total £
Negative film stock						
Developing						
Printing						
Magnetic stock -shooting						
-transfers						
					Total (1)	£

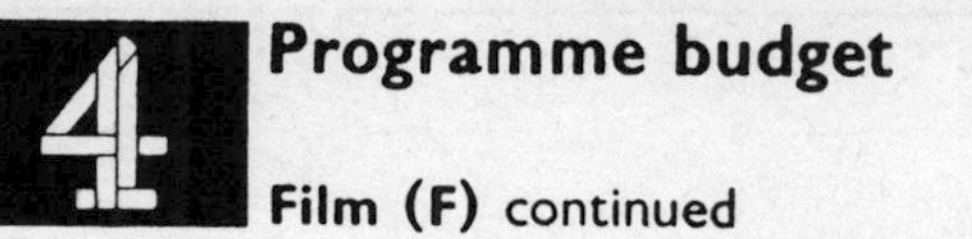

Programme budget

Film (F) continued

Schedule 16 (b)

2. Editing	Details (where appropriate)	Units	Quantity	Rate (£ per unit)	Total £
Numbering					
Spacing					
Reprints					
Magnetic stock					
Optical sound negative stock					
Stock shots or archive material					
Cutting copy dupe					
Opticals					
Special effects					
Graphics and artwork					
Titles					
				Carry forward	£

Programme budget

Film (F) continued

Schedule 16 (c)

2. **Editing** continued	Details (where appropriate)	Units	Quantity	Rate (£ per unit)	Total £
	Brought forward				
Negative cutting					
Optical sound developing and printing					
First answer print					
Second answer print					
Transmission print					
Colour reversal internegative (CRI)					
Less: rebates					( )
discounts					( )
				Total (2)	

3. **Editing facilities**	Details	
Cutting room	at ______ for ______ hours/days @ £ ______ per hour/day	
Dubbing theatre	at ______ for ______ hours/days @ £ ______ per hour/day	
	at ______ for ______ hours/days @ £ ______ per hour/day	
	Total (3)	
	Total this section, (1 + 2 + 3)	

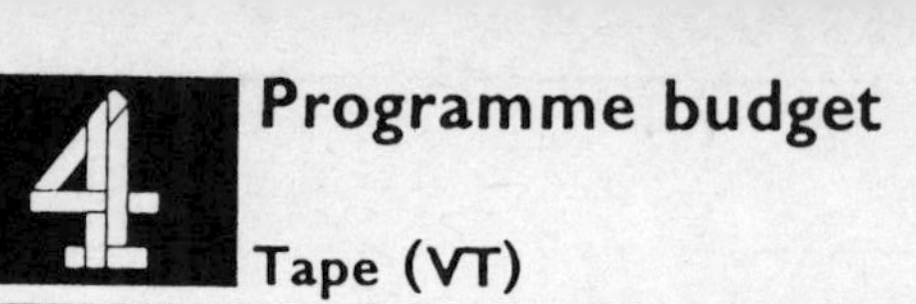

Programme budget

Tape (VT)

Schedule 16 (d)

Shooting company if different from production company ______

I. Tape - stock	Details (where appropriate)	Format	Tape length mins.	Number of tapes	Cost per tape £	Total £
Shooting - video tape						
Shooting - audio tape (multitrack)						
Other video tapes						
Edited masters						
Others (specify)						
Less: rebates for wiped tapes						( )
					Total (I)	

Programme budget

Tape (VT) continued

Schedule 16 (e)

2. **Editing**, including facilities	Company ______ Details (where appropriate)	Total £
Editing - visual	____ hours/days @ £ ____ per hour/day using ____ machines ____	
	____ hours/days @ £ ____ per hour/day using ____ machines ____	
Editing - sound		
Stock shots or archive material		
Titles		
Audio dubbing		
Special effects		
Caption generator		
Others (specify)		
	Total (2)	
	Total this section, (1 + 2)	

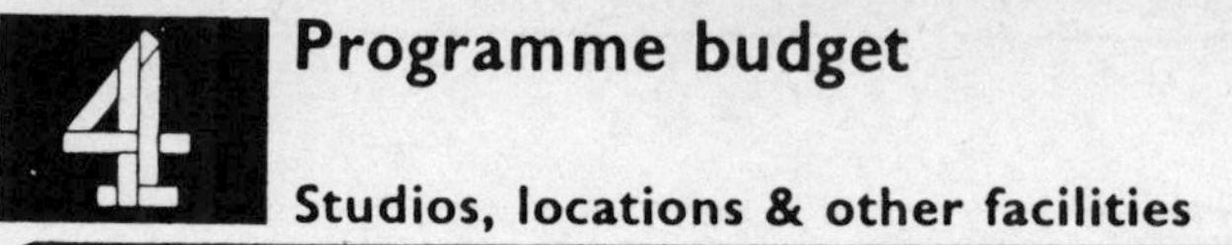

Programme budget

Studios, locations & other facilities

Schedule 17 (a)

Details	Schedule - weeks/days				Rate per week/day £	Total £
	Pre-production	Production	Post-production	Total		
1. **Studios, etc.** (specify) Venue						
Rehearsal rooms						
Music recording						
Production office						
Others						
2. **Locations** (specify)						

Carry forward £

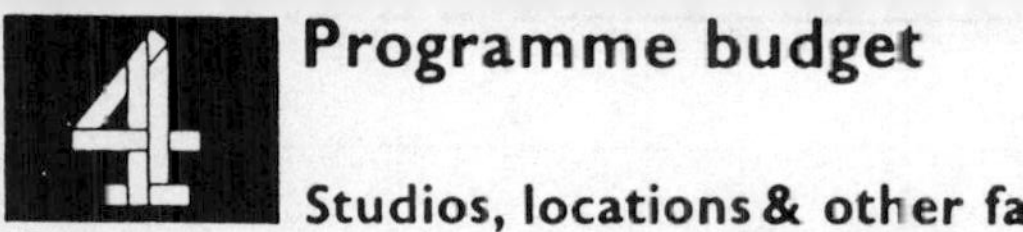

Programme budget

Studios, locations & other facilities

Schedule 17 (b)

Details	Schedule - weeks/days				Rate per week/day £	Total £
	Pre-production	Production	Post production	Total		
Brought forward						
3. **Other facilities** - include o.b. units, etc. (specify)						
Note: Details required. Use additional schedules where necessary.					**Total this section**	£

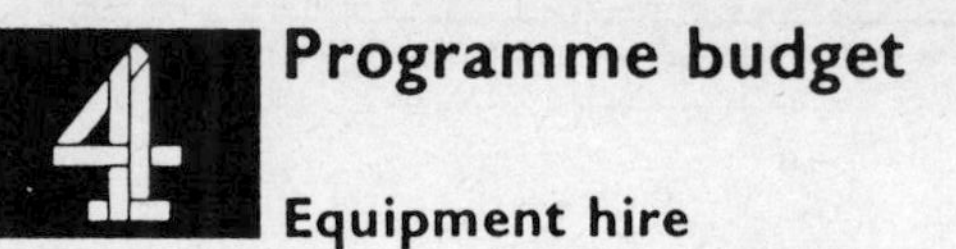

Programme budget

Equipment hire

Schedule 18

Details	Schedule - weeks/days				Rate per week/day £	Total £
	Pre-production	Production	Post-production	Total		
1. **Cameras & accessories** (specify)						
Dollies, tracks, special lenses, etc.						
Camera crane						
2. **Lighting equipment**						
Lamps						
Generators						
3. **Sound equipment**						
Tape recorders						
Microphones						
4. **Other equipment** (specify)						
					Total this section/carry forward	£

Programme budget

Travel and transport

Schedule 19 (a)

Details		Rate per day £	Pre-production		Production		Post-production		Total £
			Days	£	Days	£	Days	£	
1. Location Reconnaissance									
Transport to/from location - unit									
- artistes									
- equipment									
								Carry forward	£

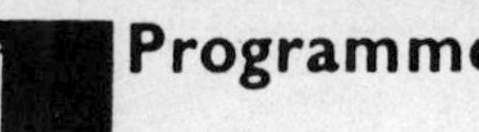

Programme budget

Travel and transport

Schedule 19 (b)

Details		Rate per day £	Pre-production		Production		Post-production		Total £
			Days	£	Days	£	Days	£	
	Brought forward								
Local transport - hired vehicles									
- fuel & oil									
- drivers' wages									
- other local travel and transport									
Sundry charges									
								Carry forward	£

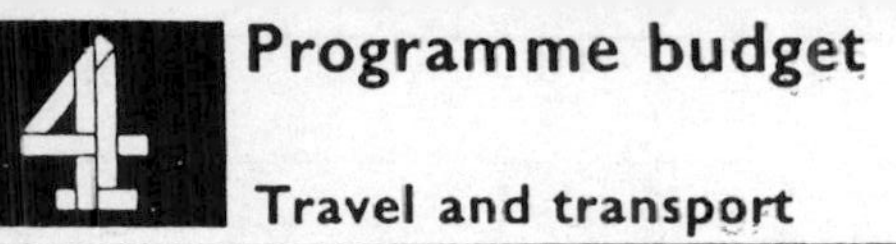

Programme budget

Travel and transport

Schedule 19 (c)

	Details	Rate per day £	Pre-production		Production		Post-production		Total £
			Days	£	Days	£	Days	£	
	Brought forward								
2. **Studio** Fares and mileage allowances									
Hired vehicles									
Fuel & oil									
Drivers' wages									
Other (specify)									
								Total this section	£

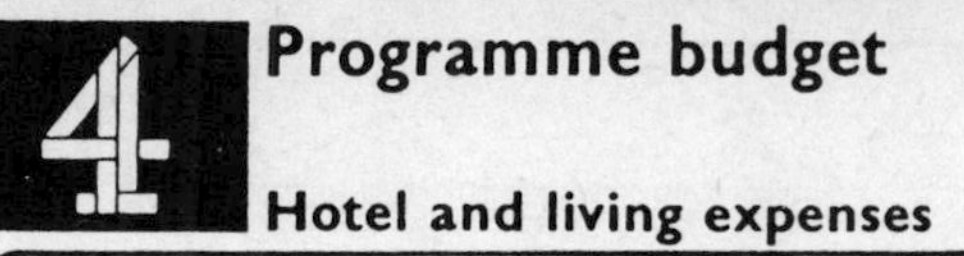

Programme budget

Hotel and living expenses

Schedule 20 (a)

	Details	Rate per day £	Pre-production		Production		Post-production		Total £
			Days	£	Days	£	Days	£	
1. **Location** Reconnaissance									
Accommodation - unit - artistes									
Catering - unit - artistes									
								Carry forward	£

Programme budget

Hotel and living expenses

Schedule 20 (b)

Details		Rate per day £	Pre-production		Production		Post-production		Total £
			Days	£	Days	£	Days	£	
	Brought forward								
Living expenses									
Other (specify)									
2. Studio Catering (specify)									
								Total this section	£

Programme budget

Other production expenses

Schedule 21

	Details	Rate per day £	Pre-production		Production		Post-production		Total £
			Days	£	Days	£	Days	£	
1. **Power/fuels** Electricity									
Other fuels									
2. **Other** (specify)									
								Total this section	£

Programme budget

Salary/wage related overhead

Schedule 22

	Details	Pre-production £	Production £	Post-production £	Total £
1. Artistes					
N.I.					
Holiday credits					
2. Salaried staff					
N.I.					
Holiday credits					
3. Others					
N.I.					
....					
....					
....					
....					
....					
				Total this section	£

Programme budget

Insurance, finance and legal fees

Schedule 23

1. Insurance	Total £	2. Finance and legal fees	Total £
Policies (specify)		Loan interest	
		Loan of £ ______ at ______ % per annum	
		for ______ months from ______	
		Loan of £ ______ at ______ % per annum	
		for ______ months from ______	
		Audit fee	
		Legal fees	
		Other fees and commissions (specify)	
Total (1)		Total (2)	
		Total this section (1 + 2)	

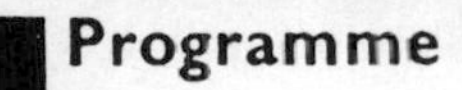

Programme budget

Other expenses

Schedule 24

Details		Rate per day £	Pre-production		Production		Post-production		Total £
			Days	£	Days	£	Days	£	
1. **Publicity** Salaries Expenses									
2. **Subscriptions & fees** (specify)									
3. **Telephones & postage**									
4. **Printing & stationery**									
5. **Other expenses**									
								Total this section	£

PROGRAMME AS COMPLETED FORM

MUSIC
CUE SHEET

PAGE NO

IMPORTANT
N.B. EACH USAGE OF AN ITEM MUST BE TIMED SEPARATELY.
MUSIC ON FILM CLIPS MUST BE INCLUDED AND ORIGIN STATED.
MUSIC AUDIBLE TO THOSE APPEARING IN PROGRAMME IS VISUAL.
MUSIC NOT AUDIBLE TO THOSE APPEARING IN PROGRAMME IS BACKGROUND.

DESCRIPTION OF USE
IB INSTRUMENTAL BACKGROUND
VB VOCAL BACKGROUND
IV INSTRUMENTAL VISUAL
VV VOCAL VISUAL
ADD 'SIG' FOR SIGNATURE TUNE OF SERIES

CHANNEL FOUR

PROG TITLE SUB TITLE	TX DATE	C4 CONTRACT NO	PRODUCTION COMPANY & TEL. NO

MUSIC TITLE	COMPOSER	ARRANGER	PERFORMERS	PUBLISHER	IF APPLICABLE		DESCRIPTION OF USE (see above)	DURATION
					RECORD LABEL/NO/ TITLE (If different from MUSIC TITLE)	RECORD PREFIX/SUFFIX SIDE/BAND		MIN SEC

PLEASE RETURN **ALL** THESE COPIES TO **CHANNEL FOUR TELEVISION**, 60 CHARLOTTE STREET, LONDON W1P 2AX.

APPENDIX TWO

Addresses

(i) General
(ii) Grant-making bodies
(iii) Television companies
(iv) British trade associations
(v) Cable networks
(vi) American film unions
(vii) American regional public television networks
(viii) Major film and television festivals

General

Association for Business Sponsorship of the Arts (ABSA),
2 Chester Street,
London SW1
Tel: (01) 235 9781

British Board of Film Certification (BBFC),
3 Soho Square,
London W1V 5DE
Tel: (01) 439 7961

British Copyright Council,
29–33 Berners Street,
London W1P 4AA
Tel: (01) 580 5544

British Film Institute (BFI),
127 Charing Cross Road,
London WC2H 0EA
Tel: (01) 437 4355

British Screen Finance Consortium Ltd (BSFC),
22 Southampton Place,
London WC1A 2BP
Tel: (01) 831 7561

Charity Commission,
14 Ryder Street,
London SW1
Tel: (01) 214 6000

Children's Film and Television Foundation (CFTF),
Thorn EMI Studios,
Borehamwood,

Herts WD6 1JG
Tel: (01) 953 1600

Co-operative Development Agency,
Broadmead House,
21 Panton Street,
London SW1Y 4DR
Tel: (01) 839 2988

Co-operative Union,
Holyoake House,
Hanover Street,
Manchester M60 0AS
Tel: (061) 832 4300

Federation Against Copyright Theft (FACT),
St Margaret's House,
19–23 Wells Street,
London W1P 3FP
Tel: (01) 637 9567

Industrial Common Ownership Movement,
7–8 The Corn Exchange,
Leeds LS1 7BP
Tel: (0532) 461 737

International Institute of Communications (IIC),
Tavistock House South,
Tavistock Square,
London WC1H 9LF
Tel: (01) 388 0671

National Film Development Fund (NFDF),
22 Southampton Place,
London WC1A 2BP
Tel: (01) 831 7561

National Viewers' and Listeners' Association (NVLA),
Ardleigh,
Colchester,
Essex CO7 7RH
Tel: (0206) 230 123

Television Users' Group,
29 Old Compton Street,
London W1V 5PL
Tel: (01) 734 5455

Video Copyright Protection Society (VCPS),
15–19 Cavendish Place,
London W1
Tel: (01) 580 8152

Grant-making bodies

The Arts Council of Great Britain,
105 Piccadilly,
London W1V 0AU

Regional Arts Associations

Eastern Arts Association,
8–9 Bridge Street,
Cambridge, CB2 1UA
Tel: (0223) 357 596

East Midlands Arts Association,
Mountfield House,
Forest Road,
Loughborough
Leicestershire LE11 3HU
Tel: (0509) 218 292

Greater London Arts Association,
25–31 Tavistock Place,
London WC1H 9SG
Tel: (01) 388 2211

Lincolnshire and Humberside Arts,
St Hugh's,
Newport,
Lincoln LN1 3DN
Tel: (0522) 33555

Merseyside Arts Association,
6 Bluecoat Chambers,
School Lane,
Liverpool L1 3BX
Tel: (051) 709 0671

Northern Arts Association,
10 Osborne Terrace,
Jesmond,
Newcastle-upon-Tyne,

NE2 1NZ
Tel: (091) 281 6334

North West Arts Association,
12 Harter Street,
Manchester M1 6HY
Tel: (061) 228 3062

South East Arts Association,
9–10 Crescent Road,
Tunbridge Wells,
Kent TN1 2LU
Tel: (0892) 41666

South West Arts Association,
Bradninch Place,
Gandy Street,
Exeter EX4 3LS
Tel: (0392) 218 188

Southern Arts Association,
19 Southgate Street,
Winchester,
Hants SO23 9EB
Tel: (0962) 55099

West Midlands Arts,
Brunswick Terrace,
Stafford ST16 1BZ
Tel: (0785) 59231

Yorkshire Arts Association,
Glyde House,
Glydegate,
Bradford BD5 0BQ
Tel: (0274) 723 051

Television companies

BBC

British Broadcasting Corporation (BBC),
Television Centre,
Wood Lane,
London W12 7RJ
Tel: (01) 743 8000

BBC TV Programme Acquisitions,
Centre House,
56 Wood Lane,
London W12 7RJ
Tel: (01) 743 8000

Independent Television

Independent Broadcasting Authority,
70 Brompton Road,
London SW3 1EY
Tel: (01) 584 7011

Anglia Television,
Anglia House,
Norwich, NR1 3JG
Tel: (0603) 615151

Border Television,
Television Centre,
Carlisle CA1 3NT
Tel: (0228) 25101

Central Independent Television,
Central House,
Broad Street,
Birmingham B1 2JP
Tel: (021) 643 9898

Channel 4 Television,
60 Charlotte Street,
London W1P 2AX
Tel: (01) 631 4444

Channel Television,
Television Centre,
St Helier,
Jersey
Tel: (0534) 73999
and
Television Centre,
St George's Place,
St Peter Port, Guernsey
Tel: (0481) 23451

Grampian Television,
Queen's Cross,

Aberdeen AB9 2XJ
Tel: (0224) 646464

Granada Television,
Granada Television Centre,
Manchester M60 9EA
Tel: (051) 236 3741

HTV,
Television Centre,
Culverhouse Cross,
Cardiff CF5 6HJ
Tel: (0222) 590 590
and
HTV West
Bath Road,
Bristol BS4 3HJ
Tel: (0272) 778 366

Independent Television News,
ITN House,
48 Wells Street,
London W1P 4DE
Tel: (01) 637 2424

London Weekend Television,
South Bank Television Centre,
Kent House,
Upper Ground,
London SE1 9LT
Tel: (01) 261 3434

Scottish Television,
Cowcaddens,
Glasgow G2 3PR
Tel: (041) 332 9999

S4C Sianel Pedwar Cymru,
Sophia Close,
Cardiff CF1 9XY
Tel: (0222) 43421

Television South West (TSW),
Derry's Cross,
Plymouth PL1 2SP
Tel: (0752) 663322

Thames Television,
306–316 Euston Road,
London NW1 3BB
Tel: (01) 387 9494

TV-am,
Breakfast Television Centre,
Hawley Crescent,
London NW1 8EF
Tel: (01) 267 4300

TVS,
Television Centre,
Vinters Park,
Maidstone,
Kent ME14 5NZ
Tel: (0622) 54945

Tyne Tees Television,
Television Centre,
City Road,
Newcastle-upon-Tyne, NE1 2AL
Tel: (0632) 610 181

Ulster Television,
Havelock House,
Ormeau Road,
Belfast BT7 1EB
Tel: (0232) 228 122

Yorkshire Television,
Television Centre,
Leeds LS3 1JS
Tel: (0532) 438 283

British trade associations

Association of Cinematograph, Television and Allied Technicians (ACTT),
111 Wardour Street,
London W1V 4AY
Tel: (01) 437 8506

Association of Independent Cinemas (AIC),
Theatre One Cinema,
Ford Street,

Coventry
Tel: (0203) 20446

Association of Independent Producers (AIP),
17–18 Great Pulteney Street,
London W1R 3DG
Tel: (01) 437 9191/734 1581

Association of Professional Video Distributors,
PO Box 25,
Godalming,
Surrey GU7 1PL
Tel: (04868) 23429

British Academy of Film and Television Arts (BAFTA),
195 Piccadilly,
London W1
Tel: (01) 734 0022

British Academy of Songwriters, Composers and Authors (BASCA),
148 Charing Cross Road,
London WC2H 0LB
Tel: (01) 240 2823

British Actors' Equity Association (Equity),
8 Harley Street,
London W1N 2AB
Tel: (01) 636 6367

British Film and Television Producers' Association (BFTPA),
Paramount House,
162–170 Wardour Street,
London W1V 4LA
Tel: (01) 437 7700

British Industrial and Scientific Film Association (BISFA),
102 Great Russell Street,
London WC1B 3LA
Tel: (01) 580 0962

British Videogram Association (BVA),
10 Maddox Street,
London W1R 9PN
Tel: (01) 499 3131

Broadcasting and Entertainment Trades Alliance (BETA),
King's Court,
2–16 Goodge Street,

London W1
Tel: (01) 735 9068

Cable Television Association,
295 Regent Street,
London W1R 7YA
Tel: (01) 637 4591

Composers' Guild of Great Britain,
10 Stratford Place,
London W1N 9AE
Tel: (01) 499 4795

Designers' and Art Directors' Association,
Nash House,
12 Carlton House Terrace,
London SW1Y 5AH
Tel: (01) 839 2964

Directors' Guild of Great Britain,
56 Whitfield Street,
London W1
Tel: (01) 580 2256

Educational Television Association,
The King's Manor,
Exhibition Square,
York YO1 2EP
Tel: (0904) 29701

Electrical, Electronic, Telecommunications and Plumbing Union (EETPU),
Hayes Court,
West Common Road,
Bromley, BR2 7AU
Tel: (01) 462 7755

Film and Television Lighting Contractors' Association,
20 Darwin Close,
New Southgate,
London N11
Tel: (01) 361 2122

Film Artistes' Association (FAA),
61 Marloes Road,
London W8 6LF
Tel: (01) 937 4567

Guild of British Camera Technicians,
303–315 Cricklewood,
Broadway,
London NW2 6PQ
Tel: (01) 450 3821

Guild of British Film Editors,
c/o Alfred Cox,
Travair,
Spurlands End Road,
Great Kingshill,
High Wycombe,
Bucks
Tel: (0494) 712313

Guild of Television Cameramen,
72 St Augustines Avenue,
Wembley Park,
Middlesex HA9 7NX

Incorporated Society of Musicians,
10 Stratford Place,
London W1N 9AE
Tel: (01) 629 4413

Independent Film and Video Makers' Association (IFVA),
79 Wardour Street,
London W1V 3PH
Tel: (01) 439 0460

Independent Film Distributors' Association (IFDA),
55 Greek Street,
London W1
Tel: (01) 434 2623

Independent Programme Producers' Association (IPPA),
50–51 Berwick Street,
London W1V 3RA
Tel: (01) 439 7034

Independent Television Companies' Association (ITCA),
Knighton House,
56 Mortimer Street,
London W1N 8AN
Tel: (01) 636 6866

International Songwriters' Association (ISA),
22 Sullane Crescent,
Raheen Heights,
Limerick,
Ireland
Tel: (010) 353 61 28837

Joint Industrial Relations Service (JIRS),
Paramount House,
162–170 Wardour Street,
London W1V 4LA
Tel: (01) 437 7700

Mechanical Copyright Protection Society (MCPS),
Elgar House,
41 Streatham High Road,
London SW16 1ER
Tel: (01) 769 4400

Musicians' Union (MU),
60–62 Clapham Road,
London SW9 0JJ
Tel: (01) 582 5566

Music Publishers' Association,
Kingsway House, 7th Floor,
103 Kingsway,
London WC2B 6QX
Tel: (01) 831 7591

National Organization of Workshops (NOW),
2 Soho Square,
London W1V 6DD
Tel: (01) 437 8506

National Union of Journalists (NUJ),
314 Grays Inn Road,
London WC1X 8DP
Tel: (01) 278 7916

Performing Rights Society (PRS),
29–33 Berners Street,
London W1P 4AA
Tel: (01) 580 5544

Society of Authors Broadcasting Committee,
84 Drayton Gardens,

London SW10 9SB
Tel: (01) 373 6642

Society of Film Distributors (SFD),
72–73 Dean Street,
London W1V 5HB
Tel: (01) 437 4383

Society of Television Lighting Directors,
46 Batchworth Lane,
Northwood,
Middlesex HA6 3HG

Women's Film, Television and Video Network (WFTVN),
23 Frith Street,
London W1V 5TS
Tel: (01) 434 2076

Writers Guild of Great Britain,
430 Edgware Road,
London W2 1EH
Tel: (01) 723 8074

Cable networks

Aberdeen Cable Services Ltd,
303 King Street,
Aberdeen AB2 3AP
Tel: (0224) 649 444

British Cable Services Ltd,
Lombard House,
Leighton Road,
Leighton Buzzard,
Bedfordshire
Tel: (0525) 376 110

Bolton Telecable Ltd,
33 Bradshawgate,
Bolton BL1 4QB
Tel: (0204) 26255

Cabletel Communications Ltd,
10 Field Way,
Greenford,

Middlesex
Tel: (01) 575 9000

Clyde Cablevision,
40 Anderston Quay,
Glasgow G3 8DA
Tel: (041) 221 2917

Cotswold Cable Television Company Ltd,
The Quadrangle,
Imperial Square,
Cheltenham,
Glos. GL50 1YX

Coventry Cable Ltd,
Blackburn House,
Whitley Village,
London Road,
Coventry CV3 4HE
Tel: (0203) 505 070

Croydon Cable Television Ltd,
Royal Oak House,
Brighton Road,
Purley,
Surrey CR2 2BG
Tel: (01) 660 6092

East London Connections Ltd,
Limehouse Studios,
Canary Wharf,
West India Dock,
London E14 9SJ
Tel: (01) 987 2090

Merseyside Cablevision Ltd,
Joint Computer Unit,
Royal Liver Building,
Pier Head,
Liverpool L3 1NG
Tel: (051) 227 5234

Shaw Cable Ltd,
11 Bruton Street,
London W1Y 7AG
Tel: (01) 409 2570

Swindon Cable Ltd,
Newcombe Drive,
Hawksworth Estate,
Swindon SN2 1TU
Tel: (0793) 615 601

Ulster Cablevision Ltd,
40 Victoria Square,
Belfast BT1 4QB
Tel: (0232) 249 141

Westminster Cable Company Ltd,
87/89 Baker Street,
London W1M 1AH
Tel: (01) 935 6699

Windsor Television Ltd,
5 High Street,
Windsor SL4 1LD
Tel: (07535) 56345

Rediffusion Cable Networks,
Head Office:
British Cable Services Ltd,
187 Coombe Lane West,
Kingston-upon-Thames,
Surrey KT2 7DJ
Tel: (01) 942 8900

36 offices throughout the country

American film unions

American Federation of Musicians (AFM),
1500 Broadway,
New York,
New York 10036

Directors Guild of America (DGA),
7950 Sunset Boulevard,
Hollywood,
California 90046

International Alliance of
Theatrical Stage Employees (IATSE),
1515 Broadway,
Suite 601,

New York,
New York 10036

International Brotherhood of Electrical Workers (IBEW),
1125 15th Street NW,
Washington,
District of Columbia 20005

International Brotherhood of Teamsters (IBT),
25 Louisiana Ave NW,
Washington,
District of Columbia 20001

National Association of Broadcast Employees and Technicians (NABET),
224 South Michigan Avenue,
Chicago,
Illinois 60604

Screen Actors' Guild (SAG),
7750 Sunset Boulevard,
Hollywood,
California 90046

Screen Extras Guild (SEG),
3629 Cahuenga Boulevard West,
Los Angeles,
California 90068

Screen Writers Guild of America (SWGA),
East: IMC 555 West 57th Street,
New York,
New York 10019
West: IMC 8955 Beverly Boulevard,
Los Angeles,
California 90048

American regional public television networks

Central Educational Network,
4300 West Peterson Avenue,
Chicago,
Illinois 60646

Eastern Educational Network,
131 Clarendon Street,

Boston,
Massachusetts 02116

Pacific Mountain Network,
2480 West 26th Avenue,
Denver,
Colorado

South Educational Communications Association,
PO Box 5966
Columbia,
South Carolina 29250

Major film and television festivals

American Film Market,
Suite 402,
8899 Beverly Boulevard,
California 90048
Held: March

Banff Television Festival,
Banff Centre,
PO Box 1020
Banff, Alberta,
Canada
Held: 2–8 June

Berlin Film Festival,
International Film Festival,
Budapester Str. 50,
D 1000 Berlin 30
Held: February

British Industrial and Scientific Films and Videos,
120 Long Acre,
London WC2E 9PA

Cannes Advertising Film Festival,
International Advertising Film Festival,
Screen Advertising World Association Ltd,
103a Oxford Street,
London W1R 1TF
Held: 24–29 June

Cannes Film Festival,
71 rue du Faubourg St Honoré,

75008 Paris
Held: 8–20 May

Celtic Film and Television Festival,
Library,
Farraline Park,
Inverness IV1 1LS
Held: March

Chicago International Film Festival,
415 North Dearborn Street,
Chicago,
Illinois 60610
Held: November

Edinburgh Film Festival,
Film House,
88 Lothian Road,
Edinburgh EH3 9BZ
Held: 10–25 August

Edinburgh International Television Festival,
17 Great Pulteney Street,
London W1R 3DG
Held: mid-August

Filmex,
Berwin Entertainment Complex,
6526 Sunset Boulevard,
Hollywood,
California 90028
Held: March

London Film Festival,
National Film Theatre,
South Bank,
London SE1 8XT
Held: 14 November–1 December

London Market,
33 Southampton Street,
London WC2E 7HQ
Held: 30 September–4 October

MIFED,
Largo Domodossolal,
20145 Milan
Held: October

MIP TV/International Television Programme Market – Cannes,
179 Av. Victor Hugo,
75116 Paris
Held: 20–25 April

International Television Festival of Monte Carlo,
Palais des Congrès,
Av. d'Ostende,
Monte Carlo,
Monaco
Held: 9–16 February

Montreal,
World Film Festival,
1455 Blvd de Maisonneuve West,
Montreal,
Quebec HG3 1M8
Held: August/September

Montreux Television Festival,
Direction du Concours de la Rose d'Or de Montreux,
PO Box 97,
1820 Montreux
Held: May

International Munich Film Festival,
Munchen Filmwochen GmbH,
Turkenstrasse 93,
8000 Munich 40
Held: June

NATPE,
30 East 42nd Street,
New York,
New York 10017
Held: January

Oxford International Film Festival,
123 South Bank House,
Blackfriars Road,
London SE1

Pacific International Media Market,
PO Box 478,
South Yarra,
Australia 3141

Rio de Janeiro Festival Internacional de Cinema, Televisaeo e Video,
Direcão Geral,
Hotel Nacional,
Av Niemeyer 769,
São-Conronda,
Brazil CEP 22450
Held: November

San Sebastián International Film Festival,
Apartado Correoas,
397 Reina Regenta s/n,
San Sebastián,
Spain
Held: September

Taormina International Film Festival,
Via PS Mancini,
12–00196 Rome
Held: July

Tokyo International Film Festival,
Dentsu Inc.,
15 Hanover Square,
London W1R 9AJ
Held: 1987 September

Tyneside Film Festival,
Tyneside Cinema,
10–12 Pilgrim Street,
Newcastle-upon-Tyne,
Held: 16–27 October

Venice Film Festival,
La Biennale di Venezia, Sectore Cinema & Spettacolo Televisio,
Ca Giustinian,
San Marco,
301 Venice
Held: August/September

Vidcom – Cannes,
179 Av. Victor Hugo,
75116 Paris
Held: 20–24 October

APPENDIX THREE

Further Reading

Periodicals

Published by the trade associations:

AIP and Co.	Association of Independent Producers, 17 Great Pulteney Street, London W1R 3DG Tel: (01) 439 2684
In Focus	British Film and Television Producers Association, Paramount House, 162–170 Wardour Street, London W1V 4LA Tel: (01) 437 7700
IPPA Bulletin	Independent Programme Producers' Association, 50–51 Berwick Street, London W1V 3RA. Tel: (01) 439 7034
Views	Independent Film and Video Makers' Association, 79 Wardour Street, London W1V 3PH. Tel: (01) 439 0460

Other:

Broadcast	100 Avenue Road, London NW3 3TP Tel: (01) 935 6611
The Business of Film	24 Charlotte Street, London W1P 1HJ Tel: (01) 580 0141
The Hollywood Reporter	57 Duke Street, London W1 Tel: (01) 629 6765
Independent Video	The Media Centre, Southhill Park Arts Centre, Bracknell, Berkshire. Tel: (0344) 27272
Screen Digest	37 Gower Street, London WC1E 6HH Tel: (01) 580 2842

Screen International	6–7 Great Chapel Street, London W1V 3AG. Tel: (01) 437 5741
Sight and Sound	127 Charing Cross Road, London WC2 Tel: (01) 437 4355
Stills	6 Denmark Street, London WC2H 8LP Tel: (01) 836 0445
Television and Video Production	PO Box 109, MacLaren House, Scarbrook Road, Croydon, Surrey CR9 1QH Tel: (01) 688 7788
Televisual	60 Kingly Street, London W1R 5LH Tel: (01) 437 4377
Variety	49 St James's Street, London SW1. Tel: (01) 493 4561
Video Business	Hyde House, 13 Langley Street, London WC2H 9SG. Tel: (01) 836 9311
International Media Law	Longman Group Ltd, 21–27 Lambs Conduit Street, London WC1N 3NJ Tel: (01) 242 2548

Yearbooks

AIP Production Handbook	pub. Association of Independent Producers annually. Includes markets and film festivals, agents, distributors and discussion of current film funding options and policy.
BFI Film and Television Yearbook	pub. annually by the BFI. Review of current BFI policy and British cinema. A comprehensive directory of trade associations, distributors, workshops, video labels and periodicals, with press contacts for film, television and video.
Screen International Film and Television Yearbook	ed. P. Noble. pub. annually. Includes a directory of trade associations, film studios, agents and distributors, and contact numbers for many leading people in the industry.
The Television Yearbook	ed. Dick Fiddy. pub. annually, Virgin Books.

Other reading

Martin Auty and Nick Roddick, *British Cinema Now*, BFI, 1985

John Boorman, *Money Into Light*, Faber and Faber, 1985

Broadcasting Research Unit, *A Report from the Working Party on the New Technologies*, 1983

Committee on Photographic Copyright, *A Brief Guide to Photographic Copyright*, 1983

Leslie Cotterell, *Performance*, John Offord (Publications), 1985

Bill Curtis, *Video Production; Notes on the Theory and Practice of Lo-Band U-matic Equipment*, The Albany, Douglas Way, London SE4

Michael Flint, *A User's Guide to Copyright*, Butterworth, 1985

Gregory Goodell, *Independent Feature Film Production*, St Martins Press (New York), 1982

IBA Programme Guidelines, IBA, 1985

H. I. L. Laddie, Prescott and Vittoria, *The Modern Law of Copyright*, Butterworth, 1980

Henry Lydiate, *The Visual Artist's Copyright Handbook*, Artlaw Services, 1983

David McClintick, *Indecent Exposure*, Columbus Books, 1983

National Council for Civil Liberties, *Civil Liberty*, 1981

Geoffrey Robertson & Andrew G. L. Nicol, *Media Law, The Rights of Journalists and Broadcasters*, Oyez Longman, 1984

Harris Watts, *On Camera*, BBC Publications, 1984

Brian Wenham, ed., *The Third Age of Broadcasting*, Faber and Faber, 1982

Linda Wood, ed., *Film and Video Production and Funding*, BFI, 1984

INDEX